Murder is not my business, even though I am a private investigator. Nor is it my hobby. I n fact, I rarely even read detective stories. I don't care what the butler did, why the dog didn't howl in the night, what Mrs. McGillicuddy saw, or who shot Cock Robin. I'm more interested in retrieving misdirected funds, tracking down missing persons, plugging holes in security systems, and exposing fraudulent business deals. I am repelled by dead bodies, nervous about carrying a firearm, and haven't physically struck another person since I was a teenager. I have a strong aversion to violent death, particularly my own. Unfortunately, violent death seems perversely partial to me.

MANAGANSETT PRESS

Don D'Ammassa is the author of:

Horror
Blood Beast
Servant of Chaos*
Caverns of Chaos*
Wings over Manhattan
The Gargoyle
That Way Madness Lies*
Little Evils*
Passing Death*
Date with the Dark*
The Devil Is in the Details*
Living Things*

Science Fiction
Scarab*
Haven*
Narcissus*
Translation Station
The Sinking Island*
Alien & Otherwise*

Mysteries
Murder in Silverplate
Dead of Winter*
Death at the Art Gallery*
Death on the Mountain*
Death on Black Island*

Fantasy
The Kaleidoscope*
Elaborate Lies*
Perilous Pursuits*

Nonfiction
The Encyclopedia of Science Fiction
The Encyclopedia of Fantasy and Horror
The Encyclopedia of Adventure Fiction
Masters of Detection Vol I & II*
*Published by Managansett Press

DEATH ON BLACK ISLAND

Don D'Ammassa

Managansett Press First Edition 2015

DEATH ON

BLACK ISLAND

Murder is not my business, even though I am a private investigator. Nor is it my hobby. I n fact, I rarely even read detective stories. I don't care what the butler did, why the dog didn't howl in the night, what Mrs. McGillicuddy saw, or who shot Cock Robin. I'm more interested in retrieving misdirected funds, tracking down missing persons, plugging holes in security systems, and exposing fraudulent business deals. I am repelled by dead bodies, nervous about carrying a firearm, and haven't physically struck another person since I was a teenager. I have a strong aversion to violent death, particularly my own. Unfortunately, violent death seems perversely partial to me. Some things are hard to get used to.

Nor am I the most sociable person you will ever meet. When I was younger and worked for someone else, I always tried to skip office parties, or if they were completely unavoidable, I'd put in a token appearance and slip away at the first opportunity. It's not that I'm antisocial, but this kind of gathering always strikes me as artificial, awkward, and potentially a source of friction, particularly if alcohol is involved. Now that I'm the boss, I find that my participation is mandatory. Every Christmas I rent a private room at some local restaurant. There are around fifteen direct employees at Birch Investigations, plus a few wives and husbands. Most of my regular staff are college kids or recent graduates who haven't found a better job yet. They spend their days tracking people down via computer. Most of them are unmarried, but naturally a lot of them bring dates. And there are about a dozen people I use on a job by job basis, and most of this group is married, so we get as many as sixty people altogether. I stay through the meal, make a very brief speech, and sneak out soon after, unless Dusty is having a particularly good time, in which case we stay around longer. Dusty has this incredible ability to have a good time even in the least likely situations so for the past two years we've stayed almost to the end.

One night a year isn't too bad, but this year a confluence of events conspired against me. For one thing, we had made a lot of money that winter. The biggest chunk came from Eblis Manufacturing, whose contract with me stipulated a bonus based on the amount of money we recovered after they'd discovered their

CFO was an embezzler. Neither we nor they were expecting this to be a large sum, but Nicholson wasn't very bright, had left an almost luminescent money trail, and we recovered nearly all of the three million dollars he'd stolen. Ten percent of that added to our usual charge made this our most profitable year to date, and it was only March. A couple of other choice jobs fell into our collective lap – the publicity resulting from my involvement in a major murder case hadn't hurt – and for the first time I could remember we had only one client in arrears. I was so cash rich that I gave everyone who worked for me a spring bonus.

I frankly felt that the bonus was sufficient, but my senior staff each in their own way had other ideas. The first betrayal came from Merrilee Brubaker, who manages the "kids" on our second floor, tracking down missing persons, delinquent dads, parole violators, lost heirs, and reluctant witnesses. Each of them worked at a computer terminal all day and the turnover rate was pretty high, mostly because the college students were raising money for the following year's tuition and the rest were marking time while they looked for a job with more upward mobility. Merrilee came down to my office one day to advise me that two of her charges were getting married in a few weeks, having met because they shared adjacent cubicles.

"That's great." She told me their names and I thought I remembered the young man, but wasn't sure if his bride to be was the redhead or the one with coal black hair that fell to her waist. "I'll have Steve send flowers for the wedding."

"It doesn't sound like it's going to be that kind of wedding." Merrilee obviously disapproved of whatever kind of wedding it was going to be.

"Not a church wedding, I gather," I said, not really caring either way.

"They have no money, and no family either. They're talking about having a judge marry them in his chambers."

I was starting to suspect where this was going and I was ready to jump off the bus at the first opportunity. "I'm sure they'll be fine."

Merrilee ignored me. "That doesn't sound like any kind of wedding to me. They ought to have at least a little bit of ceremony to remember later."

I sighed. Merrilee always reminded me of the pictures of Aunt Jemima that used to decorate boxes of pancake mix when I was a kid. I loved pancakes and so, by the law of magical contagion, I loved Aunt Jemima as well. On the other hand, Merrillee's soft exterior concealed a core of iron. "If we did something for them, it would be discriminatory, Merrilee. I can't pay for everyone's wedding reception."

"No," she sighed, turning to leave. "It's a shame though."

That might have been the end of it, but then I asked Steve, my secretary, when he planned to take his three weeks of vacation. "I was thinking about going out to my uncle's place in June for a week. He owns a string of cabins out on Black Island. The season doesn't open until the first of July so it's nice and quiet."

I had never been to Black Island so I asked what it was like.

"Pretty laid back. Even during the season it's usually quiet. Half the island is a state park and wildlife preserve. There are only about five hundred year round residents. The tourist business isn't big but it supports two hotels plus Uncle Ted's cabins and a few people rent rooms or houses. The ferry makes four round trips per day during the season, once a day the rest of the year. Most of the residents have their own boats. "

"What draws the tourists?"

Steve shrugged and settled back in his wheelchair. He had lost both legs to an IED in Afghanistan. "There are a few gift shops, but they're only open during the season. A couple of nice restaurants and some cheaper places. Mostly people come there to walk on the beach, look at the scenery, or visit the lighthouse. The pace of things is a lot slower than in the city. I like to sit out on one of the cliffs facing the ocean and read a book. It's very restful."

"I could use some restful."

"You should come out some time. Uncle Ted will give you a discount, particularly if it's not during his busy period."

"I'll keep it in mind."

I mentioned the conversation to Dusty when I got home that evening. "That'd be nice. I've never been on an island. Well, Manhattan is an island, I suppose, but you know what I mean."

The elements of the trap were closing around me.

The next veiled attack came from Barry Shaw, my forensic accountant. Barry would like to be my partner; at times he already acts as though he's my boss. I sometimes wonder if he'd balk if I actually offered him a partnership. Despite the bravado, Barry doesn't like to make decisions, although he doesn't mind taking credit for them when they turn out well. He's by nature a follower, but one who thinks he ought to want to be the leader. Sometimes he convinces himself that he's in the wrong role, but more often he probably knows that it's all an act. He just doesn't realize that the rest of us all recognize the truth. Or maybe he does but just doesn't care.

Barry is also very very good at what he does for the company. He has a kind of sixth sense about numbers. On one occasion he told me that he reads financial statements for amusement and can often detect problems even where the bottom line appears to be positive. "Sometimes too big a profit is as bad as too little. It might mean that a company isn't reinvesting adequately, or that its personnel are underpaid and likely to be restless or resentful."

Anyway, Barry had recently uncovered a nifty little scam at a local plating company. The purchasing agent and the warehouse supervisor would log in and authorize payment for fifty ounces of gold, but only forty eight would actually be delivered. The other two were assigned to an escrow account with the vendor for a supposed subsidiary that was actually owned by the purchasing agent and the warehouse supervisor, who resold the gold and pocketed the entire proceeds. Since the gold that was actually delivered was dissolved into the plating solution and used in a process that could not be measured to that degree of accuracy, their little scheme had been going smoothly for several years. Barry matched the requisitions from the factory floor to the issues from the warehouse, noted an interesting pattern of slight discrepancies, and their golden goose laid no more eggs. They were currently considering the consequences while residing at the Adult Correctional Institution. Arthur Weston, owner of the plating company, had been ecstatic and he and Barry had become best friends forever.

"Hey, boss," Barry said lightly as he entered my office. "Want to go on a cruise?"

"Not particularly." I've never actually understood the attraction of boating. I mean, once you're out of sight of land, there's nothing to see except water, and it all looks alike. And what's with fishing anyway? "I've been to Bermuda and Cancun and didn't care for either of them."

"Not that kind of cruise. Just around Narragansett Bay or maybe out to Cape Cod. You remember Arthur Weston?"

Of course I did. He'd paid promptly and without quibbling. That's less common than you might think. Most of my clients want to negotiate after the contract is complete, because they've already got what they wanted.

"How is Arthur doing?"

"Making money hand over fist. His two biggest competitors both went belly up and no one's stealing from him anymore. He finally got restitution, partial at least."

The property of the purchasing agent and his cohort had been seized and held pending litigation, which I presumed was now complete. "Good for him. I hope he left them without a penny."

"Pretty much. And he used the check as down payment on a yacht. A nice big one. Sleeps twelve plus crew. Says he could take it to Europe if he wanted to. The point is, he offered to let us borrow it sometime."

"Neither of us knows anything about sailing a yacht," I said. Did yachts sail? Didn't they run on motors?

"Of course not. It's got a full time professional crew. We'd just tell the captain where we wanted to go and he'd take us there."

"How about Albany? My college roommate keeps asking me to visit."

"You're missing a great opportunity."

"I'll recover from the disappointment."

Three days later, Tina Kirk unwittingly joined the conspiracy. Tina is my computer person. She keeps the network running but more importantly she can read source code or whatever it is that makes a program run as well as Barry can peruse a spreadsheet. On more than one occasion she has spotted hacks that diverted funds clandestinely from a client or holes in company fire walls. She's a workaholic and rather intense and I'd been trying unsuccessfully to keep her from coming in weekends to check things that didn't need to be checked or to do things that she could just as easily have done during regular work hours. She lived alone and was a textbook case of the person with no life outside work.

It was a Monday morning and I had come in early. All my senior staff have keys but the building was locked when I arrived. I noticed Tina's car in its usual place and wondered what had brought her in so early. I found her asleep on the couch in the waiting room. She had clearly been there for several hours.

"I was working on something and I felt sleepy so I thought I'd just take a nap." She wouldn't meet my eyes.

"So you slept here all night?"

"Well, most of it, I guess. I was working until well after midnight. I'll just go home and change and be right back."

"No, Tina. Go home and go to bed. Take the day off. You're spending too much time here."

She looked positively shocked. "Oh, I couldn't do that. There's so much that needs to be done."

I insisted and she actually stayed away, almost until lunch time. I threatened to kidnap her and lock her up some place if she didn't start taking more time for herself and she looked positively frightened. "I'm kidding, Tina. But you need to relax." She went away, and I realized I was starting to get a little worried about her. I had Steve pull her records for me and found what I expected. She hadn't taken any vacation days in over three years. I told myself I needed to do something about that, but then things got busy and it got shuffled to the back of my mind.

All of the elements were in place but I might still have escaped if it hadn't been for Dusty.

Dusty is my significant other. We'd been living together at my oversized house for well over a year and were still getting along. I attributed most of this to the fact that we were both just excellent people, considerate of others, well suited to one another, and sexually compatible. Part of it was probably also the fact that the house was so large that we could pursue our own interests without interfering with each other, even when those interests required a lot of space. My space was mostly books and videos. I was currently reading the complete works of Thomas Hardy, which held no appeal for Dusty, and watching the Charlie Chan movies, which she loved. I have no explanation for the fact that I dislike detective novels but love the old noir films. They must resonate in different parts of the brain.

Dusty is a novelist, under her own and other names, and her current project was the final volume of a fantasy trilogy, which she had almost finished. She required a physical manifestation – at least symbolically – of her setting, so most of the space in the walk-in attic had been transformed into the landscape of her mythical world of Pullemia. The story had expanded beyond the desert locale of the first two novels, so the expanse of sand had contracted to make room for the Meadowlands – a swath of deep piled green carpet – and the Caverns of Chaos, a structure resembling an anthill which Dusty had constructed by taping small cardboard boxes together. Her protagonists had been exiled from the city of Solenia at the end of book two and were now exploring a world they had known only from legends.

Dusty was just getting out of her car when I arrived home that evening and she had a back seat full of shopping bags. Some of them held groceries. Others were obviously from the thrift store. "Those are going to the attic," she told me. "I'm upgrading."

We distributed the groceries and I volunteered to help with the rest. Dusty led the way up the narrow staircase to the attic, where I could see that some major modifications were under way. The Caverns of Chaos had been shifted to the back wall to clear up some floor space for the manifestation of the ever expanding Pullemia. "What are you building now?"

"The last third of the book takes place in the Palace of Eternity. If all goes well, I should have the first draft done by the first week of June." Whenever Dusty finishes the first draft of a novel, she takes a week off to let things settle before doing the final editing.

I started emptying bags. The contents seemed totally random. I held up a fancy ice cube tray. "Those are sleeping pods for the Immortal Ones." A glass egg was the Orb of Forgetfulness, a Doctor Strange action figure was the Wizard of Forevermore, and a piece of rubber tubing was the Gilded Serpent, even though it was pale gray. I pointed this out and was told I had no imagination. I spent the rest of the unpacking time describing my problem with Tina.

"We ought to kidnap her to a deserted island some weekend and force her to relax."

"I think we'd have to keep her tied up or she'd use coconut shells to construct an abacus and start writing programs for it."

"Didn't you say you'd been invited out to an island? Martha's Vineyard or someplace like that?"

"Black Island. It sounds primitive. I don't even know if they have cell phone coverage. Martha's Vineyard is probably full of computers."

And so it started. We talked about it jokingly over supper and I even mentioned Barry's suggestion that we borrow Arthur Weston's yacht. In my defense, I wasn't taking any of this seriously. Neither was Dusty at first; I'm not sure just when the transition took place. At some point I realized that Dusty was talking about this as an actual project and alarm bells started going off in my head. "Dusty, we can't really kidnap Tina, you know."

"No, I suppose not. But maybe you could just order her to go. Or trick her into thinking there was some job out there that only she could handle."

As much as I love Dusty, she sometimes gets set on a course of action so determinedly that she cannot be diverted. Often I am happy to go along, but sometimes the destinations aren't wisely chosen. She tricked me into letting her pose as one of my employees once and it almost got both of us killed. So I decided to change the subject while there was still a chance of distracting her. Unfortunately, I started telling her about our two lovebirds and how sad it was that they had no family and apparently too few friends to justify even a mildly festive wedding.

All of the factors seemed to me discrete and unrelated, but Dusty was a lumper where I'm a splitter and through some process I will never understand she suddenly had a unified plan.

"Don't you see? It all fits together!" We'd opened a second bottle of wine by then and some of her enthusiasm may have come out of the bottle. In my case, all of the reasonable objections I hoped to propose seemed elusive, and that might also have been because of the wine, because they did emerge the following day, when it was far too late.

"That's just it. There are too many things that have to coincide. It's like trying to put together an amateur stage production. You can never find a night when everyone's available to rehearse." A former girlfriend had been a theater student and she'd talked me into my one and only acting role. It had been a disaster. The whole production, I mean, not just me.

"Oh, you're just being obstructionist. Let me organize things. I'll find a way."

"Be my guest." I was confident that she could never pull
things together.

But she did. I should have known.

So one hot, muggy, overcast Friday in early June Dusty and I
were driving to Newport with Barry Shaw – enthusiastic – and Tina
Kirk – sulking – in the backseat of my car. The Brubakers were
bringing the bride and groom to be and the rest of her kids – except
for a couple who had begged off – were making their way
separately. Our answering service could reach us in the event of an
emergency and cell phones did work on the island – most of the
time. We were all supposed to meet at the marina before boarding
the unfortunately named *Calamity Jane*. Arthur Weston's ex-wife
was Jane. They had an odd relationship and still dated. Steve was
already on the island.

I wasn't exactly in shock but I was a bit stunned. The yacht
was available to take us over and bring us home at the end of our
stay. Steven's uncle only had two units rented so he could take us all
with no difficulty and at a very reasonable price, which was good
because I was paying for everything except food and drink. There
was a Unitarian minister on the island who would perform the
wedding in his chapel. Steve had adjusted our schedules so we were
all free until Tuesday. Tina had been forbidden to bring her laptop
and Dusty had threatened to search her luggage. Dusty had even
finished her first draft so this was her rest week. After realizing how
neatly everything had been planned, I decided that if I ever needed
an office manager, Dusty would be my first choice. Even Steve, who
was a wizard for organization, had expressed his admiration. "She
really knows how to get things done."

We weren't the first to arrive. The Brubakers had preceded us
and Kevin Wise and Laura Marzocchi were leaning against the fence
that surrounded the long term parking area. They were holding hands
and staring out at the ocean. I had tried to learn the names of all of
Merrilee's kids in advance, but just to be safe I had an index card in
my pocket with names and a couple of descriptive words. Maria
Gomes and Carl Celluci were sitting on benches over near the
vending machines but very pointedly not together. Carl was smoking
a meerschaum pipe with a dragon motif and looked a little like a
juvenile Sherlock Holmes. The Brubakers were sitting on a bench

watching a sailboat drift past. Herman had an obviously expensive camera in his hands and was peering through the lens, apparently taking pictures of the three fishing boats moored nearby. None of them looked picturesque to me, but I've never really understood photography.

The parking was all prepaid, thanks to Dusty, and almost as soon as we had our suitcases out of the trunk, the caravan arrived, three more cars with the remainder of our party. Only two people had declined the invitation, so there were seventeen of us, not counting Steve. There were only two non-employees. Emily Granger had brought a female friend and Dennis Malden had brought a rather pretty blonde whose high pitched voice hurt my ears. I didn't know either of their names. There were some hasty introductions as we all gathered into a bunch. The *Calamity Jane* was the largest of the dozen or so yachts in the marina so we did a final headcount and set off in that direction.

The captain was Barbara Wayne, a woman about my age and almost as tall. She and one of the two crewmen were on deck when we arrived and she waved us aboard. She was neither friendly nor unfriendly although she was polite enough. The crewman showed us where to store our luggage for the trip. "We're technically over our capacity but there are some extra lifejackets in the locker just outside the observation deck." She gave us a quick tour, her words coming so glibly that I was sure she had done this before.

"I assume everyone's here." I was quite sure she had counted us while we were boarding, but I nodded confirmation. "Then we'll be underway in about ten minutes. Crossing time to Black Island should be just over an hour. There's a little bit of chop today. You're welcome to use any of the enclosed areas except the bridge but if anyone is prone to seasickness I recommend they stay out in the fresh air."

Ten minutes later, almost to the second, we started to back out into the narrow channel. Five minutes after that we were past the breakwater and headed out to sea. Since our destination was fifteen miles off the coast, we wouldn't be able to see it for some time yet so the horizon was unbroken unless we looked sternward, where the mainland began to shrink to a thin dark line in the distance.

Black Island was first explored by colonists from Newport in 1649. Although there was evidence that it had been visited by the

Niantic Indians, it was totally uninhabited when Jebediah Black landed and claimed it. Black established a small community largely with members of his own family and it was known as Black's Island until sometime during the 18th Century when the possessive was dropped. The Blacks were an enterprising group who engaged in fishing and hunting and some legitimate trade although the bulk of their income probably came from smuggling and piracy. The latter often involved driving captured ships onto the rocks that fringed the north side of the island, although some of the many ships who died there were probably legitimate salvage. The lighthouse wasn't built until the 1830s. The British attempted to capture the island as a base during the American Revolution, but were lured onto the rocks, suffered some damage, and decided to try elsewhere.

The Black family eventually died out but the name stuck. The population had stabilized at around five hundred. There was a limited tourist trade from July through September, but since the park and wildlife preserve gobbled up almost half of the island's seven square miles, there wasn't enough room to develop a more robust industry and most of the residents were relatively poor. The waterfront was beautiful, however, so tourists still came over in large enough numbers to make the local economy viable, although many of the residents spent their winters on the mainland. The rest hunkered down to wait out the icy squalls and frequent windstorms that swept in from the ocean. Poaching was the most common crime. There were deer in the preserve, although not many anymore.

The first signs of tension among us showed up early. Tina and Herman Brubaker went inside, Tina to sulk, Herman looking for coffee for himself and his wife. Barry was sporting a white captain's cap which made him look rather silly and was striking a pose on the forward deck; at least he was until the promised wind snatched it away. I was tempted to yell "Hat Overboard" but refrained. Dusty was talking to a foursome that I correctly identified as Dennis Malden and his date, whose name I still hadn't caught, and Emily Grainger and her date, whom she'd introduced as Ashley Sternberg. James Brock, our newest hire, was standing by himself glaring around as though he thought the whole idea of traveling over water was somehow offensive. Merrilee had told me that she was probably going to let him go after his thirty day trial. "There's something very angry inside that boy and I don't want to be around when it all comes boiling out."

Eric Rogers and Claire McCurdy were on the level above us, Claire hanging onto her dark red hair as the wind tried to undo her efforts to keep it in order. They were both employees but had been dating since before we hired them. He was almost as dark as Merrilee and kept his hair cut so short he might as well have shaved his head. I'm not sure where the bride-and-groom-to-be spent the trip; they must have found a secluded corner somewhere. Carl Celluci had gone down to stand near the stern railing, still puffing on his pipe; Maria Gomes joined him after a while, although they didn't seem to be talking. Dusty and Merrilee and I sat in a little open air lounge facing sternward where we could enjoy the brisk air without being blown around.

"Are they a couple?" I asked Merrilee, glancing toward the stern.

Merrilee made a sound halfway between amusement and disgust. "No, but not because she hasn't tried. She makes cow eyes at him all day and used to find excuses to go to his cubicle until I told her to knock it off."

"Not his type, I suppose. She's not unattractive."

"His heart belongs to another. Unfortunately, the other is getting married tomorrow."

"Laura?"

"The one and only. They dated a few times before we hired Kevin but I think she was already looking around. Laura was on a short leash with her parents until she finally found the courage to move out. She wasn't looking for another dad."

"And Carl wanted to be the boss," suggested Dusty.

"Absolutely. Always thinks he knows best and can't understand why anyone would disagree. Every once in a while he tries to tell me how I could manage people better." She sighed. "But he's our most productive worker. Took to the job right away."

"I imagine it gives him a feeling of power. Some of those people are trying to stay hidden but he comes along and exposes them in a matter of minutes."

"He probably tells his friends he's a private detective," said Merrilee, chuckling. "If he has any friends, which I seriously doubt."

Herman showed up with two Styrofoam cups of coffee, both black. "Sure I can't get you two something? They have donuts and pastry." He slapped his ample belly. "Which didn't tempt me at all, of course."

It was just about then that Carl Celucci turned toward Maria Gomes and said something we couldn't hear. Whatever it was, she raised the back of one hand to her mouth, then turned and fled somewhere out of sight. It was definitely fleeing, even though she didn't run. I could tell by the set of her shoulders and they way she kept a hand in front of her face that she was upset.

"Looks like there's trouble in paradise," said Dusty.

"If things go badly this weekend, just remember that none of this was my idea." I meant it humorously but just at that moment I was very close to serious. If I'd known just how badly things were going to go, I might have jumped overboard and risked swimming back to shore.

The second sign that things weren't destined to be idyllic occurred while Captain Wayne was negotiating the wharf at Blackston, the only settled area on the island. The view had been picturesque as we approached but once we were close enough to see details, it became obvious that the village was not as prosperous as it might have been. There were maybe a dozen shops facing the ocean but at least half of them had yet to open for the tourist season and one of them had boarded windows that appeared to be there for the long term. I could see two hotels, both small, but Dusty told me that the Breakwater was not accepting guests until the end of the month. There was a crew washing windows on the Oceanview, presumably so that it could live up to its name.

Kevin and Laura had emerged from wherever they had been hiding and were standing not far from us. Except for Carl and Maria, everyone had come forward to watch the docking procedure, even Tina. Emily Granger and her friend were quite close to us but to one side, so I think I was the only one who noticed that Ashley was staring daggers at Kevin. That puzzled me because as far as I knew they had never met, but since Ashley didn't work for me, I decided it wasn't a problem worth worrying over. So much for my keen detective instincts.

Dusty and I lingered while the others went ashore, waiting for a chance to thank Captain Wayne for what had been a reasonably smooth trip, considering the weather. She was noticeably more relaxed when she was finished with whatever captains do and I attributed this to the fact that none of us had gotten seasick and vomited all over her spotless decks. She confirmed that she'd return by ten in the morning on Monday to take us back, weather permitting. "We 're looking at some possible squalls around then but if there's anything serious I have Ms. Rhodes' cell phone number. Reception out here is spotty but I can always leave a message at the Beachcomber office."

The unimaginatively named Beachcomber Cabins was where we would all be staying.

We variously carried or trundled our bags over a stretch of cracked pavement that led up to the main road. It was probably called Main Street but I never found out for sure because there were no street signs. Dusty led us along the road to our left and up a little rise. I glanced back at that point and saw the *Calamity Jane* already moving back toward the open ocean. For a brief moment I felt as though we'd been deserted like convicts set ashore in Australia a couple of centuries earlier. Then we were headed down the gentle slope as it curled around a stand of tall trees and back toward the shoreline. There were a couple of structures half hidden there, including a diner – "open every day 6AM-10PM" – that currently had no customers.

At the foot of the hill was a narrow dirt road with a sign reading "Beachcomber Cabins". There was a smaller neon sign over the office door, but it wasn't operating. We could see the cabins scattered around through a couple of acres of pine trees, fairly widely separated from one another. Each cabin was actually a duplex, two complete units equipped with propane stoves and small refrigerators. Bathrooms were separate, one sitting at each end of the property. There were ten duplexes arranged in a roughly crescent shape, and they alternated facing north and south vs east and west. We were taking six of them, although two units would be empty. None of us were in the four duplexes closest to the street, but only three of those units were occupied. I noticed a man with a heavy beard glaring at us from the unit closest to the office, but he disappeared a moment later.

Steve and his uncle were waiting for us inside. Although he'd only been out here for a couple of days, Steve already looked noticeably more tanned than when I'd last seen him. There was a good deal of family resemblance. His Uncle Ted looked like an older, grayer, but more relaxed version of my receptionist. He greeted us heartily, asked if we'd had a good trip out, and except for a fleeting moment when he seemed to be distracted, he radiated charm and cheeriness. "You folks will be in units three through eight. 8B is empty and 4b is closed up until I can get the roof patched. Had a big tree limb come down in a storm this past winter. The rain ruined the kitchen before I got the hole plugged."

I thought we were just going to grab keys at random, but Ted Welch handed them all to Dusty, who pulled a diagram out of her bag. It showed the layout of the cabins and had names typed next to each . "All right, boys and girls, here are your room assignments." She called off names while Ted Welch issued keys and I felt like I was back at summer camp. She'd given some thought to the arrangements though. Kevin was in 3A by himself. Laura was temporarily in 3B with Maria Gomes, although she'd change rooms after the wedding. This wasn't prudishness; it was tradition. Or at least so I had been told.

Brock and Celluci – both unattached males - would share 4A, the undamaged side of that cabin. Dusty and I were in 5A and the Brubakers in 5B. Barry and Tina each had one side of building 6. That put all of us old fogies squarely in the center and made me feel like a chaperone. Emily Grainger and Ashley Sternberg had 7A while Dennis Malden and Donna Goodrich – I surreptitiously added her name to my index card when she was identified this time - would be in 7B. Eric Rogers and Claire McCurdy rounded out our group in 8A. Brock didn't look happy, but then he hadn't stopped scowling since he'd arrived at the dock on the mainland. Everyone else seemed pleased if not actively excited, except Tina who was obviously feeling awkward and out of place.

Once she had finished, Dusty pinned the diagram to the bulletin board on the office wall.

"Maybe we should have let Tina bring her laptop," I whispered to Dusty.

"Stay strong. It's for her own good. Think of it as an intervention."

The cabins were nicer than I expected, though a bit musty. Each front door opened onto a roomy sitting room with seats for half a dozen people. Each had a fake fireplace. No television. No telephone except a pay one in the office. There was a small kitchenette to the left in our unit, but in some it was on the right. Two small bedrooms filled the back corners with a large storage closet between and smaller ones elsewhere. No bathrooms, but there were showers in the two restrooms. The beds were king sized so we could sleep together or separately as the mood struck us. I was pretty sure I knew how the mood would strike us. Everything was clean and in a good state of repair, although some of the chairs could have used reupholstering. There were pictures on the walls, all prints of sailing ships or seagulls.

We unpacked and put everything away. There was supposed to be a laundromat nearby but we had enough clothes with us to last until we got home. I had brought along a couple of books to read and I'd noticed that the bookstore back in the village was open for business, so I had a fallback. I looked through the cupboards in the kitchenette and found what you'd expect, some battered but serviceable cookware, a half dozen plates that matched and a dozen assorted coffee mugs and drinking glasses which did not. The silverware was made in Taiwan. The refrigerator was empty, there were posted instructions for operating the propane stove, and there was even a small microwave oven.

It took Dusty a little longer to unpack, not because she had brought a lot more things, although she had, but because she didn't believe in haphazardly unloading suitcases into drawers and onto hangers. There had to be a system to it and sometimes it took her awhile to figure out what that system should be. But she emerged at last, looking pleased with herself.

"So what's on the agenda for the rest of the day?" I asked.

"We're all pretty much on our own. The wedding party is supposed to have a rehearsal at the chapel, but that won't take long. Uncle Ted is going to organize a campfire when it gets dark and tell us stories about the island." Dusty had made Ted Welch her honorary uncle at some point. "I suggest we do the tourist thing in the village."

I was amenable if not necessarily excited, and I also suspected it wouldn't take long. The problem with visiting out of season was that it was in fact out of season. The businesses patronized by the permanent residents would be open, but little else.

It was one of my more accurate predictions. There was a combination drug and grocery store that also sold alcoholic liquors under a special license from the state. Rhode Island normally required that food and strong drink be sold separately. The general store had a few items clearly aimed at tourists – embossed shirts and jackets, nautically themed knick knacks, salt water toffee, and so forth – but most of their stock was more practical. The diner was open for business and looked clean. The menu posted outside was uninspiring. The ice cream shop and four souvenir shops were closed. We spotted a bar down a side street, across from a moped rental place, currently locked up. A doctor, a dentist, and a realtor shared what looked to be a converted house. The visitors' center was closed and, ominously, there was an emergency room right across the street.

They were still working on the windows at the Oceanview. We peeked into the lobby, which was deserted except for a bored looking desk clerk. The book store was tiny but had an interesting assortment of titles and I noticed they had the morning papers from the mainland. Another side street offered a gift shop specializing in Polynesian style items, a branch bank with an ATM in the lobby, and a barber shop. Excuse me, a hair salon.

The fanciest restaurant on the island was The Moby Dick, which wasn't serving until evening. Its only real competition was The Pirate's Den, which had opened at noon. Both had posted menus, dominated by sea food. There was also a sandwich place where Dusty and I had a surprisingly good meal. We decided to walk by the chapel on the way back, which would take us a little out of the way. The road was narrow, no shoulder, and some kind of tall grass grew prolifically on both sides so that it felt like we were passing through a tunnel.

The village was quaint and faintly rundown but the island itself was beautiful. I had just made a rather uninspired comment about the ability of humanity to turn beauty into ugliness when we stumbled onto a perfect example of the latter. Because the road curved so sharply, we could hear someone coming our way before we could see them.

"At least she's with her own kind." It was a male voice, thick with anger.

"But they're just not right for each other. He's smart and funny and she's just a stick in the mud." Female, also angry. "And she's going to marry someone else anyway, so why doesn't he just get over it and move on?"

Dusty and I had both unconsciously slowed down, but the other couple had no idea that we were there and we all sighted each other simultaneously. It was Maria Gomes and James Brock, who were not a couple insofar as I knew. Brock was a big guy, heavier than I am and almost as tall with his light hair cut short. I would have described him as ruggedly handsome but somewhat aloof. He was the one Merrilee was probably going to let go. Maria had been with us well over a year. She was the classic introvert, quiet, somewhat withdrawn, good at her work. They stopped talking as soon as they saw us. Maria looked guilty, James belligerent. We nodded greetings as we passed but no one spoke.

"What do you suppose that was all about?" asked Dusty as soon as we were safely out of earshot.

"Someone's not thrilled about the wedding."

"She's not, but he wasn't talking about the same people."

"Young love. Who can fathom its mysteries?"

She punched me on the arm and we went on.

The chapel was a bit shabby on the outside, although this was mostly masked by the vines and shrubbery that covered everything except where they'd been trimmed back from the windows. The doors were open, however, so we stepped inside. An older woman was vacuuming the carpet but she paid us no attention as we looked around. The interior was much nicer, tastefully done with a small, relatively plain looking podium. The windows were clear glass but there were some nice paintings, or prints, on the walls, none of them with obvious Christian motifs but more an air of generic mystical spirituality. I estimated that the pews would hold fifty people, which was more than enough for our group. Dusty nodded approvingly.

The rest of the wedding party arrived a few minutes later, and Chaplain Morrison arrived and explained the choreography. It took about fifteen minutes and then we all drifted off.

Dusty and I stopped back at the cabins briefly. Steve was in the office – he was staying with his uncle in his house a short distance away from the camp. There were no ramps for his wheelchair but the ground here was hard enough that he had no trouble getting around. "I can't really use the beach though. Not enough traction. "

"We could push you," I offered.

He laughed. "We tried that once. It took four able bodied men to get me back to solid ground. Thanks anyway."

We hadn't seen the beach yet so we walked past our cabin and down a very gentle slope that suddenly became very steep. The water was closer than I'd realized and judging by the curve of the beach had obviously carved away a considerable piece of land. It was one of two usable beaches on the island, although there were so many rocks that you had to be cautious in the water. The other one ran in front of the two hotels, not surprisingly. The Brubakers were sitting in adjacent lounge chairs and both appeared to be napping. Barry Shaw was wading and talking to Emily Grainger and Ashley Sternberg. Eric Rogers and Claire McCurdy were lying on a blanket and I could see Dennis Malden and Donna Goodrich walking along the shore in the distance.

Barry spotted us and came out of the water. I have to admit he looked pretty good in a bathing suit, at least for an accountant. I always though accountants were supposed to be wimpy and pasty white. Barry looked fit and energetic, and I'd have sworn his skin was already perceptibly darker than it had been when we arrived.

"Where's Tina?" I asked. "Not moping in her room is she?"

"I don't think so. The love birds collected her for lunch. I haven't seen any of them since."

"It looks like everyone's enjoying themselves," said Dusty.

Barry blinked. "Well, almost everyone."

"Trouble in paradise?" I asked.

"The big blonde kid had words with the black one. I'm not sure what it was about but he stormed off in a huff. I thought there was going to be a fight for a few seconds. One of the girls went after him. I don't know her name either. The mousy one."

"We ran into them," I said.

"Then Celluci started sulking so hard that he might as well have had a sign around his neck. The fluffy blonde girl said something to him and he stalked off. Haven't seen him again either." The fluffy blonde was Claire. "And those two young ladies," Barry turned his head to indicate the pair he'd just left, "really like the bride-to-be but they aren't so fond of the groom."

    "I'm pretty sure they're a couple," said Dusty. "They might just be objecting to the latest manifestation of a patriarchal culture." She kept a straight face.

    "This was a little more intense than feminist unity." Barry laughed. "And they seem to tolerate me."

    "You're one of the bosses," I pointed out. "Don't confuse tactful self interest with approval."

    "I'm sure it was my natural charm that won them over." I didn't know a lot about Barry's private affairs. He had never mentioned having a woman in his life and I would not have been surprised to learn that he was gay. But he hadn't mentioned a man in his life either. I thought of him as pretty much self contained, almost asexual, which was almost certainly not true. I didn't think he'd try to hit on any of the junior employees, although he might flirt with them a little. It would be inconsistent with the image he was trying to project.

    We didn't have the beach entirely to ourselves. There was an older couple sitting under an umbrella and the man with the heavy beard had reappeared and was standing on top of a dune from which point he was, I suspected, clandestinely watching the females in our party. I took off my shoes and walked down into the edge of the water, but it was too cold and I beat a hasty retreat. Ashley and Emily had come back onto the sand by then and I noticed that neither of them was wet from the waist up. They were both shivering.

    The beach was well equipped. There were at least a dozen lounge chairs, each chained to a stake driven presumably quite deeply into the beach sand. There was a lifeguard's tower, currently unoccupied, set to one side with a good view down the length of the shore in both directions. The base of the tower was enclosed so that life saving equipment could be stored inside, although I didn't know that until later. Back at the tree line, a small trash dumpster sat in shadow beside a gravel road that ran behind the farthest cabin, down past the office, and eventually to the house where Steve was staying with his uncle.

    Dusty and I found chairs and she promptly went to sleep with her straw hat pulled down over her face. I tried to do the same but I was restless and decided to get one of my books and read for a while. The Brubakers were trudging back as well and Merrilee stopped and waited for me to catch up.

"I confess that I had my doubts about all of this, but everyone seems to be having a good time."

"Almost everyone," I said. "The new guy is upset about something."

"James." It wasn't a question; she knew I was talking about him. "I told you James is an angry young man. He has talents but I don't think he's a good fit for us."

"Why is he upset about Kevin and Laura?"

She looked surprised. "I wasn't aware that he was." I repeated the remark we'd overheard and she frowned. "He was talking about Eric and Claire. He doesn't approve." Her tone was caustic.

"Because it's interracial."

She nodded. "He's an odd duck. I don't think he minds working for me. His prejudice probably allows for exceptions to the rule. He might even have voted for Obama. But I suspect he doesn't hold with mixing."

"He'd better get used to it. What about Maria then? Isn't she supposed to be the maid of honor?"

"Oh, she doesn't have any problem with the wedding. She and Laura were college roommates and Laura got her the job with us. And she likes Claire too. I don't think she's bothered that she's with Eric. Her problem is Carl."

"Carl? The moody one?"

Merrilee nodded. "It's a lover's rectangle. Carl seems to have fallen for Laura, although I can't imagine why. They don't seem to have anything in common and she's never encouraged him, at least not that I know of. They went out a couple of times but it never seemed to get serious, at least on her part. But Carl doesn't like being denied anything he wants. I knew he was infatuated with her and I was actually surprised when he agreed to come out here, but maybe he's hoping everything will fall apart at the last minute."

I was beginning to see the light. "And Maria has the hots for Carl."

"She sure does. You should have been a detective."

"Has he encouraged her?"

"I doubt it. I don't even think he's aware of her interest. She's too shy to say anything outright."

"How about Emily and her partner? Barry says they aren't thrilled about the wedding either."

Merillee frowned. "I only met the Sternberg girl today, but Emily never seemed bothered about it. I haven't sensed any bad feelings between her and either half of the couple. They've always gotten alone all right at work."

"Maybe they just don't like having another sister subjugated to the Man."

Merrilee sighed. "Well, with any luck it won't matter much by this time tomorrow." She was right, but for the wrong reason.

I found my book and trudged back to the beach in time to witness some more drama. Dennis and Donna had returned from their walk, and Carl had reappeared as well. Emily and Ashley were back in the water, but only knee deep. Barry had gone over to talk to the bearded man about something, and the latter stood up abruptly and walked away, clearly angry. Barry stood with his hands on his hips, watching until the man was out of sight.

"What was that all about?" I asked.

"Just responding to some discourtesy." I could hear anger in his voice. I don't think I'd ever previously seen Barry more than mildly irritated. "The girls were being a little affectionate and our hairy voyeur called out something rude." He glanced back toward the water, where Ashley and Emily were now holding hands. "I don't think they heard it."

"We'll have to keep an eye out. I'm pretty sure he's staying in cabin nine." That was where he had been standing when we'd first arrived.

Carl had settled down beside Dennis and Donna and they seemed to be talking amicably. I was starting to feel apprehensive about the weekend. We had barely arrived and there were already multiple signs of discord. So far we had the four way lovers' problem, some racial tension, and a disapproving voyeur, not to mention Tina's potential meltdown and whatever bad feeling Emily and Ashley held about Kevin.

I settled down beside Dusty and opened my book. I think I managed about ten pages before I fell asleep.

I felt oddly disoriented when Dusty shook my arm to waken me. The sky was beginning to darken as clouds moved in and it was noticeably cooler. I sat up and looked around. Eric and Claire were rolling up their blanket. Carl was over near the lifeguard tower talking to James Brock. No one else was in sight.

"What's up?"

"You are, I hope. I let you sleep as long as possible but we need to get back. Campfire, remember?"

I stood up and stretched. "What are we doing for supper?"

"Toasting hotdogs over the fire. I knew you weren't listening when I told you all this."

"I was so confident that you had everything under control that I didn't feel I needed to be involved."

"Yeah, right."

It became decidedly chilly once we were out of the sun. I had wisely packed a sweater which I retrieved while Dusty changed from shorts to slacks. It was much darker under the trees and a handful of lights came on outdoors. When we went back outside, we found about half of our group standing around the large fire pit centrally located at a safe distance from the crescent of cabins. Ted Welch was down near the office talking to a policeman, whose car was parked in the driveway, and I felt a sudden rush of irrational anxiety. They were out of earshot but it didn't appear to be anything serious because the officer left a few seconds later.

Steve was apparently in charge of the logistics of firewood placement and the arrangement of the food on two long folding tables. There were two large bags of uncooked hotdogs, several packages of rolls, condiments, and several bowls of what turned out to be potato salad. His minions were Eric and Claire and, to my surprise, Tina. She was even smiling despite what was probably a bad case of digital withdrawal.

Uncle Ted started the actual fire which caught quickly thanks in part to a brisk little breeze. We were all handed freshly cut willow sticks with which to impale and cook our hotdogs. I started counting heads and noticed that Kevin, Laura, and Carl were still unaccounted for, a combination that troubled me mildly. Then I told myself that they were, after all, adults and that it wasn't my responsibility to worry about their social interaction. That didn't make me feel any better.

It was all quite festive. Barry sat flanked by Ashley and Emily and I wondered what strange chemistry was at work there. Tina and Claire somehow put themselves in charge of making sure everyone had what they needed. The rest had found comfortable places to sit before the fire reached its peak and had to retreat before the rising heat, but other than an occasional charred hotdog and one that fell into the flames, there were no mishaps. Tina started distributing marshmallows as the fire subsided, falling in on itself, and the last few pieces of wood were thrown in to keep it going.

Ted Welch was a natural born storyteller. He regaled us with a considerably enhanced version of the island's history, emphasizing the less reputable activities of the Black family. Some of it seemed pretty unlikely to me, but it made good theater. Then a voice called out requesting a ghost story, and to my mild surprise it was Carl who had spoken up.

Ted Welch paused and let his eyes pass over his audience. "Well, there is one legend connected to Black Island, but maybe I shouldn't talk about it. It happened right down there on the beach. I wouldn't want to scare you away."

Predictably this elicited a chorus of mixed catcalls and encouragement. It was obvious that he was going to tell the story, and this is the story he told, minus some flourishes I don't remember.

Jebediah Black was born in Plymouth shortly after the colony was founded in 1620. He was frequently in trouble with the local authorities all through his childhood and he left the colony when he was fifteen. He showed up in Providence in 1638 where he reportedly killed a man in a fight and ran off to live with the Pokanoset Indians. He lasted there for six months before offending the chief and fleeing to Newport, where he signed on to a merchant vessel trading between Newport and the Massachusetts Bay Colony. Apparently life at sea suited him and by 1645 he had his own ship, the *Freelancer*. There was ample trade at the time, but rumors persisted that he engaged in occasional acts of piracy.

Black and his crew were blown out to sea by a powerful storm in 1649. While making repairs to their rigging, they spotted the island which would eventually bear his name. Black found a sheltered cove – where the hotels would later be built - and led a party ashore. Having determined that the island was unoccupied, he moved his wife and children there from Newport, along with the families of most of his crew and a few other cronies he knew he could trust. There were less than a hundred settlers but the land was fertile, as were the women in the group, and within five years the population had doubled, the harbor was home to half a dozen ships, and Jebediah had become a relatively wealthy man.

Although the Black family and their followers fished and traded on a regular basis, there were growing rumors that some of the ships that ended up on the rocks on the south side of the island had been driven there deliberately after they were boarded, their crews murdered, and most of their cargo offloaded. The remarkable efficiency with which the Blacks recovered "salvage" from the wrecks was highly suspicious. There was talk of a punitive expedition but the larger colonies were all feuding with one another and concerted action was not a high priority. But then Jebediah made a mistake. He raided a Pequot village on the mainland and personally killed the sachem's son while trying to carry off the boy's sister, whom he fancied. Unfortunately, she also perished, shot down by one of the raiders before Jebediah could capture her.

The sachem, one Ninigret, was a wise and powerful man whose family had adopted the squid as a kind of totem. Ninigret beseeched the great sea spider to avenge his son's death. Jebediah was unaware of the curse that had fallen upon him, but one night he was walking along this very stretch of beach when a giant squid rose to the surface and dragged him under. In the morning, his sons came looking for him and found nothing except for the marks where he had been dragged through the sand to his doom.

"And to this very day," Uncle Ted concluded, "it is said that if a man who lusts after a woman to whom he has no right should walk this beach at night, he might well find that Ninigret's curse will rise from the sea and carry him away."

There was a brief pause before Ashley spoke up. "Would that include a man who won a woman's heart by lying about his past?" I saw Emily punch her friend on the arm and even in the dancing light from the fire I could tell she was embarrassed.

No one responded to the question and conversation became general again. The fire was dying quickly now and it was getting decidedly chilly. Dusty stood up and brushed off her jeans before raising her voice. "You're all on your own tomorrow, but I trust you'll all be on time for the ceremony." It was almost nine o'clock, fully dark, and about half the group started toward their respective cabins. A few others drifted over to the coolers where most of the ice had melted around bottles and cans of beer.

I didn't want another beer, but Dusty had gone off with Merrilee and Tina and I was restless so I wandered in that direction. Barry intercepted me. "We have an audience." He gestured with his head and I turned to look toward the office. For a few seconds I couldn't see anything unusual, but then there was movement and I realized someone was standing under a tree, watching us. "I think it's the guy with the beard again."

"He's staying here. We can't very well tell him to go away. He hasn't really bothered anyone, except maybe you."

"He makes my skin crawl."

Then raised voices caught our attention. I knew that Kevin and Laura had been living together for a while, and that she was staying with Maria Gomes temporarily as a nod to the tradition that the groom shouldn't see the bride the day before the wedding. She had gone off with Maria when things had started to break up, but Kevin had remained behind. He had had a couple of beers, but he wasn't even close to being drunk. Carl Celluci had also been drinking beer, but I'd noticed him sipping from a flask a couple of times and I assumed it was something with more bite. Although I couldn't see him, he was clearly having words with Kevin. I picked out his voice easily enough. It was brittle, high pitched, and excited.

I didn't find out until later what the argument had been about but I did see Kevin rear up and reach for Carl. Carl threw a punch, but he stumbled and it was nowhere near his target. Eric Rogers stepped between them quickly and said something too low for me to hear. James Brock seemed to appear out of nowhere and there was a scuffle of some sort. By the time Barry and I got there, Eric and James were glowering at one another, Kevin was rubbing the knuckles of his right hand and looking puzzled, and Carl was sitting on the ground shaking his head. He started to get up and staggered a bit. I caught his arm in part to steady him while Barry interposed himself between Carl and the others. I hadn't realized before just how slight Carl was; I doubt he weighed 120 and the top of his head barely cleared my shoulder. That didn't make him easy to handle though. He pulled away roughly and gave me a dirty look, but common sense must have finally prevailed because he dropped his arms and took a deep breath.

"This isn't over." It might have seemed melodramatic if Carl hadn't been slurring his words.

"Maybe we should all call it a night," I suggested as neutrally as possible.

Carl looked as though he wanted to argue further, but then he shrugged. "You caught me by surprise, Kevin, but I'll have my turn. The night is young." He started walking toward the cabins. I watched him while Ray convinced the others to go back to their rooms. I was still watching when Carl turned away from cabin four and took the path to the beach. I thought about going after him, but he was an adult, even if he didn't act like it. With luck, he'd sleep through the ceremony in the morning.

So I went to bed.

"What kept you?" asked Dusty.

"Nothing of any significance," I answered. But I was wrong again.

I had no trouble sleeping that night and as usual Dusty was asleep when I slipped out of bed and put on a robe and my sneakers. It was still cool outside but the wind had died so it was actually pleasantly invigorating as I walked to the restroom farthest from the office, wearing only a short robe and with a towel thrown over one shoulder. Inside were the promised showers but no hot water, and the usual array of sinks and toilets. James was lathering up at one of the sinks and mumbled a polite reply to my greeting. I shaved and took a quick shower – quick because it felt colder than the ocean had the evening before. Brock was gone by then but Kevin was looking at the other shower stall somewhat dubiously.

"Today's the big day," I said cheerily. I'm not at my witty best until I've had coffee.

Kevin nodded. "We really appreciate you going to all this effort, Mr.Birch. Laura said she wasn't interested in anything formal but I think she's really pleased."

"I hope you'll both be very happy."

When I stepped outside, I saw James leaning against a tree, smoking a cigarette. He had brought his clothes with him so he was completely dressed. I started to walk by but he straightened up. "Carl never came back last night."

I thought for a second. "Maybe he bunked with someone else." I realized immediately that wouldn't work. The only solo tenants were Barry and Tina, and I couldn't see either of them taking Carl in. But then it occurred to me that the couples would all have potentially had an empty bedroom. Dennis Malden and the two girls and or Eric Rogers might each have let him move in with them. For that matter, Maria and Laura probably slept separately. Laura obviously wouldn't share with Carl but Maria might well jump at the chance for a little snuggling.

I was concerned but not worried. Chilly or not, Carl could have slept outside. He'd had a lot to drink and might have passed out. I secretly hoped he'd be too sick to come to the wedding. If he made a scene it might make things memorable for all the wrong reasons. "Could be." James settled back against the tree and concentrated on his cigarette. I mentally ratified Merrilee's decision not to keep him on. He was too moody. It suggested an unnatural reserve, if not outright resentment.

Dusty was up when I got back. "How are the showers?"

"Cold."

She groaned. "Whose idea was this anyway?"

"Mostly yours." I pulled on my clothes and started for the door.

"Where are you off to?"

"Carl didn't go back to his cabin last night. I'm going to take a look around."

"He's probably sleeping off a hangover on the beach."

"That'd be my guess."

When I stepped outside, I saw Maria Gomes coming toward me, fully dressed. "Have you seen Carl this morning? I just spoke to James and he said Carl never came to bed last night."

"He probably slept on the beach. I was just going to go look."

"Why would he do that? It got really cold last night."

"He had a sweater, and he'd had more to drink than the rest of us. And it wasn't that cold." I found myself growing irritated not just with Carl but with Maria as well.

I started toward the path and she fell into step beside me. "Carl acts like a jerk some times, but he's really a good guy." I wasn't sure which of us she was trying to convince so I limited myself to an ambiguous grunt.

The beach was very much as we had left it but the tide was obviously near its high point. There was no one in sight, but if Carl was slouched down in one of the chairs, we might not have been able to see him. We had almost reached the nearest cluster of them when I noticed something sparkling in the sand ahead. Another few steps provided confirmation that Carl was not on the beach, and identification of the silvery object in the sand. It was a hip flask, probably the one Carl had been carrying the night before. I picked it up. The cap was off and it was empty.

I was so focused on the flask that I didn't notice the other odd feature until Maria let out a gasp. My eyes snapped up and I saw that a line of disturbed sand led from the side of one of the lounge chairs more or less straight toward the water, disappearing where the sand had been washed smooth. It looked very much as though some heavy object had been dragged down to the shore and into the ocean.

I remembered the ghost story Ted Welch had told at the campfire, suppressed a very brief surge of superstitious awe, and then smiled to myself. Someone, almost certainly Carl Celluci, was perpetrating a rather silly practical joke. Then I realized its only purpose could be to disrupt the wedding and I was no longer amused. I glanced at Maria and saw her staring out to sea, her face chalk white, and I realized her thoughts had run parallel to mine, except that she was stuck on the story of a vengeful sea creature. Young people are too gullible these days. I blame the internet.

"It's a prank," I told her as reassuringly as possible. "Uncle Ted made up that story. I think Carl is just trying to ruin the wedding."

She got back some of her color, but shook her head energetically. "He wouldn't do anything like that, Mr. Birch. I know he's cranky, but he's really nice once you get to know him."

"Well, I'm sure that he didn't get carried off in the night by a giant squid."

"Then where is he?"

"I have no idea. If he didn't stay here, he might have gone back into town and gotten a room at the hotel."

She pondered that. "Or he might have stayed with friends. He told me he knew someone who lived out here."

"See. Everything has a sensible explanation." I was relieved to see that her expression had changed from alarmed to puzzled.

"But where are his tracks? If he made those marks and then walked away, where are his footprints?"

I did some mental calculations. The tide had reached its high point sometime after we left the beach the previous day. It would have wiped out all of our tracks except those furthest from the water, including the area around the chairs. But except for the drag marks, the beach sand looked completely untouched.

"I can think of two explanations," I said at last. "He might have used something to brush away the tracks behind him when he left." I wasn't sure how good a job he could have done in the darkness. "It would have been even easier to make that trail down to the water, then walk along the wet part of the beach in either direction until he reached the rocks over there," I pointed to the right, "or the retaining wall for the town pier in the other direction."

Maria craned her head to examine each possibility. "I guess that would work."

I refused to let Carl's petulance take up any more of my time. "Aren't you supposed to be the maid of honor?"

She blushed. "Yes I am. It was really nice of Laura to ask me."

"Then shouldn't you be helping her get ready for the big day?"

"I guess so." She finally managed a smile. "Thanks, Mr. Birch. I guess I was just being silly." She turned on one foot and started back.

I stayed behind for another minute or two, staring at the tracks. I don't like pranks.

The wedding went without a glitch. The minister was young, friendly, and rather good looking. Dusty and I came to the chapel early to see if there was anything we could do and found Tina arranging flowers and actually talking to Reverend Morrison about something that didn't involve technology. Dusty double-checked the musical program, which meant making sure that she'd brought the CD she'd burned, and then joined me in the pew. The others drifted in well before the ceremony was due to start, most of them coming from breakfast at the nearby diner. Dusty and I had had coffee in our room, with some croissants we'd bought on the way to the *Calamity Jane*, which we had never gotten around to eating.

Maria came and got me when it was time. I was the surrogate father and gave away the bride. Laura was calm but seemed very preoccupied. Her eyes were red and I suspected that she had been crying, but it wasn't any of my business so I didn't ask. I managed to give her to Kevin without tripping and Dusty patted my knee approvingly when I returned to my seat. Ashley had a coughing fit and left early on and we didn't see her again until almost the end. The service was probably very nice, but I didn't hear much of it after that. I had a vague feeling of uneasiness that I would like to credit to my gift for uncovering the truth, but which was more likely the result of sleeping in a strange bed after witnessing a series of interpersonal tensions, followed by the still unexplained absence of Carl Celluci. I still believed that my proposed explanation was at least pretty close to the truth, but I had to admit there was a possibility that I was wrong. Carl seemed to me more confrontational than subtle.

The applause startled me out of a darker reverie and I rose with the others while the newly minted Mr. & Mrs. Wise left the chapel. As far as I could tell, Donna Goodrich was the only one who cried, which was rather odd since she'd met neither bride nor groom until the day before. There was no beribboned car to take them away on their honeymoon, but by unspoken agreement, we all let them walk back to cabin 3A, or wherever they decided to go, without an audience.

"So that's done." Dusty's voice betrayed a sense of relief that I shared. I had told her about the mysterious tracks on the beach and I was sure Maria Gomes had talked to some of the others, which probably meant that everyone knew my theory about Carl's practical joke. Except that I wasn't as confident now as I had been. What was the point if not to cause some disruption of the wedding, which had not in fact occurred?

Dusty and I went back to the campground with Steve but almost everyone else drifted off into the town to get lunch. I brought Steve up to date, but he didn't seem particularly worried. "I'll ask Uncle Ted to call the Oceanview and see if Carl checked in." Dusty went along with him but I walked down to the beach.

The water was higher and had wiped out more of the drag marks. The older couple was back and they were polite but cautious when I described Carl and asked if they'd seen him. "A half dozen young people came through a little while ago, but I don't think your friend was one of them." The man introduced himself as Norman Davies, a retired civil engineer. His wife Roberta nodded or shook her head and didn't speak a word while I was there.

"You might ask Mr. Reynolds. He spends a lot of time on the beach. He was here just a few minutes ago."

"I don't think I know him."

"Heavy set fellow. Doesn't talk much. Big, bushy beard."

"Oh, I think I have seen him."

"Not the friendly type, but he's always out watching people."

Dusty met me as I was walking back to the cabin. "No one checked in at the Oceanview last night except an Australian couple who came over in a private boat. But didn't you say he knew someone on the island?"

I had, but for the life of me I couldn't remember who had told me at that moment. I felt a sudden surge of frustration. "Carl had better have a damned good explanation if he wants to keep his job."

"Ted's going to call the police and ask them to keep an eye out. He'll turn up eventually."

It was as if she'd summoned him by invocation. Ted Welch rounded the corner of the cabin and waved as he approached. "I had a talk with Constable Parish. He said he'd keep an eye peeled for your wandering friend. I'm sorry if I started any trouble with my little ghost story."

"Don't worry about it, Ted." I was still feeling grumpy but it wasn't his fault. "I have a feeling this was all prepared in advance. If it hadn't been your story, we would have found a puddle of blood or something else to make us think something had happened. He just improvised."

Ted rubbed his chin. "I don't suppose anything's missing from his cabin? Something he would have to have taken with him? A change of clothing or something like that?"

"I don't know. The most likely explanation is that he's staying with a friend. He supposedly knows someone local."

"He did look familiar. I think I've seen him on the island before, but he never stayed here."

Past his shoulder, I saw a police car pull in from the road. "There's the police. Maybe they found him already."

They hadn't. Constable Parish had just stopped by to see if we had a picture. Obviously we didn't but I thought Maria might. "I'll ask her when she gets back."

Parish was a handsome looking man in his late-twenties, slender but well muscled. His manner was professionally reassuring but a bit distant. "I can't spare much time for this, I'm afraid. Except for a couple of part timers, I'm the entire police force and my job is mostly to herd drunk kids off the beaches, make the poachers keep their heads down, and hand out parking tickets. If anything more serious happens, the state police send out their launch."

"We appreciate your help, officer, and I'm sorry about the trouble. Carl has been going through some emotional trauma recently and I'm afraid it's affected his judgment." Why was I making excuses for Carl?

"It's no real trouble. Truth is things get pretty boring around here most of the time. Looking for a missing person will give me something to talk about for a while." He turned to Ted. "You mind fetching your master key, Ted? I'd like to take a glance at the boy's room."

"You know damned well it'd be just as fast to use a credit card to pop the lock," said Ted somewhat shamefacedly. "You broke into them often enough when you were a kid. They all have deadbolts for night time and I usually warn people not to leave anything valuable unattended."

Dusty spoke up. "Here comes his roommate. He'll have a key."

It was in fact James Brock, alone, walking rapidly with his head down. I don't think he even noticed us until he was almost within reach. "James, this is officer Parish. He'd like to take a look in Carl's room."

James looked a little uncomfortable, but he nodded. "Sure thing. I went in there this morning to see if he'd come back while I was asleep, but there was no sign of him."

He led the way and we all followed. Their cabin was much like our own, with the kitchenette on the opposite side. Both bedroom doors were shut and James hastily pointed to the one on the left. "That's where he was supposed to sleep."

Parish opened the door and stepped inside. From where we were standing we could see that there was some discarded clothing on the bed and a pouch of tobacco sat on a tiny night table next to a lamp, but the rest of the room was out of sight. The constable moved out of our line of sight for a moment, and then James stepped through the door and glanced around. I heard him inhale sharply.

Parish came back into view, his expression neutral. "Is something wrong?" he asked.

James hesitated. "I think someone's been in here since this morning. I remember his suitcase was in the closet, but now it's on the floor beside the bed."

Parish called from inside the room. "Are you sure of that?"

James seemed to gather himself together. "Yes I am. Someone must have moved it while we were at the wedding."

Parish reappeared and his expression was more serious. "I don't suppose you know anything about this?" He held up a handkerchief that was stained dark brown. There was a large fleur de lis in each corner.

"Is that blood?" asked Ted.

"Looks like," said Parish.

"Maybe he had a bloody nose. I know he had an allergy problem. He was taking something for it. He had a real bad sneezing fit yesterday."

"This was on the floor behind the bed. Was it here when you looked in earlier?"

James bit his lip. I had never seen him so ill at ease. "I don't think so, but it might have been. I just glanced around to see if he'd come back to change clothes or something. I'm sure about the suitcase though. It was definitely in the closet this morning."

Parish glanced in my direction. "I wouldn't get alarmed just yet but I think I'll look a bit closer when I do my rounds, ask around a bit. Can you talk to the rest of your party and see if anyone else has seen the boy?"

"Of course," I said. "They'll probably be coming back from lunch in fits and starts. I'll let you know if anything turns up."

Ted Welch was shaking his head. "I don't know. I don't like this. Don't you think we should call the mainland and get some help, Dan?"

Parish shook his head. "Not just yet. The boy is an adult. He might be playing a prank or he might just have gone off with his local friends. The only indication of foul play," he held up the handkerchief, "is pretty flimsy. I'll hold onto this for now though."

Nobody said much after that. Parish went back to his car and drove off. Ted muttered something about never having had trouble before and headed back to the office. Dusty and I walked over to the ash strewn fire pit. "You looked worried," said Dusty.

"I am a bit, and not just about Carl."

"James didn't want us in their cabin, did he?"

"No. And he was very relieved when we left."

"Do you think he was lying about the suitcase? Could he be in league with Carl?"

I shrugged. "Maybe. Or he might just have wanted to distract us so we didn't look too closely at something else."

The first group of people appeared a few minutes later. Tina was walking arm in arm with Ashley and Emily. I have absolutely no idea what Tina's sexual orientation might be. If pressed, I'd say she was asexual, although that's probably unfair. She never seemed to have time for emotions or personal alliances, but maybe that was just because she was wary of them. Ashley and Emily had no such compunctions. They were openly affectionate without being over the top. I found it rather refreshing. Dennis and Donna should have taken notes; I had seen his hand under her bikini top on the beach the previous day, although I had pretended not to.

Dusty waved them over. "What's up?" asked Tina, with an unfamiliar expression on her face that I realized was a smile.

"We're still looking for Carl. He hasn't turned up." I noticed a quick, surreptitious exchange of glances between the two younger women.

"Is that why the cop was here?" asked Ashley. "We saw him driving away."

"We've asked him to take a look around."

"You don't think something has happened to him, do you?" Emily's voice sounded odd, as though she were reciting a line rather than reacting spontaneously. "I mean, could he have gone in swimming and gotten carried away or something?"

I was about to say that an accident was a possibility but Dusty spoke up first, shaking her head firmly. "Apparently not. I asked Uncle Ted about that this morning and he says the current there isn't strong enough and there's some kind of reef just off shore.

If you throw something in the water along here, it always ends up back on the beach or floating in plain sight unless there's a strong wind or a storm, and last night was dead calm."

"We still think he's just gone off somewhere in a snit," I said. "But we need to know if any of you saw or heard anything during the night that might help us figure out where he is."

Emily and Ashley both shook their heads, but Tina spoke up. "Well, I don't know if it had anything to do with Carl, but there was certainly a lot of running around going on after I went to bed."

"Oh?" Dusty and I sounded off in stereo. Emily and Ashley immediately looked so guilty it was almost comical.

"What kind of running around?" I asked.

"Well, someone ran past my door crying. And two other people were arguing. And then I heard a door slam. And someone else was swearing. I don't sleep very well when I'm not home."

"Whoa! Who were these people and when did all this happen?"

Tina looked flustered. "I don't know who they were. I was half asleep. It was a woman crying, and I think it was a guy swearing."

"What time was this?"

She screwed up her face. "I think the crying was pretty early. Before midnight anyway. I don't know when the rest happened. I don't have my alarm clock with me."

Tina was sounding a bit stressed so I forced myself to answer calmly. "Well, it's probably not important, but if you remember anything else, please let me know."

"Right, boss." But her smile was gone. Ashley took her arm and the three of them walked away.

Dusty looked up at me. "You think something happened to Carl, don't you?"

I thought about it. "I'm not sure if Carl is the one we should be worried about, but yes, I think something happened last night that shouldn't have."

Dennis, Donna, Eric, and Claire arrived next, all in a group. Dennis was talking animatedly to Claire, and I sensed that both Eric and Donna were a bit uncomfortable. I couldn't read Claire at all. Merrilee had almost let her go at the end of her probationary period because she had occasional days when she couldn't seem to concentrate on her work. There hadn't been any viable candidates to replace her at the time so her probation had been extended. Eventually she'd knuckled down although she was still our least productive employee.

None of them could tell us anything about Carl, and none of them would admit to being out of their cabin after the campfire party had broken up. The Brubakers were next. "We were asleep ten minutes after we reached our room." Merrilee suggested getting everyone together and threshing things out but I talked her out of it.

"We don't want to make this bigger than it already is."

Maria Gomes straggled back at the end. She told us that Kevin and Laura had gone straight to their cabin and as far as she knew hadn't moved since. For obvious reasons, we decided not to knock on their door.

"Did you hear anything unusual last night, Maria?" asked Dusty.

"Like what?" She looked apprehensive, but not guilty.

"Anyone up and about. A couple of people said they heard voices."

"I don't think so. Laura and I stayed up for a while. She had the last minute jitters. You know, her last night as a free woman. She isn't used to alcohol, I guess. She was a little weepy."

"So what time did the two of your call it a night?"

"Oh, about ten o'clock I guess, or a little later. I was pretty tired so I gave up first. Laura said she was going to take a short walk outside to clear her head and I went to bed. I fell asleep so fast I never even heard her come back."

I was tempted to roust out Mr. & Mrs. Wise, but decided it could wait. If something had happened to Carl, it was too late to do anything about it now. If he was all right, he wasn't being held prisoner by two newlyweds even if they did have good reason to be annoyed with him. Dusty tapped my arm. "How about we go get something to eat?"

"Good idea."

We had a nice lunch but I was edgy. I had the feeling that things were happening just beyond the limits of my perception. Carl had disappeared sometime after ten o'clock and before dawn. There had been several people out and about during the critical period.

Tina had heard more than one and we knew that Laura had gone for a late night walk. Kevin, who had the most obvious reason to resent Carl, was staying alone and could easily have slipped out. So could James Brock who would have been alone if Carl was out on the beach. And I hadn't specifically asked the others if they'd remained together after the party broke up.

As soon as we got back I told Dusty I was going to knock on the door of cabin 3A but it turned out to be unnecessary. Kevin, wearing a bathing suit and clogs, was just coming out. "Good morning, Mr. Birch." He didn't sound particularly elated for a newlywed, but then again, he and Laura had already been living together for several months.

"Afternoon, actually. Kevin, I need to talk to you and Laura."

His eyes immediately became wary. "Why? What's happened?"

"I'm not sure. Maybe nothing, but Carl didn't sleep in his room last night and no one has seen him yet today."

Kevin nodded. "I noticed he wasn't at the chapel."

"Did you expect him to be?"

"Not really. He wasn't very happy about us. Laura and I. It wasn't so bad before even though we were together, I guess, because he figured we might split up and that he'd have a shot. He never had a chance though. Laura thinks he's creepy, but then she feels guilty about feeling that way so she was extra nice to him to compensate. And then he misinterpreted that and thought he still had a chance and that creeped her out even more."

"I sympathize, but there's a chance that he hasn't just one off in a huff so we need to talk to everyone. Is Laura inside?"

He shook his head. "No, she went down to the beach a few minutes ago. I'm supposed to bring the towels." They were folded under his arm. "I'm sure she doesn't know anything."

"How about you? Were you out of your cabin any time last night?"

"No, I went straight to bed after the party. I'm not a big drinker and I was a little tipsy." Kevin's eyes had skittered away and I knew he was lying.

"Are you sure? Could you have stepped outside for a smoke or gone to the restrooms?"

"I stopped on my way to the cabin, and I quit smoking a couple of years ago."

"You didn't hear anything during the night? People talking outside, anything like that?"

"No, I pretty much passed out."

He spoke with more confidence, but he wasn't telling me the truth. "Well, let's go see if Laura knows anything." And we walked down to the beach in silence.

The Brubakers were back in their preferred seats. The bearded man – Reynolds - was down beyond the lifeguard's tower staring out to sea. Eric and Claire were lying on a blanket but they weren't talking. Claire was reading a magazine and turning the pages with a quick flipping motion that suggested restrained violence. Laura was down at the waterline, arms wrapped around her shoulders. The waves splashed her feet and she retreated slightly but didn't change position otherwise.

Kevin called her name and beckoned to her when she turned. She seemed almost reluctant, particularly when she saw me, but her face was neutral.

"Mr. Birch wants to know if we saw or heard anything last night. Carl's gone missing." Kevin blurted it all out quickly, as though he wanted to warn her of something.

"Kevin was pretty angry when he left the campfire last night," I said.

Laura had a mildly hunted look but she nodded. "He wasn't happy about Kevin and I getting married. I never encouraged him, honest, but we dated a few times before I started going with Kevin and I guess he just couldn't let go."

"Did you talk to him later that evening, after the rest of us went to bed?"

She shook her head. "Absolutely not. I never said a word to him after we got off the boat." Her chin was up and her eyes locked on mine. I was pretty certain she was telling the truth, at least at the moment.

"Did you see or talk to anyone else later on? Maria said you went for a walk."

"I couldn't sleep. I know it's silly but I was nervous about the wedding."

"Did you walk down to the beach?"

"No," she answered quickly. "There are no lights down there. I walked along the coast road away from the town center, then came back the same way. I stopped and had a quick shower, then came back to the cabin and went to sleep."

"And you didn't see anyone else?"

"I heard voices from over near the office building but I don't know who they were."

"Male or female?"

She shook her head. "They kept their voices low. It was pretty late by then."

"What time was all this?"

She thought about it. "I think I went out around ten. When I came back to get a towel for my shower, Maria was asleep, but it must have been close to eleven by then. It probably took me about fifteen minutes to wash and dry myself. Maybe a little more. What's this all about?"

"Carl is missing. The favored theory right now is that he's pouting somewhere or trying to scare us, but there's always the chance that there's been some kind of accident."

"I'm sorry. I don't know anything else and I'm not feeling very good. I think I'll go back to the cabin and lie down for awhile."

"What's wrong?" asked Kevin with obvious concern.

"Nothing. Just a headache." She walked off.

Kevin hesitated a minute. "I'd better go check on her," he said apologetically. And he left as well.

Thoroughly frustrated I went back to my cabin to vent my feelings but Dusty wasn't there, so I wandered over to the office instead. Steve was behind the desk with his uncle. They both had serious expressions. My immediate reaction was to assume they'd heard something dire about Carl, but I was wrong. It was another guest they were worried about.

"Mrs. Sanford over in cabin two has been complaining about Mr. Reynolds in cabin nine," explained Steve.

I drew a map inside my head. "They're about as far away from one another as they could be."

"Not far enough," said Ted with a sigh. Oliver is a little strange but he's been staying with us so long he feels like family. And he pays the rental fee every week and in cash. It's almost the only income I've got during the winter."

"He stays here in the winter?"

Ted nodded. "Oliver's been staying here for almost two years. He's a native. Used to have a house out near the lighthouse. Sold it after his daughter died. Terrible thing. She had a boyfriend on the mainland and used to take their skiff back and forth all the time. She was a pretty little thing. Half the eligible bachelors on the island were in love with her. One day she went to see him up on the mainland and never came back. The boyfriend told the police she'd never shown up. They found the boat adrift a couple of days later but the body was never recovered."

"Was there any suspicion of foul play?"

Ted shook his head. "I guess they questioned the boyfriend but he stuck to his story. A couple of people claimed to have seen a couple that looked like the two of them at a coffee shop, but they couldn't be sure and the waitress didn't remember them. Oliver took it pretty hard. He shut himself up for three or four months, then got arrested for attacking some tourist down in the village. Called him a murderer. It was a complete stranger though, down from Canada. The second time it happened, they made him see some doctors on the mainland and they put him in some kind of hospital. A few months later he was back home, but it was like someone had cut out the core of what made him a person. He sold the house and everything else and asked me to rent him a cabin, both sides. He uses one to store everything he kept when the house was sold. He's been here ever since."

"Is he the man with the bushy beard?"

"That's Oliver. Spends most of his time pretending to be a beachcomber or sitting in his cabin. Doesn't talk much and when he does, he's usually arguing with somebody. I discourage him from going down to the beach when people are around. Sometimes a young girl flirting with someone will set him off."

"Has he attacked anyone else?"

"No, he seems harmless. But sometimes his language is a bit, uh, rough, if you know what I mean. And Mrs. Sanford has sensitive ears, I guess."

"How long are they staying?"

"Till the end of the week. I guess I'll have to try to talk to Oliver. He was a real pain during the season last year. I had three of four complaints. If it happens again, I'll have to tell him to go someplace else. Hate to do that though, and not just because of the money. He used to be a really nice guy. Maybe I should have the constable try talking to him. They were pretty close at one time. Oliver half raised Mitchell when his dad died. The mother was a lush. They haven't been as close since Mitchell became constable but I'm sure they're still friends."

I asked if he had heard anything from Constable Parish about Carl. "Nope. He called a while ago to ask if anything had turned up here and I told him no."

"This moved past the amusing stage a long time ago. I apologize for any trouble we're causing. Carl is going to be in big trouble when he gets back."

Steve looked up at me. "Do you really think he's coming back?"

"I hope so, because if he hasn't been strangled already, I want to do the job myself."

I went back to my cabin. When Dusty showed up a few minutes later, I was sitting at the narrow table writing in a notepad. "What are you up to?" She sat down across from me.

"I'm trying to come up with a timeline."

She was quiet for a few seconds. "So you really do think something has happened to Carl?"

"Don't you?"

It took another few seconds, but she nodded. "I don't know him that well, but I recognize the type. If it was a prank, he'd have shown up by now to see how we were reacting. Carl is impulsive, emotional, and lacks discipline. He wouldn't be able to stay away."

"That's what I think too."

"Do you think he's dead?"

"I hope not." But I wouldn't have given odds on it.

"So what do we know?"

"Not an awful lot. Sometime between 8:30 and 9:00, Carl left the campfire and went down to the beach. He probably never came back to his cabin, but we can't be sure of that. Between 10:00 and 11:00 Laura went for a walk. According to her, she headed up towards the farms on the east end of the island, then came back, retrieved a towel from her cabin, and took a shower before going to bed. No one else has admitted being outside from that point on –

although we haven't specifically asked everyone. Tina heard an argument and someone else crying but she doesn't remember what time or in what sequence, both probably after midnight. This morning Maria talked to James and found out that Carl hadn't come back to the cabin. She and I went down to the beach and found his flask and drag marks leading down to the water. Everyone except Carl attended the wedding from about 10:00 until almost noon, after which we asked Ted to notify the local police. The constable found what appeared to be a bloody handkerchief in Carl's room, and James insists that someone had moved things while we were all at the chapel."

"Not much to go on." She let out an unhappy sound. "If you're right, you realize that this means someone in our group might be a murderer."

"Not necessarily." I told her about Oliver Reynolds. "I don't want to go around pointing fingers at anyone, but apparently he has a recent history of violence directed toward young men Carl's age. And I suppose for completion's sake we should include the Sanfords and Uncle Ted on the list of potential suspects."

"Not much to go on."

"No. I think I'm going to have to talk to everyone again. For one thing, Laura was lying earlier. "

"Do you think she saw something while she was out walking?"

"I don't know, but she was hiding something. I think she needs to realize this is serious."

Dusty came with me. Kevin answered the door when we knocked and we could see Laura sitting at the table inside. She looked upset. Kevin clearly didn't want us to come in but he couldn't think of a good reason to refuse and I suspect he was so used to deferring to me that it was hard for him to break the pattern. Laura glanced up and then quickly down.

"We need to talk."

Kevin closed the door behind us. "Laura's not feeling well. Can't this wait until later?"

"Later she might have to talk to the police. I thought it might be less stressful if we did this informally."

Laura's head snapped up and I could see the fear in her eyes, but she remained silent. "Have they found him yet?" asked Kevin.

I gave him a hard look. "Are you expecting them to?"

He recovered quickly enough. "Sooner or later he'll have to come out of hiding. He's not planning to spend the rest of his life on this island, is he?" The words were right but the tone was wrong. Kevin knew more than he was saying. I think that was the moment when I realized that Carl Celluci was dead. It had seemed likely earlier, but now I was certain.

"I think we all know that this isn't a practical joke. Something happened to Carl last night and both of you know something about it."

They didn't look at each other, which I thought was strange. Kevin finally answered. "It does sound bad. But neither of us knows anything else. We've told you everything."

Laura hadn't answered. Dusty reached across the table and touched her wrist. "Laura, do you have something to tell us?"

She recoiled as though she'd been burnt. Her head came up and her eyes were bright with tears. "I don't know anything! Just leave me alone!" And she stood up abruptly and crossed to the nearest bedroom, slamming the door behind her.

"I think you should go." Kevin was obviously trying to balance tactfulness around his boss with firmness in protecting his wife.

"You don't have to talk to us, Kevin, but the police won't back off."

He lifted his chin as we stood up. "We're not afraid of the police. We're not hiding anything."

I shook my head. "Even I can tell you're both hiding something and the police are a lot more experienced at this sort of thing than I am. What if Carl's still alive but because you wouldn't say anything he dies? How are you going to live with that?"

But at that point I don't think he was even listening to us anymore. "I think you should leave now."

"Well, that didn't go well." We had walked down to the beach for want of a better plan. There was a party of young people I didn't recognize playing some kind of ball game. The Sanfords were back, as were the Brubakers, all ensconced in chairs facing the ocean. I glanced down the beach but there was no sign of Oliver

Reynolds. I almost didn't see her but Maria Gomes was sitting on the sand huddled into herself. No one else from our group was present.

For want of anything better to do, I started toward Maria. Dusty surprised me by going off to greet the Sanfords. I squatted down beside Maria, who jumped a little, then gave me a tentative smile. "Oh it' s you, Mr. Birch. You startled me."

"Sorry. I understand you're fond of Carl." I deliberately used the present tense.

She gave a sort of half shrug. "He's okay. There's nothing going on between us though." There was the hint of a sigh at the end.

"He and Kevin didn't get along, I gather."

Maria laughed briefly. "They used to be friends until Laura left Carl for Kevin. I don't think Carl even cared about her really, but he didn't like someone taking something that he thought was his. I mean, Laura's a nice person and all that, but she's hardly a beauty and she's kind of, I don't know, repressed. She always feels guilty if she's having fun."

"Aren't the two of you friends?"

She made an uncertain gesture. "Sort of. I introduced her to Carl originally, before I worked for you, I mean."

I let almost a full minute tick by. "You said Laura went for a walk last night."

"Yeah. She was nervous about the wedding. Maybe she was having second thoughts." Maria unfolded her arms and grasped her knees. "Carl said something to her earlier that upset her. He probably made a last desperate effort to talk her out of it."

"She did seem a little withdrawn during the ceremony." She had stumbled on the way down the aisle and I'd caught her elbow. She'd been trembling.

"Kevin loves her. He'll be good for her."

"You were asleep when she got back?"

"Yeah, I guess so. We had separate rooms, you know? She might have slipped in before I dropped off but I don't think so."

"Any idea how late you were up?"

"The last time I looked at my cell phone, it was just half past ten. I don't think I lasted very long after that."

"How was she in the morning?"

"Scared. She was already up and dressed in her sweats when I woke. She said she'd gone jogging. She was all sweaty and went off to shower. "

"Did she say where she'd been?"

"No, just out running. I could tell she was a little on edge so I gave her as much space as I could."

"And you didn't go out last night at all?"

"No. I'm not good about going out at night by myself."

I couldn't think of anything else to ask her, so I stood up slowly. She stayed where she was. "Do you think something bad has happened to Carl, Mr. Birch?"

"I honestly don't know, Maria. Let's hope for the best."

"Yeah, that's about all we can do, right?"

I assumed the question was rhetorical.

Dusty must have seen me coming because she said something I didn't hear to the Sanfords and then started across the sand to intercept me. "How's Maria?"

I shook my head. "Pretty shaken. I think she fears the worst."

"As do we."

"How are the Sanfords?"

"Pleasant, and irritated. They were happy to tell me why."

"Reynolds?"

"Got it in one. It seems that Mrs. Sanford is a very light sleeper. She was disturbed last night by a string of foul language coming from just outside their bedroom window."

"Tina heard someone swearing as well. Mr. Reynolds may have had a busy night."

"And a long one. Mrs. Sanford went to the window and saw him standing just outside. He was facing away but she's convinced he was looking in through their window before she woke up."

"A Peeping Oliver?"

"Maybe."

"I don't suppose she knows what time this all took place?"

"It didn't occur to her to check." Dusty smiled. "But she woke up her husband and he says his watch read ten minutes after four."

"Mr. Reynolds is an early riser."

"Or a night owl."

"Did they confront him?"

"No. By the time Mr. Sanford got to the window, Reynolds was gone, and he didn't think it would be a good idea to go after him."

"Sensible man."

Constable Parish came by about mid-afternoon. Dusty and I were back in our cabin when we heard a knock. He was with Ted Welch. We invited them in.

"I've been asking around about your missing friend. I don't suppose anyone in your group can tell us who he knew locally?"

"I don't think so. You might ask Maria Gomes." I remembered now that she was the one who mentioned Carl had an island connection. "She was the closest to him."

"Steve already suggested that and we stopped to see her on our way here. She has no idea except that he mentioned once that he'd been out here a couple of years ago to stay with a friend. She doesn't think he's been back recently, until now anyway."

"One of the others might know something, but no one else was particularly close to him." Except Laura, I thought to myself. She had dated him for awhile and he might have told her. I'm not sure why I didn't say anything to Parish, but I found it hard to cast Laura in the role of murderer and was feeling illogically protective of her, even though she was obviously hiding something. I think I wanted her to have time to come forward herself, rather than have her break down in front of a police officer asking peripheral questions.

"How about family?" asked Parish.

"Merrilee might know. She hired him."

"And how can I get in touch with her?"

"Follow me."

The Brubakers were still on the beach, although they were gathering their things together when we arrived. I made the introductions. "Constable Parish is looking for some background information about Carl."

Merrilee looked Parish over as though trying to decide whether or not to hire him. "How can I help you?"

"Does he have a roommate or anyone back on the mainland that we could speak to? Someone who might know if he'd been planning to do a disappearing act?"

Merrilee shook her head. "He lived with two other young men when he first came to work for us, but that didn't last long. He changed his mailing address a few weeks after he started. As far as I know he was living alone."

"Do you know if his parents are still living in the area?"

"They relocated to Florida about a year ago. I don't think it was a close family."

"Any siblings?"

Merrilee shook her head. "He didn't list an emergency contact when he filled in his medical information. Told me no one cared whether he lived or died. I tried to get him to use his parents but he wouldn't tell me their address."

"You were his supervisor?"

"Indeed I am." The change of tense was emphasized but Parish ignored it.

"Has he ever done anything unusual before? Practical jokes, unexplained absences, anything like that?"

"Not to my knowledge. His attendance record was good and he was an above average worker. Rather moody at times and not particularly sensitive to other people's feelings, but I wouldn't say that he was actually cruel. Immature, I suppose, but he was more likely to blow up in someone's face than plot a devious way to get back at them."

"So you don't think this is all a prank?"

"No, I think something happened to the boy. Maybe an accident, maybe something more in your line."

Parish considered that. "Thank you, ma'am."

He asked if there was any way that I could get our whole party together. "I've got some questions but it would save time if I didn't have to ask them over and over again."

"We're supposed to hike over to the lighthouse this afternoon about four o'clock." That was only an hour or so away by now. "Just about everyone should be here."

"Except us," said Merrilee. "Herman and I are past our hiking days."

"We'll be assembling in front of the office. That's probably your best bet."

"All right, I'll stop by. Thanks again for your help."

Dusty and I were on our way back to our cabin when Dennis Malden intercepted us. "Hi, Mr. Birch. I wondered if I could talk to you for a minute."

"Sure," I answered. "What's up?"

There was an awkward pause which Dusty read correctly. "I have to change before we go hiking. If you gentlemen will excuse me?"

Dennis waited until she was out of sight and then spoke quietly and quickly. "I don't want to get anyone into trouble and this is none of my business, but I know people are started to get worried about Carl and I don't know if what I heard matters anyway but it might."

"Whoa! Slow down. Do you know something about what happened to Carl?"

"No, not really. But I heard him talking with someone last night."

"What time last night?"

"It was just before midnight. Donna was asleep but I had a headache so I got up to find some aspirin. It was in my backpack in the front room. I have sinus problems a lot so I always keep some with me. There was enough light from outside that I didn't need to turn on the lamp and I knew right where it was so I was taking it out when I heard them." He was still talking too fast but I didn't say anything this time.

"Who did you hear?"

"Two people talking as they walked past the cabin. It was a girl talking at first. I didn't hear all of it, but then she said 'You've always been an asshole, Carl' or something like that. Then she laughed, giggled really. Then I guess he answered but his voice was so low I couldn't make out the words. Then she said 'Maybe you're finally going to make yourself useful.' But by then they were moving away so I don't know if he answered or not."

"Did you see who the woman was?"

Dennis shook his head. "No. I looked out the window but they were behind the trees. There was something moving but I didn't get a good look."

"How about the voice? Do you know who she was?"

Dennis looked more uncomfortable than ever and shifted his eyes away. "I don't want to get anyone into trouble," he said again.

"If anyone gets into trouble over this, it won't be your fault. And you might be able to help us straighten things out."

"All right, but can you not tell anyone who told you?"

"Unless it's absolutely necessary, yes."

"Well, I'm not completely sure because they were sort of whispering but it sounded a lot like Emily."

Emily and her partner Ashley were about the last people I would have expected to find keeping company with Carl, but then again, I didn't know any of these people particularly well. I felt slightly guilty about that. After all, they worked for me and it wasn't as though I had scores of people to keep track of. I made a resolution to do better.

I left Dennis and went looking for Emily and Ashley, almost missed them as I took a shortcut through the trees to the beach just as they were walking back along the main path. I spotted them and shuffled across the sand, calling Emily's name. They both stopped and waited for me.

I hadn't had time to plan a strategy so I just asked Emily outright if she'd been out of her cabin the night before. She and Ashley exchanged wary looks. "I might have stepped outside for a few minutes," she admitted.

"You didn't meet Carl walking back from the beach?"

Ashley didn't react but I saw Emily flinch. "No," she said at last.

"Are you sure? Someone claims to have seen you with him just before midnight."

The two exchanged another glance. Something was definitely up. "Ashley was with me all the time last night, Mr. Birch. We were together from the time we left the party until we went to bed." Ashley nodded confirmation.

There was a precise, artificial manner in her speech that meant either that she was lying to conform to a pre-arranged story, or that she was treading a careful path so that she told no outright lies while omitting things she didn't want me to know.

"Emily, this could be very important."

I thought I sensed indecision, but Ashley reached over and took Emily's hand and the moment passed. It was Ashley who spoke up. "The two of us did leave our cabin last night. We were feeling hot and sweaty and we decided to go rinse off in the ocean. It was dark enough that we didn't bother with bathing suits, which is why we didn't want to talk about it."

Emily still didn't speak but I saw her suppress a guilty grin and decided this much, at least, was true. "Did you see Carl while you were there?"

Both shook their heads. "There was no one on the beach except us, Mr. Birch. At least, we didn't see anyone. But we were only there for a few minutes because the water was too cold."

"What time was this?"

"It was after eleven when we left the cabin. We weren't much more than a half hour."

"How about when you came back? Was anyone walking around near the cabins?"

They shook their heads. "We were only wearing towels so we weren't looking for company,' explained Emily.

"Did you come straight back up the path?"

Emily had a blank look which probably meant she wasn't sure how she was supposed to answer that question. Ashley, whom I now realized was the dominant member of the pair, filled in the gap. "No, we walked down the beach a way, almost to the lifeguard tower. Then we came back through the trees."

"But you're sure no one else was around?"

Ashley tried to look abashed but it didn't work. "We were kind of preoccupied with each other. I suppose someone else could have been there. But we didn't speak to anyone and no one spoke to us."

Emily nodded. I was tempted to push it, but I had the feeling that neither of them would budge from their story in the other's presence. It might be useful to get them apart on some pretext, but I suspected Ashley would be watching for that. "All right, but if you remember anything else you've forgotten to tell me, please let me know."

By now I was pretty sure that something bad had happened involving Carl Cellucci. He might have been the victim or the perpetrator, but I was leaning toward the former. I was also sure that some members of our little outing knew more than they were telling, if they weren't actively lying, and that last night had been more eventful than it had seemed. But it didn't follow from that that everything was related.

Dusty was in shorts, a halter top, and comfortable shoes when I arrived at the cabin. I changed my footgear while summarizing what I'd heard from Dennis, Ashley, and Emily. "They're obviously not trying to hide the fact that they're a couple," she observed. "But it sounds like they did a little more than just go skinny dipping. I did notice that they don't like Kevin very much."

"I wondered about that myself. Merrilee says he and Emily are fine together at work."

"So something happened recently."

"Or it involves Ashley somehow. Those two are tight but she's the one calling the shots."

"Did she know Kevin before yesterday?"

"I have no idea."

Barry, Tina, and the newlyweds were standing in front of the office when we arrived. The latter seemed to have regained their equanimity but neither of them would meet my eyes. Eric showed up without Claire, who had a headache, but otherwise only the Brubakers were missing. Black Island's only police cruiser pulled up while I was telling them that the constable wanted to ask a few questions before we left. Parish was looking a bit harried but he went out of his way to put people at ease. "I don't want anyone to start worrying unnecessarily because this could still simply be a misguided joke, but just in case your missing friend has had some kind of accident, I'd like to ask a few more questions."

"Could he have gone swimming and been swept out to sea?" asked Tina.

"It's not likely. The tides along this side of the island tend to throw things up on the shore rather than wash them away. I can't claim that it's impossible, but I'd say the likelihood is pretty low." Parish ran through approximately the same general line of questioning that I'd pursued already, and elicited the same answers. Ashley and Emily glanced at me before admitting that they'd gone down to the beach for a late night swim but insisted they hadn't seen or heard anything. Laura recited her story about her solitary walk and shower, but she looked pale, a detail I suspect Parish noted although he didn't pursue the issue. Dennis reluctantly volunteered a version of his own story, saying that he'd heard someone talking to Carl at around midnight but that he hadn't recognized the voice. He gave me an apologetic glance as he did so and I didn't give him away.

I paced back and forth behind the group because that sometimes helped me to think more clearly, and it was just by chance that I was passing the newlyweds when Kevin took out his handkerchief and blew his nose. It was a casual act, requiring only a few seconds, but it gave me a whole new bit of information to worry about. I was almost certain that the corners of his handkerchief were decorated with fleur de lis, just like the one Parish had found in Carl's bedroom.

Parish seemed to be running out of steam. "Did any of you notice anything else on the beach that was out of place?"

That's when I remembered Carl's flask. I must have put it in my room at some point, but I didn't remember seeing it after I'd picked it up from the sand. Maria had seen it as well but she seemed to have forgotten about it. I waved my hand and mentioned my visit to the beach with Maria. "I completely forgot about finding it, and I'm not absolutely certain it was his. At the time I had no reason to think anything was wrong. It's in my cabin somewhere."

Parish nodded. "Anyone else?"

We all looked at one another but no one volunteered.

"Can someone tell me what Carl was wearing when you last saw him?" Several people confirmed that he was dressed in cutoff jeans and a tee shirt, but there were some differences of opinion about the color of the latter.

"There has been some indication that Carl might have had friends on the island. Can anyone remember anything that he said that might help us identify who those people were?"

Maria raised her hand. "I don't know if it helps, but he told me he'd been out here a few years ago but hadn't liked it much. He isn't really an outdoorsy type person. I don't think it was a girl, but I'm not sure."

"Did he mention any names?"

She shook her head. "No. Not to me anyway. He might have said something to Laura."

All eyes were on Laura and Kevin. "No," she said promptly. "We didn't know each other very well."

Parish let a hint of frown cross his face. "Didn't you date him for awhile?"

Laura was suddenly flustered. "We went out a couple of times but we weren't really a couple. I didn't know anything about him outside of work."

Parish asked a couple of the same questions in a different way but without learning anything new. He thanked us all, put away the notebook into which he had not written anything, and told us to enjoy our hike to the lighthouse. It had all been very low key, but after he drove off, I could tell the mood had darkened considerably.

I had recommended that everyone bring a hat because we'd be out in the sun almost all the way and almost everyone had taken my suggestion. We set off in a somewhat ragged line, with Barry and Tina leading the way and perforce setting the pace. It was impossible to get lost. As soon as we passed through the commercial district we went up a gentle incline and the top half of the lighthouse was visible. This was the highest point on Black Island outside the preserve and gave us a good view of the western half. Little Salty, the smaller of two inland salt water ponds, was visible through a thin screen of trees. Big Salty, the wildlife refuge, was further east but the denser forest that spread south from the residential district completely concealed it. Little Salty was in the state park; its bigger brother was off limits without a permit. The beach was to our right as we passed the hotels, and it was bigger and better maintained than the one we were using, but still not crowded. There were two or three children wading and perhaps a dozen adults scattered around.

The road forked just ahead. We turned right so that we could walk along the shore rather than take the interior road. There were a few private residences here and a handful of small piers with boats tied up. In a few cases it looked like people were living aboard them. A sign offered to take people water skiing or fishing or sightseeing, but no one was around. The season hadn't started yet, after all.

The lighthouse was open for regularly scheduled tours during the season and by appointment out of season. Dusty had called and set things up. The small snack bar was closed but there was a white truck and a rather overweight man selling frozen lemonade and popsicles. It had warmed up considerably and by the time we arrived, everyone was thirsty so we put a substantial dent in his inventory. A moped was the only other vehicle, which we discovered belonged to Elaine Whitby, our tour guide, head of the local chapter of the Rhode Island Historical Society.

"Actually the chapter consists of three of us, two if my husband goes to bed early. Most of the downtown was wiped out by the hurricane of 1938 so we don't have much in the way of historical buildings left." She told us that the current structure had been built in 1879, replacing an older light that had been located closer to the cliffs. "The west side of the island is particularly vulnerable to erosion. When I was a child there were trees and picnic tables over there," she gestured toward the edge of the bluff overlooking the Atlantic. "Fifty years from now the place where we're standing will be at risk."

Although it was largely automated now, the lighthouse had sleeping quarters for up to four people, but no restroom. "There are portajohns outside if anyone needs them." Not everyone was willing to climb the tight spiral staircase to the light itself, and even then we were separated from it by a metal screen door that was locked shut. "The crystal was brought down from Portland, Maine when they rebuilt one of their lights on a bigger scale. It dates from the 1840s."

We all nodded appreciatively but there really wasn't much to see. There was a small observation deck and we took turns looking out to sea and then back over the island. Big Salty was visible from this height but it wasn't very impressive seen from this distance. Mrs. Whitby asked for questions and there were a few polite ones before we began the descent. I'm not usually bothered by high places but I admit that I felt a lot better when we were back on solid ground.

It was after five o'clock and everyone was on their own for supper. Tina started back with Ashley and Emily; they seemed to enjoy each other's company even though Tina was almost ten years older than the other two. James and Dennis decided to take a look at Little Salty, so they set off in the opposite direction. Maria was sitting at one of the two picnic tables talking to Barry while Eric and Claire wandered over to the edge of the bluffs to look down at the water eating away at the face of the cliff. Mrs. Whitby started up her moped, waved, and was quickly out of sight. "What happened to Kevin and Laura?" I asked.

Dusty glanced around. "They were here a minute ago."

We walked around the curve of the lighthouse but there was no sign of them. Then we heard Laura's voice, thick with stress. "I don't want to talk about it!"

We still couldn't see them but the explanation was apparent. A little path led down into a hollow that was almost completely concealed by thick shrubs. From there it rose and went directly to the edge of the cliff, where it disappeared from sight.

"We can't just pretend that nothing happened." That was Kevin. There was an audible hint of anger.

Dusty and I looked at each other. It wasn't our business to interfere, but I was sure that this had something to do with Carl's disappearance. We were still hesitating when Laura appeared, head down. I don't know if she even saw us as she walked quickly away. A second later Kevin emerged, his expression unhappy. He saw us but made no effort to cover up. Dusty turned and went after Laura.

"Is everything all right, Kevin?" I asked.

"I honestly don't know."

"Would it help to talk about it?"

Kevin shook his head. "Thanks, Mr. Birch, but I don't really understand what's going on well enough to try." He turned and started walking away and I let him go.

Dusty and Laura were out of sight already. Feeling rather useless, I made my way around the periphery of the lighthouse pretending to be sightseeing. Maria and Barry were gone, and Eric and Claire were coming back from the cliff edge. "We're heading back." Eric put his arm around Claire. "Someone has a craving for lobster." They ambled off in no hurry, arms around one another.

I was feeling restless and unfairly annoyed at having been abandoned when Dusty and Laura reappeared. "We need to talk," said Dusty. "Laura has something to tell you."

Laura looked as though talking to me was her least favorite thing in the world right now but I led the way over to the now abandoned picnic table. Laura sat down facing me with Dusty beside her. "What's wrong, Laura?"

For a full minute I didn't think she was going to say anything. Then she drew a deep breath and spoke, but kept her head down so I couldn't see her eyes. "I saw Carl when I went out last night. I thought he was dead, but now I'm not so sure."

I can't say that I didn't suspect that she knew more about Carl's disappearance than she was letting on, but this revelation still came as a bit of a shock. "Maybe you should start at the beginning."

"All right." She took a deep breath. "You know that Carl was jealous of Kevin."

"That's been pretty obvious. I saw the fight at the campfire."

"Oh, that was nothing. It's been getting worse every day. We thought the wedding would finally make him accept the way things are, but once we set a date it only seemed to make him more desperate. He was always pretty angry. The last time we dated, he almost hit me. That's why I stopped going out with him. It's like there's this fire inside that sometimes flares out of control."

"Did he threaten you?"

"No, but he said some things to Kevin that were scary. Kevin's pretty cool about that kind of stuff, but Carl started to get under his skin. Someone keyed his car a few weeks ago and he decided it was Carl, so he let the air out of the tires on Carl's jeep. Kid stuff, but it was kind of ugly."

"You could have gone to the police and gotten a restraining order."

"That would have been kind of hard to do since we all work together." She shrugged. "And I think Kevin thought that would be wimping out. He's still a little boy in some ways. We talked about it but decided to wait and see if the wedding changed things. I didn't think Carl would even come on the trip."

"But he did."

"Yes. He made some snide remarks on the way over here and he was snippy with everyone all day yesterday. I knew he was drinking a lot and he doesn't usually do that, so I was hoping he'd pass out and be too sick to come to the chapel. Then he picked a fight with Kevin last night, and when we came back to the cabins he was there waiting for us. It was the worst scene yet even though they didn't raise their voices. They started pushing each other and Carl threw a punch but he was drunk and Kevin knocked him down. Then we both went inside. I stood there for awhile listening, but I guess Carl just went away because when I peeked out a while later he was gone."

She fell silent, but I knew there had to be more so I just waited.

"This is hard," she said at last, her voice almost inaudible.

"You'll feel better when you've told him," said Dusty.

I'm not sure Laura was convinced of that, but at length she took up the narrative. "Like I said I couldn't get to sleep. I decided to go jogging on the beach. I figured no one else would be there and I'd have some privacy. But as soon as I got to the end of the path, I saw that someone was sitting in one of the lounge chairs. It was clear and light enough that I could tell it was Carl. I almost turned and went back then, but I guessed he'd calmed down or fallen asleep so I went over to see him. I thought just maybe that I could say something that would get him to accept the situation. I was close enough to touch him when I saw the blood."

My gut clenched, even though I'd been expecting something like this. "Where was the blood?"

Laura turned and looked out over the ocean. "The side of his face and the top of his head near the back. I didn't realize what it was at first and I reached over and touched it. It was still sticky and I got it all over my hands." Her voice caught but she swallowed and resumed. "I turned and started to go for help but then I realized who might have the best reason to want Carl dead."

"Kevin," I said quietly.

She nodded. "I wasn't thinking straight. I went back to the body with some vague idea that I could make things right, but of course there wasn't anything I could do. I tried to clean off my hand while I was thinking, but I just made it worse."

A thought occurred to me. "What did you use to clean yourself?"

She looked up, surprised. "Oh, one of Kevin's handkerchiefs that I'd borrowed. I'm not sure what happened to it. I looked for it later but I must have dropped it someplace."

"Did you notice Carl's flask?"

She shook her head. "It might have been around somewhere. I didn't think to look for it."

"So what did you do?"

Laura licked her lips and set her shoulders back and for the first time she seemed relatively composed. "I was afraid that someone would think Kevin had killed him. There'd been at least two fights that day and everyone knew how awkward things were with us. I guess I wasn't thinking straight but I decided to hide the body."

I suspected it was a little more than that. She was afraid that Kevin had in fact assaulted Carl. "So you dragged him down into the ocean?"

"No, I wouldn't have done that. I just wanted to put him where no one would know things were wrong until the wedding was over with."

"Why the wedding?" asked Dusty.

"Because if they were married she couldn't be compelled to testify against Kevin," I said easily. "You thought Kevin had killed him." Maybe she still did.

"No, of course not. Kevin's not violent." I wasn't sure who she was trying to convince but I didn't press the point. "I decided to drag him down the beach behind the rocks. Then I'd find an excuse to go down there after we were married and find the body. I figured it might look like he'd slipped and fallen on the breakwater. Everyone knew he was drunk." She looked back and forth between Dusty and I. "If he was already dead, it wasn't going to hurt anyone if I kept quiet for a few hours." Dusty and I both kept our faces neutral. "Anyway, he was heavier than I expected, but it was easier dragging him across the smooth sand where it was wet, and I didn't want to leave tracks to the body where someone might find him too soon."

"We looked around the rocks this morning," I told her. "Carl's body wasn't there."

"No, I never got that far. I stopped to rest near the lifeguard tower and I noticed that the door underneath was unlocked. There was nothing inside but more of those folding chairs and some life preservers and there was plenty of room so I dragged him into a corner and sort of boxed him in. Then I went back the way I had come so that I wouldn't leave any more tracks. I took a shower to get the blood off and I stood there for a long time crying. It all hit me at once then and I knew I'd done something stupid, but it was too late now. I couldn't very well drag him all the way back."

"Are you telling me that Carl's dead body was lying hidden there while we were looking for him?'

"No! And now I don't know if he's really dead at all. Dennis' girlfriend told me that he heard Carl talking to a girl sometime around midnight. So I guess he was just unconscious when I found him. I feel so bad about that! But before she talked to me, I went back to look because it all seemed like some kind of a dream and Carl wasn't there so I didn't know what to think."

"When was this?"

"I don't know. Early, around seven this morning. I ran down first thing before Maria woke up. Everything was the way I remembered except no Carl."

"Any tracks in the sand?"

"I don't know. Maybe. I thought it had all been some weird dream, except that the inside of the tower looked just like I remembered it. I came back and saw James outside and asked him if Carl was all right. He gave me a funny look, like I shouldn't have been asking for Carl I guess, and said he hadn't seen him. Then I went back to my room to start getting ready."

"Is that everything?"

"Yes." Her face told me that it wasn't but I was prevented from asking any more questions when Kevin reappeared.

"We should start back," he said calmly. "I'm starting to get hungry."

"All right." She stood up, gave us both an enigmatic look, and went off to take his arm.

Dusty and I looked at each other. "She thinks Kevin tried to kill Carl," said Dusty.

"She might be right," I answered. "But if so it sounds like he didn't make a thorough job of it. And if we assume that Carl recovered sometime during the night, went back to his room with the bloody handkerchief, then where is he now?"

"He might have had a concussion."

"Which means he could have wandered off and lost consciousness." I shook my head. "But that doesn't explain how he could have been overheard later that night."

"How far could he have gone on his own?"

"Who knows?" I took out my cell phone.

"Who are you calling?"

"Constable Parish, or whoever is answering his phone. I have to tell him we might have an injured man lying somewhere on the island."

Parish answered on the third ring. "Island Police. How can I help you?"

"Constable Parish? This is Paul Birch. I have some new information about our missing man."

"Good news I hope."

"I'm not sure. There's a chance that he sustained a head injury last night and might have wandered off and collapsed."

There was a short pause. "Where are you located at the moment, Mr. Birch?"

"We're just starting back from the lighthouse."

"Great. I'm close by. If you come back along the main road, I'm at the third driveway on the left. There's a big conch shell mounted on the mailbox."

"All right. We'll be there shortly."

Five minutes later we were standing at the end of an unpaved driveway that led down to a sheltered cove. The Island Police cruiser was parked just off the road. There was a rickety looking pier there with a good sized power boat moored at the far end and a small wooden shed flanked by two benches. Constable Parish was trudging up the hill toward us and we waited for him.

"Moving time," he said, gesturing at the backseat of the cruiser, which was filled with cardboard boxes. "When my father died, he left me his house and enough cash that I indulge myself with a boat big enough to serve as my fair weather home. During the season I move in and sometimes I rent the house out to tourists."

"Sorry to bother you off duty."

He laughed. "Oh, I'm still on duty. Technically I'm never off except when I leave the island. Being on call gives me a few perks though. As long as everything gets taken care of, nobody asks questions when I take some time for myself. So what do you have for me?"

I gave him a somewhat edited account of Laura's confession. He was frowning by the time I was done. "Well, that answers a few questions. The young lady showed pretty bad judgment."

"No argument about that," I admitted.

Parish glanced up at the sky. "It's going to start getting dark soon. I'm not sure how much good we can do searching in the dark."

"I don't suppose the Coast Guard could help?"

"Might be able to get a chopper to fly over with a searchlight. There's a lot of cover though."

"He might still be alive."

Parish was obviously concerned about that very fact. "I'll go back to the office and talk to the Coast Guard people, see what they suggest. Can I give you two a ride back?"

Yes, indeed he could.

We were having a quiet supper at the Pirate's Den when Parish called back. "They're going to make a couple of passes over the island later tonight, but if he was out in the open somewhere, chances are he would have been spotted already. This isn't that big an island, and I can't believe he wandered as far as the preserve. We can organize some of the locals to search the fields in the morning and I can use the police launch to check the rocks out beyond the beach. It's a bit risky in the dark and if he fell off one of the bluffs, he's likely dead anyway. Sorry to be so blunt."

"No apology necessary. I appreciate whatever you can manage."

"I'm going to have to speak to the young lady."

"I figured you would."

"That can wait till morning as well. If the boy was still alive when she left him, the state police might want to press charges."

"She's pretty shaken up."

"Doesn't change anything."

"No, it doesn't. If you find him, please let me know, no matter what time it is. I'm not going to get much sleep tonight either way."

"I guess neither of us is."

When we got back to the Beachcomber, everyone was there. I imagine Laura had finally told Kevin about her night time adventure, if she hadn't previously, but although neither of them was likely to have passed it on, there was a palpable atmosphere of imminent tragedy. The various couples sat by themselves, mostly not talking. Even Ashley and Emily had toned down their act. Steve was sitting with the Brubakers and Merrilee was looking somber. Most of them glanced in our direction as though waiting for us to make some kind of awful announcement, but I didn't have much to say to them so I pretended I didn't notice the attention we were getting.

There was a cooler outside the office – payment by honor system into a tin can with a slot cut in the top – and I overpaid for two cans of soda. I was stalling and the others were drifting toward us. Obviously I was going to have to say something, so finally I did.

"There's been some indication that Carl might have suffered a concussion last night. If true, then he may have wandered off in a daze and collapsed somewhere. The Coast Guard is sending a helicopter to fly over the island and in the morning the police are going to organize a search. If any of you want to help, it would be appreciated."

There was some murmuring and a few people said they would volunteer and asked where and when they should show up. "I don't know yet. I'm supposed to get a call later tonight, but it will probably be shortly after sunrise. That's all I know right now."

Somehow they had all coalesced into a crescent facing me and they shifted into smaller groups but didn't really disperse even when it became obvious I had nothing more to tell them. I gestured to Tina and she came over to where Dusty and I were standing.

"Tina, you said you heard people talking outside your cabin last night."

"Yes, more than once. But I couldn't tell you who they were or what they were saying. I was really tired out. I'm not used to a lot of physical activity."

"Do you know when you heard them?"

She thought about it but shook her head. "Sorry, boss. I can't even tell you for sure what order they were in. I know I heard a woman crying and I'm almost positive one of them was male." She frowned. "It wasn't Eric, if that helps. He has a really deep voice."

"Could it have been Kevin?"

"Sure, but it could have been Barry, or you, or even Emily's friend Ashley. Her voice is pretty husky. I just don't know. Is it important?"

"Probably not. But there seems to have been a lot of people running around last night and chances are somebody saw something."

"Do you think Carl's still alive?"

"I just don't know."

Dusty and Steve were talking by themselves and I went over to the Brubakers. Herman was looking solemn. Merrilee repeated Tina's question and I gave her the same answer. "Carl could be a pain in the ass sometimes." She let out a prolonged sigh. "He was one of those boys my mother would have said was born to be hanged. But he did a good job for us and he was one of my kids. If this was an accident, I'll say a prayer for him and feel sad for awhile. But if someone else did it, I want them to pay."

I thought about stalling but Merrilee would see through me in an instant. "I'm pretty sure this wasn't an accident."

She nodded. "I guessed as much. Do you know who's responsible yet?"

"No. It could be any of them."

"Another of my kids?"

"Seems most likely. Thieves don't usually mug someone sitting on a beach wearing a bathing suit with no wallet."

"There are other people staying here." I knew she was thinking about the peculiar Mr. Reynolds.

"True enough."

"You'll find out the truth, won't you?"

I'd been trying to avoid thinking about that. "If there's been a crime, the police will investigate."

"But if they don't find out the truth?"

"Then, yes, I guess I'll give it a try."

"If you try, you'll find out. You can't walk away from a puzzle."

"Now you're sounding like Dusty."

"That's because we're both smart women."

I had been aware for some time that James Brock was hovering nearby, all by himself, but obviously watching me. I figured if he was waiting for a chance to get me alone so I decided to provide the opportunity and see what came of it. Without looking around, I walked past the line of cabins to the head of the path to the beach, where I leaned against a tree and pretended to be thinking. Actually, I suppose it wasn't a pretense, except that I tried to appear unaware that I had a shadow. He must have been undecided because several minutes went by before I lost patience and straightened up. Perhaps realizing that his opportunity was slipping away, James stepped out of the shadows.

"I was wondering if I could talk to you, Mr. Birch."

"Sure. What's up, James?" I wondered if he had ever been a Jim, or even a Jimmy.

"Could I ask you a kind of theoretical question?"

"You might only get a theoretical answer."

"I know lawyers don't have to reveal everything they know about their clients, even when a crime is involved."

"Client confidentiality is important, but there are limits. If a lawyer knows a client is a serial killer, they're obligated to tell the authorities. Lawyers sometimes go out of their way to not know things about the people they represent, for that very reason."

"Does that hold true for private detectives?"

"It's not quite the same thing, but yes, with the reservation I just made, we don't reveal what our clients tell us."

"What if someone knew something about a crime, which he didn't commit, but which he probably should have reported to the police?"

"There can be extenuating circumstances but it's not usually a good policy to hold back information without a compelling reason."

He licked his lips and reached into his pocket, pulling out a pack of cigarettes. He offered me one automatically and I waved it off. "What if he did something with the best of intentions but it was technically wrong and he tried to undo his mistake later but couldn't?."

I had no idea where this was leading. "Well, if he broke the law under extenuating circumstances, the prosecutor might choose to let him off with a reprimand or at worse, if charges were actually filed, it would serve as mitigation during sentencing."

"Would it mean jail time?"

I shook my head. "I can't even guess without knowing what we're talking about."

He waited so long to speak again that I thought he'd decided not to. And when he did, he took off in an entirely different direction. "Do you think Kevin and Laura are good together?"

"I don't think I know either of them well enough to make a prediction, and it's really not my business anyway. What do you think?"

"I like Kevin. He and I argue sometimes but he always acts as though he takes what I say seriously. He reminds me of my little brother." There was an awkward laugh. "I say little but he's bigger than I am. He's a marine. But I'm the older one."

I was afraid that if I said the wrong thing James would clam up. He was notoriously reticent about talking about anything personal. So I kept my mouth shut.

"I like Laura too. I was thinking about asking her out back before the two of them started going together."

"She used to date Carl."

James waved that off. "That was never going to go anywhere. Carl was kind of creepy. He talked me into going on a double date with him once and my girlfriend told me she'd never go anywhere with him again. He was so rude to the waitress that the manager came over and asked us to finish our drinks and leave."

"So you didn't like Carl?"

"I don't think anyone liked him. Maybe not even Carl. And he's been getting worse. He was pretty much stalking Laura. I tried to talk to him once and he got pissed. I probably made things worse. I felt bad about that because he took it out on Laura."

"It wasn't your fault."

"I know but I felt like I owed them one. Her and Kevin, I mean. And I was tired and I'd had a few beers and none of it seemed real."

"What didn't seem real, James?"

He threw down the half smoked cigarette and ground it under his heel. "Let's take a walk."

He led the way down toward the beach and stopped at the chair where I had picked up Carl's empty flask. "I came down here last night for a smoke. There was no one around."

"What time was that?"

"It was eleven or a little later. I never go to sleep before midnight."

"And no one was here?"

"No. It wasn't bright last night but there was enough light to look around. I mean, I suppose someone could have been hiding back where the trees are or down behind the rocks, but there was no one on the beach and the chairs were all empty."

"Did you happen to see a flask lying on the sand?"

He shook his head. "I didn't notice it, but I wasn't looking for one either. Not when I saw the marks in the sand."

"What marks?"

"It looked as though someone had dragged something from here down to the water. I probably wouldn't have thought anything about it if that guy hadn't told that stupid monster story. That's what I thought it was. Not a monster, but some joke so that in the morning we'd think the monster had come up onto land."

"Any other footprints?"

"Not that I noticed."

"So what did you do?" I realized this was going to be like pulling teeth. I'd have to ease every bit of information out. If I yanked, James might balk.

"I followed them down to the water."

"Where they disappeared."

"No, they got fainter but I could still see them. They turned and ran along the edge of the water this way." He turned right and started off and I followed. As I expected he led me to a point near the lifeguard tower, then angled up toward the base. "They ended right in front of the door. It looked like a practical joke to me, so I thought I'd turn the trick around and use whatever it was to make some new marks, maybe a big smiley face just above the high tide mark. The door wasn't locked or anything."

"So you looked inside."

"Yeah. There's no light in there and at first all I could see was this big pile of folding chairs. But I knew there had to be something else so I poked around. And that's when I found him."

"Carl?"

He nodded.

"Was he still alive?"

James sighed. "I didn't think so, but now I'm not so sure. Someone said they heard Carl talking to back at the cabins after midnight. But he sure looked dead. His hair was all matted with blood and when I felt his wrist, it was cold."

"So what did you do?"

"Well, I didn't do anything at first. It was kind of hard to take in, particularly like I said because I'd had some beers. But then I started asking myself why anyone would kill Carl. I mean, he was a jerk but there are lots of jerks around. And then I remembered the fight back at the fire and I thought to myself that if anyone had a good reason to hit Carl over the head, it was Kevin."

"Whom you like."

"Yes."

"So what did you do? Move the body?"

"Yes."

"Where did you move it?"

James hunched his shoulders and I could tell this was a point beyond which he didn't want to go. But he'd gone too far to stop now. "I started to carry him back up to one of the cabins."

"Which cabin?"

"You have to realize I was half drunk and maybe a little bit in shock."

"Where did you take him, James?"

"I was going to drop him right outside cabin eight."

I did a quick mental run through of the housing plan. "That's the one where Eric and Claire are staying, isn't it?"

"Yes."

"And you don't like Eric very much."

"He's got no business being with her. He should stay with his own kind."

"And he was dating a white girl."

"Yeah."

"And you thought maybe you could get him into trouble."

"Not my best moment. I was only halfway there when I realized how stupid it was. I stopped and thought about it and I guess I started to panic. I was going to take the body back to the tower but I heard someone coming toward me and all I could think of was to get rid of it and sneak back to my cabin before anyone saw me."

"So what did you do with Carl?"

His shoulders sagged and he looked down at his feet. It would have been a comical pose if the situation hadn't been so unfunny. "I dropped him into the dumpster and ran back along the line of trees."

"Did anyone see you?"

"I don't know."

"Who was it that startled you?"

"I don't know that either." He seemed suddenly more relaxed now that he'd told his story. "So am I in trouble?"

"Probably. Moving a body – if Carl really was dead – is a crime. You also withheld information and lied to the police."

"I didn't lie. No one asked me anything that I couldn't answer truthfully. I never talked to Carl after the party and I didn't know where he was. I looked in that dumpster first thing this morning, Mr. Birch, and the body wasn't there. For awhile I wondered if I had dreamed the whole thing. And then when I heard that someone heard Carl talking after I left him, I figured that he'd climbed out on his own and wandered off."

"We're not positive that it was really Carl who was heard talking."

"I hope it was, but I don't see how he could still be alive. He was cold. I couldn't find a pulse. If I hadn't been sure that he was dead I would have called for help."

"But you went back to bed instead."

For a second or two he looked pugnacious, but then his eyes dropped. "I went back to bed. I decided it wasn't any of my business. So I was a jackass. It's not the first time. Won't be the last either."

"If Carl wasn't dead, if he recovered enough to talk to someone later that night, then where is he now?" I was talking to myself as much as to James.

"Don't people with bad concussions sometimes seem normal for awhile and then collapse later?"

"Yes. But what if you were right in the first place and he was already dead?"

"Then it wasn't him walking around later."

"Which means that when we ask people if they saw Carl after midnight, no one answers because whoever it was that Tina heard, they weren't talking to Carl. Carl was dead."

"That's what must have happened."

"Then where is his body? Are you sure you don't know who scared you off?"

"No, I never saw him. Or her. I just heard someone walking along the gravel path between the cabins."

"Does anyone else know about this?"

"Of course not. I'm not an idiot." He had the sense to think about what he'd just said. "Even if I act like it once in awhile."

"Someone moved Carl's body after you left it there."

"That's what I think. But who? And why?"

"I'll have to tell the cconstable. I imagine he'll still send out search parties in the morning, but this might alter his other plans. Carl wasn't a big guy but none of us could have carried him very far." Although two could have, I realized.

"If it was one of us. The locals have cars or trucks."

"Why would a local kill a tourist, a complete stranger?"

"But Maria said he had friends here."

I nodded. "And Carl always told the truth, right?" He didn't have an answer. "Don't mention this to anyone else yet."

"I won't. It was hard enough telling you. So how much trouble am I in?"

"That's not up to me."

"Do I still have a job?"

"Depends on how much trouble you're in."

I left him there and walked back toward the office, looking for Dusty. She was sitting with the Brubakers. Steve and most of the rest were gone. It was still early but no one seemed much in the mood for festivities. Dusty said good night, stood up and took my arm.

"I have something to tell you." For the second time recently we echoed each other's words.

"Ladies first," I suggested.

"No, mine can wait. What did you find out?"

I repeated my conversation with James. Her eyes widened slightly but otherwise she betrayed no reaction until I was done. "For a dead man, Carl had a busy night."

"That's cold."

"Writers tend to look at the world through an emotional filter."

"Really?"

"No, but it sounds good. So what do you think? Is he dead or alive?"

"If he was alive, we'd have heard something by now."

"All right, our working hypothesis is that he's dead. Who killed him, how, when, and why?"

"James thinks it was Kevin, or maybe Laura. Or both."

"Do you agree with him?"

"I think it's possible Kevin went to the beach to continue their argument and things got out of hand. I think Laura was telling the truth. The how is probably the proverbial blunt object, maybe a rock, There are plenty of them around the beach. There was blood all over his head according to Laura."

"He might have been unconscious. Scalp wounds bleed like crazy."

"I'll grant the possibility. But James is pretty sure Carl was dead when he found him."

"So who moved the body out of the dumpster, and why, and where is it now?"

"All very good questions to which I have totally inadequate answers. So what did you want to tell me?"

"A couple of little things that might not amount to much. For one thing, I overheard part of a conversation between Emily and her partner. Emily is upset about something, although she's hiding it pretty well. Ashley is taking up the slack by pretending that everything is just fine but there's a hint of panic there."

"Not surprising. In fact I'm astonished that no one decided to take the ferry back to the mainland. It left just a few minutes ago."

"Ashley and Emily split up for about half an hour last night. When Ashley came back, she suggested a moonlight swim. A little while ago she suggested another tonight and Emily recoiled visibly and said 'yeah, because the last one worked out so well' and then she went pale."

"Interesting. I'm not sure it means anything."

"Could they have found Carl's body? Before Laura did, I mean."

"I suppose, but if so, an awful lot happened down there in a very short period of time. Someone killed Carl. If they were the first to find the body and for some reason didn't say anything, then they may or may not know that Laura dragged it to the lifeguard station. After that James came down to the beach, followed the tracks, carried Carl to the dumpster, heard someone coming and dumped it, after which someone else found the body and moved it again. Or, I suppose, if Carl wasn't dead, he revived, wandered off – possibly talking to someone before disappearing."

"Could they have killed him? They might have spotted James later and moved the body again."

"Ashley and Emily? They don't seem the type and as far as I know there was no animosity between them."

"Maybe they saw the murder being committed. Let's assume it was Kevin. They might know the truth but not want to tell."

"Why not? I don't know about Emily but Ashley has been giving him dirty looks ever since we got here. She'd probably relish getting him arrested."

" If she knows he's a murderer, and Emily somehow convinced her not to say anything, that might explain why she doesn't have warm fuzzy feelings for him."

I shook my head. "She was glaring at him before we even arrived."

"Right. I don't have things ordered in my mind yet." Dusty touched my arm. "You'd better call the constable. He's organizing a search for someone who may have wandered off in a daze, not a body that someone is concealing."

"I can't do that. He'd want to know why I'm so sure Carl is dead, and then I'd have to tell him what I know."

"Shouldn't you be doing that anyway?"

"Probably, but I'm not going to. Not just yet. He'd have to arrest James and Laura and charge them both with interfering with a police investigation, maybe something even more serious. You can't move a dead body around without a damned good reason."

"So what are you going to do?"

"We'll let the search go on as planned. It might even turn something up. I'd still like to know about Carl's elusive island friends as well. There might be another and more compelling motive there."

"Do you think that's likely?"

"I don't know what to think."

"Do you think Laura and James were telling the truth?"

I nodded. "But Kevin isn't telling everything he knows, and that bothers me. There's something going on with Emily and Ashley as well. If it was Emily that the Malden kid and Tina head late last night, then they're more involved than they're saying."

Dusty frowned. "If it was them, David thought he heard them talking to Carl."

"Which doesn't make sense. Carl was almost certainly dead by then."

"It's still possible that he really was just stunned and recovered later. He might have crawled out of the dumpster and run into the girls coming back from the beach."

"Sure, but if that's what happened, why wouldn't they admit it? Not to mention that he'd have been covered with blood."

Dusty looked uncomfortable. "I think one or both of them are using drugs."

"I thought I smelled pot last night." It had been just after the fight that I'd caught a whiff. It hadn't seemed important.

She nodded. "I noticed that Ashley was acting strangely during the wedding, or as much of it as she stayed for. She couldn't sit still, she was talking faster than usual, and her eyes were bloodshot. Emily was watching to see if anyone noticed and tried to get Ashley to settle down. They put their heads together and whispered about halfway through the ceremony and that's when Ashley left."

"They'd been up late drinking. Might have been a hangover."

Dusty shook her head. "No, it wasn't that. Either she was very nervous or she was on something or both."

"It might be interesting to know where she was for the next hour or so." A wild idea occurred to me. Could Ashley have taken that opportunity to plant the bloody handkerchief in Carl's room? What purpose did it serve? Its presence there suggested the possibility that Carl had returned to the cabin after he'd been attacked. His luggage had been moved. Alternately, could he still be alive after all? He might have taken a change of clothing and slipped away to stay with his rumored friends. Possibly he wanted to get out of reach of whoever had tried to kill him, if that's what had happened. But why not just go to the police? No, it didn't make any sense. And if Ashley and Emily were somehow involved, what did they hope to achieve?

"I'd like to talk to Emily and Ashley again, but not together."

"I haven't seen them apart for more than a few seconds except at the wedding."

"Any idea how we can separate them without their suspecting why we're doing it?"

Dusty was spared answering by an interruption. We'd been walking back toward our cabin and a figure emerged from the shadows. It was Kevin and he looked unhappy. "Mr. Birch, could I talk to you for a minute?"

We had both stopped walking. "Sure. What's up?"

His eyes moved to Dusty and she took the hint. "I'll just leave you two to solve the world's problems. I'll try to come up with an answer to your question, Paul." And she walked briskly away.

"Can we go somewhere private? I don't want anyone else to hear us."

We walked out of the campground and along the beach toward the breakwater. There was no one else nearby although we could hear a party going on somewhere in the distance. Kevin sat down on a relatively smooth chunk of rock and I found another roughly facing him. For several seconds neither of us said anything and I was starting to get impatient when he finally drew in a deep breath.

"I've done something horrible. It was for the best of reasons, but I think I just made things worse."

It didn't sound like he was about to confess to the murder of Carl Celluci. He fell silent again and I was about to prompt him when he resumed.

"You know that Carl and I didn't get along."

"I know he was jealous and I saw the fight yesterday."

"I swear I never did anything to provoke him. Laura and I both ignored it when he made wise cracks in the office and it's never been physical before. We thought that once we were married, he'd cool down and accept it. We don't have any mutual friends outside the office, so it was unpleasant but manageable."

"What was the fight about?"

Kevin shrugged. "Who knows? We'd both been drinking. He made some cute remark and instead of ignoring him like usual I said something back. We went back and forth and things just got away from us. He took the first swing, but I might have hit him anyway."

"What happened after that?"

"I'm not sure where Carl went. I had another drink, which was a mistake, and then went back to my cabin. I didn't want to run into him again because I was afraid something might happen that would spoil the wedding. Laura was really excited about it, you know."

"Did you see anyone else on your way?"

"Dennis and his girlfriend were walking off together. Some of the others were still watching the fire burn out. I didn't see Carl."

He fell silent again and this time I did prompt him. "What did you do when you got back to the cabin?"

"I stretched out on the bed in my clothes and I must have fallen asleep. When I woke up, it was dark outside and I didn't hear anyone talking. I wasn't feeling so good and I decided to take a walk over to the john. I was pretty sick so I stayed there for a while in case I was going to throw up, but my stomach started to settle and I splashed some cold water on my face and started back to the cabin. But I wasn't sleepy so I walked out to the road. I wanted a cigarette but I gave them up when Laura and I started living together. She hates the smell."

"And you didn't see or hear anyone else?"

"Not at first. I could hear music from somewhere the other side of the road, but that was all. I started to feel a lot better so I walked back up the driveway and past the office. I was just coming up to the cabin where Mr. Shaw and Miss Kirk are staying when I heard something." He hesitated, but went on. "Someone was coming through the woods at the far end of the beach. I'm not sure exactly why but I slipped behind one of the big pine trees. Maybe I was afraid it would be Carl. It wasn't. It was Laura."

"Was she alone?"

"Yes. She had her arms wrapped around her shoulders and her head down. She walked right past me but never looked up. And she was crying."

"Do you know what time this happened?"

"I think it was a little before eleven. I wasn't wearing my watch."

"Where did she go?"

"Back to her cabin, I think. At least she went in that general direction."

"You didn't follow her?"

"No. I didn't know what to make of it. My head wasn't entirely clear, I guess. But I had noticed something else. There's a security light mounted on that cabin and when she walked under it I could see her pretty clearly." He paused and looked up at me. "There was blood on the hand that I could see and a little bit on her cheek, as though she'd touched it with her hand."

Kevin spoke slowly and his voice was weary, as though he was drawing each sentence up from a deep internal well. "I thought at first that she had hurt herself somehow, maybe fell on the rocks. I almost called out to her. But there was something furtive about the way she walked. She wasn't hurrying like you would if you needed help. And then she was gone and I would have to have chased after her. And I didn't."

Another prolonged silence. "So what did you do?"

"I went back to my cabin and tried to go to sleep again, but I was wide awake. After an hour or so, I got up and went back to where I'd seen Laura. I was hoping to find something that would tell me what had happened. I knew the general direction that she'd come from so I walked off toward the dumpster and the beach. I came out of the trees and it was light enough to see that no one was on the beach. I looked around a little and started to feel foolish, so I turned and walked back. That's when I saw it." He stirred easily. "Damn, I miss cigarettes."

I waited this time and he eventually started up again. "I don't know how I missed it the first time. I guess I just wasn't looking that way. But when I came back I could see it clearly. It was someone's arm hanging out of the dumpster." He looked up at me, perhaps expecting to see an expression of shock or at least surprise, but my face was set.

"I guess I should have known something was seriously wrong right away, but all I could think of was someone playing a practical joke or that it was a dummy or something. I reached out and tapped the arm but it didn't move. Then I grabbed the hand and it was cold. I boosted myself up and looked inside. He was face down but I could tell it was Carl. I think I called his name, but not very loud. I already knew that he was dead. He looked empty."

Kevin slid off the rock and stood up, shuffled his feet, and dropped his eyes. "I know that what I should have done was gone for help, or called the police, or something. I did start back toward the office but no one was there. Then I thought about waking you up, but I didn't."

"You were afraid that Laura might have had something to do with Carl's death."

"Yeah. I remembered the blood and the way she walked and I thought, maybe he tried to kiss her or something and she pushed him away and he hit his head."

"There's no way that he could have fallen into the dumpster."

"I know. But if there'd been an accident and she'd been afraid that she'd get in trouble, she might have pushed him up and over. She's stronger than she looks and he wasn't that big a guy."

"Do you think that's what happened?"

He shook his head. "Not now. But at the time I had to accept it as a possibility."

"So you covered up for her by moving the body."

"No! That's just it. I moved his arm so that no one could see him without climbing up on the dumpster and then I left. I was sort of dazed. I went back to the cabin and tried to sleep, but I only managed a couple of hours before morning."

"Did you ask her about it?"

"No, but a little while ago she told me what happened." He repeatedly what was essentially the same story Laura had told me earlier. "She's really upset because she thinks he might still have been alive when she found him and she should have gone for help."

"Did you ask her about the handkerchief?"

"What handkerchief?"

"It's nothing. What about you? Did you tell her about finding Carl's body yourself?"

He shook his head energetically. "No way. You must see how it would have sounded. Like I was spying on her and suspected that she'd killed Carl."

"It's usually better to get these things out in the open."

He pondered that. "Yeah, I guess so. But I'm not ready to do that yet. I'm still not clear myself just what I was thinking."

"You know that the body wasn't in the dumpster this morning."

"Yeah. Which means someone else moved him. Maybe whoever killed him came back."

"How would they have known where to look? According to Laura, she moved the body to the guard tower around half past ten, then went back to her cabin and the showers. T hat must have been when you saw her. Sometime during the next hour the body was moved to the dumpster." I knew that James Brock had been responsible, but I wasn't ready to tell Kevin.

"That must have been whoever killed him."

"Let's not make that assumption just yet. If the killer had wanted to conceal the body, why would he have left it in plain view on the beach for Laura to find?"

"But why would someone else move it?"

"Under the circumstances, you're really not in a position to point fingers at someone else doing something stupid."

"Yeah, right."

"So let's assume that you saw the body around half past eleven. What did you do after that?"

"Like I said, I went back to my cabin and tried to sleep." He looked away and his voice changed. Kevin was a bad liar.

"You didn't see anyone else while you were outside?"

"No. There was a light on in Eric's cabin but they weren't making any noise."

It was my turn to fall silent as I digested this new information and it was Kevin's turn to restart the conversation. "Laura says that someone heard Carl talking after midnight last night. It couldn't have been Carl, Mr. Birch. I know he was dead at least an hour before that."

"It's not clear what they heard. Someone said Carl's name and someone else answered, but we don't know who either party was. Assuming that you were right about Carl, it obviously wasn't him. It might have been something completely innocent."

"Then why haven't they said anything today? You and that policeman have been asking everyone about what they did last night."

"I don't know. Maybe they were doing something that they don't want the rest of us to know about."

"Like what?" His expression changed. "I suppose it might have been Dennis."

That caught me by surprise. "Why would Dennis and his girlfriend be wandering around mysteriously in the night?"

For a moment, Kevin looked as though he wished he hadn't spoken. "I shouldn't be telling you this, but Dennis is kind of a flirt. He and Donna aren't serious and they aren't exclusive, although I think she wants to be. He asked Laura out a couple of times before we got engaged, and he hits on Emily and Mandy all the time." Mandy was one of the people who had elected not to come on this trip. Lucky her.

"So he might have been cheating a little?"

Kevin shrugged. "It wouldn't be the first time. He told me they went out with another couple once and ended up swapping for the night."

"He doesn't seem the adventurous type."

Kevin smiled. "He's full of surprises. Look, thanks for hearing me out. Am I in big trouble or what?"

"That depends on what it is that you still aren't telling me."

Under other circumstances, Kevin's expression might have made me laugh. He was so transparently guilty of something that I was immediately confident that he hadn't killed Carl. Either he was innocent or he was the greatest actor I'd ever encountered.

"I don't know what you mean."

"It's going to come out sooner or later. If you tell me now, I might be able to help. If it comes out later, when the police are more involved than they are already, you'll be on your own."

I could see Kevin start to close down. If I didn't press him now, I might never get the truth out of him. "If you're trying to protect Laura, this isn't the way to do it."

"It has nothing to do with her."

"Then tell me what you really did after you found Carl's body."

For a full minute, I didn't think he was going to answer. He was tensed as though waiting for me to hit him, which frankly was a tempting idea. It occurred to me suddenly that Kevin was not very bright. He was a good kid, no doubt, and his intentions were probably laudable, but he just didn't grasp how the world worked. But something must have penetrated because his shoulders settled and he seemed to shrink into himself.

"I moved the body."

That was pretty much what I was expecting. I was beginning to wonder if everyone except the killer had moved Carl's body at some point. "Where did you move it to?"

"I needed time to think. I just wanted to hide it for long enough to come up with a plan. I was going to put him in his own room, but James was in the cabin and I heard someone coming so I dragged him around back and put him in the empty one."

"The one with the caved in roof?"

"Yeah."

"Wasn't it locked?"

"The locks aren't so good. I popped the door with my pocketknife and pulled him inside and left him there."

"Did you lock the door when you left?"

"No. How could I?"

I sighed. "I suppose we'd better go see."

Kevin shook his head. "He's gone. I checked back in the morning. It all seemed like a bad dream. I was going to say that I saw that the door wasn't completely closed and peeked inside and saw the body. But he wasn't there."

"You don't think he recovered and left?"

"No way. He was dead when I found him."

I was wondering what Merrilee would say if I told her to fire everyone as soon as we got back, but I stifled the thought. "What time was it when you found the body missing?"

"About six. No one else was up as far as I know. I looked around but I didn't see anything."

"No drag marks?"

"Not really. The ground is pretty hard there and there's a lot of traffic." We were both quiet for a time. "Should we tell that policeman?"

"Not yet. Tomorrow. The search still might turn up something."

"I'm really sorry about this. I just didn't know what to do."

"Well, what's done is done. We'll just have to see what we can do to minimize the damage."

"It has to be one of us, doesn't it? Someone we know killed Carl."

"That seems likely. Any ideas?"

"No, none at all. We all get along pretty well. Even the stuff between me and Carl would have blown over once he got used to it. Carl didn't like being tied down. He would never have married Laura. I think he was just pissed because she dropped him instead of the other way around."

I glanced at my watch. "It's getting late. The search party starts early in the morning."

Kevin roused himself. "Right. And I want to make sure Laura is all right. She's pretty upset." He started back toward the cabins and after another moment or two, I followed.

I was headed back to our cabin to look for Dusty but I was intercepted by Eric and Claire, who told me that Dusty wanted me to come down to the beach. I had a brief vision of her finding Carl's body back in its original position, but that seemed unlikely. On the other hand, a lot of unlikely things had already happened during the past day or two.

It wasn't as dark as it had been the night before. The sky was perfectly clear, the moon almost full, and there was a good sized yacht a little way out which was lit up like a Christmas tree, music blaring loudly, at least a dozen people visible from the shore. Several chairs had been arranged in a rough circle and I could see Dusty, Emily, Ashley, Barry, and James. James looked was holding a can of beer and looking uncomfortable. Ashley and Barry also had beers. There was an empty chair waiting for me so I took it and waved away the beer that Barry offered. Dusty gave me a look that was supposed to convey something but I wasn't sure what it might be.

The conversation was general at first – which means no one talked about Carl Celluci. Ashley didn't say much and she looked uncomfortable. Barry tried to get her to talk but she was resisting. Emily on the other hand was talking too much and there were dark circles under her eyes. James said almost nothing and kept looking out toward the party boat, then finished his beer and said good night. Barry stood up and yawned and said he was going to bed. Dusty was concentrating on keeping Emily engaged and Ashley was visibly becoming more annoyed until she finally stood up.

"It's been a long day and we have to get up early tomorrow. Nice talking to you all." She looked pointedly at Emily, who seemed momentarily disconcerted, then started to get up.

Dusty put out a hand and placed it on Emily's wrist. "Wait. I want to ask you about that antique store you were talking about earlier."

Emily looked undecided but she sat back in her chair. "It was really nice. My mom used to manage a small one on Cape Cod and she taught be a lot about it."

Ashley was clearly undecided whether to go or stay so I provided a little push. "I can walk you back to the cabin if you'd prefer some company."

The look Ashley gave me wasn't quite a glare but she was clearly insulted. "Don't bother. I can look after myself." She turned to Emily. "Don't stay too long. You know how you are when you don't get enough sleep." Once again Emily made as if to rise and once again Dusty asked her a question to distract her. Ashley turned and walked away.

As soon as she was out of sight, Emily took a deep breath. "Okay, I'm not stupid. What did you want to tell me that Ashley isn't supposed to hear?"

Dusty and I exchanged looks and I took the lead. "Actually, it's more the other way around. What is it that you don't want to tell us in front of her?"

Emily tried to look puzzled but she couldn't carry it off. "What are you talking about?"

"You and Ashley left your cabin last night, later than you admitted." She shook her head. "Someone heard you talking, Emily."

"We went to the restroom together. I didn't want to go out in the dark by myself. That's all."

"Your cabin is on the opposite side of the campground. You were heard on this side."

"I think I should go." But she made no effort to stand.

Dusty spoke up. "I know this is difficult, Emily, but you'll feel a lot better if you tell us the truth. The police won't be as understanding as we are."

Emily said something under her breath. We waited and she thought about it. "We didn't do anything wrong. Not really."

"If you lie to the police, you could be charged with a crime."

"It was so nice when it started, but then things just got out of control." She crossed her arms and closed her eyes. "We wanted to go skinny dipping after everyone else was asleep. The water was cold so we lay down on the beach and, you know, held each other to get warm."

I didn't want to hear more than I needed to. "What time was this?"

"I don't know. A little before midnight, I guess."

"And how long were you there?"

"Maybe half an hour or a little more. Then it got breezy and we decided to call it a night. We were almost back to the cabin when we heard something being dragged. Ashley pulled me down behind a bench and we tried to be quiet." She blushed. "I couldn't stop giggling. We hadn't brought any clothes with us. But then it stopped being funny."

"What did you see?"

"We saw someone dragging another person across the ground."

"Did you recognize them?"

"Yes, it was Kevin doing the dragging. We couldn't tell who the other person was, at least not just then. I thought maybe someone had had too much to drink and I would have offered to help if we hadn't been, you know, naked. "

"So what happened next?"

"Well, they disappeared around the corner of the cabin. I was going to run back to ours, but Ashley wanted to see what was happening. She's a lot braver than I am." She bit her lip. "And she doesn't like Kevin very much."

"Why not? I thought they'd never met before."

Emily shook her head. "I don't think I should say anything. You'll have to ask her. "

"All right, we will. Back to last night, what happened next?"

"Kevin got the door to the empty cabin next to yours open and pulled the body inside. He came out right away and we ducked back. When we looked again, the door was shut and he was gone. We waited a couple of minutes to be sure and then sneaked around to the door. It wasn't locked so we looked inside. That's when we saw that it was Carl. We thought he had just passed out and that Kevin had put him there to sleep it off. But Ashley saw the blood and she tried to find a pulse and told me Carl was dead." Emily's eyes were shut but she was crying.

"That must have been very upsetting." Dusty reached out and patted the back of Emily's hand.

"It didn't seem real. I thought Ashley was kidding around at first. She knew Carl a little from college and I know she didn't like him."

"Did they date?" I asked.

"God no!" Emily's eyes opened and she almost smiled. "Ashley's been out since high school. She got into the newspapers because she brought her girlfriend to the junior prom. She just didn't like him. Thought he was a weasel."

I made a mental note that Carl and Ashley were not strangers when we boarded the *Calamity Jane*. "So what happened after you knew Carl was dead?"

"I wanted to go back to the cabin, get dressed, and then call the police or something. Ashley told me to calm down. She said there was nothing we could do for Carl now and that we needed to think things through. It made more sense then somehow. She told me that Kevin had probably killed him in a fight and was hiding the body until he could figure out what to do next. I told her that was why we should tell someone right away, but she talked me into helping her move the body before he came back. I knew it was wrong but she kept insisting that we could pretend to find it the next day. I didn't realize until later what she was planning."

"And what was that?"

Her eyes closed again and she shook her head. "I can't tell you that."

I resisted the temptation to take her by the shoulders and shake her until her teeth rattled. "So you moved the body."

"We got him up and carried him between us. Ashley moved his head back and forth and pretended like he was a ventriloquist's dummy and talked to him, doing both voices. It was pretty horrible. That was probably what people heard."

"And it never occurred to you that what you were doing was wrong?"

"Of course it did! But I was scared and confused and Ashley is like this force of nature when she gets going on something. It's easier to play along than to argue. And it's not as if we were hurting him. We just wanted to make sure that Kevin got caught." She shut up suddenly and started to get up. "I have to go."

"Not just yet," I said as sternly as I could manage. "You haven't told us where you put Carl."

"The empty cabin. We knew we could get in there because the lock was broken and it was tied shut."

"The one next to Eric and Claire?"

"No, the other one. Behind where that weird old man is living. We just left him inside and tied the door back shut. I really have to go."

I had more questions, but she brushed past me and ran back toward the cabins. Dusty looked at me. "Do you suppose Carl is still there?"

"Only one way to know for sure."

It wasn't a long walk and it seemed a lot shorter because we weren't looking forward to what we might find. The door was as they'd described it. The doorknob was missing and a rope had been looped through the empty hole and tied to a nail driven into the frame. I untied it and then drew a deep breath. Dusty covered her mouth and nodded for me to open the door. But just as I reached for it, a voice came out of the darkness.

"Don't bother. He's not there anymore. I checked during the wedding this morning. Someone took him away."

Dusty and I turned in unison as a tall, slender figure emerged from the shadows. It was Ashley.

"Emily told me she'd spilled the beans. I figured you'd be coming here next. Whatever you found, or didn't find, you'd want to talk to me next. Am I right?"

"You might have saved us all a good deal of time if you'd acted a little more sensibly last night."

"You mean if I'd been a good little girl and not made any trouble?"

"That's not how I would have phrased it, but basically yes. What were you thinking?"

"I wanted to make sure that bastard got what was coming to him."

"Which bastard would that be? Kevin?"

"I know he pretends to be a very nice boy and everyone likes him, but I know what he's really like. This was a chance to make sure he didn't slide off the hook again."

Dusty figured it out faster before I could. "You were going to plant some evidence, weren't you? What was it going to be? A handkerchief maybe? Something that the police would trace back to him?"

"It was what he deserved. He killed a man."

"You don't know that," I said. "All you saw was Kevin hiding the body. And we have reason to believe he was already dead when Kevin found him."

"Of course you believe what he says. People always believe what he says. And if Emily and I told the police what we saw last night, he'd deny it and his lawyer would say it was dark so we couldn't be absolutely sure and there would be reasonable doubt and he'd get off free just like he did before."

"What are you talking about? I thought you hadn't met Kevin before yesterday."

Ashley put her hands on her hips and tossed her head back. "We were never formally introduced and I doubt he remembers me, but yes we've met. I was a freshman and he was a couple of years ahead of me. Frat boy, full of himself. Some of his friends invited my friend and me to a party and we went for the free beer. We were pretty naïve."

"They got you drunk," said Dusty.

Ashley laughed. "We should have been so lucky. They drugged us. I woke up naked in a room upstairs. I guess I'm lucky I didn't come to sooner. My friend got pregnant, dropped out of school, and never spoke to me again."

"You went to the police?"

"I reported it to the college. They ran some kind of hokey investigation, but it was an obvious cover-up. They suspended the frat's party privileges and slapped a few wrists."

"How about Kevin?"

"Claimed he didn't know a thing about it."

"What makes you think he did?"

"He was the one who gave us the beers."

"Suggestive but not conclusive."

Ashley's face twisted with sarcasm. "That's what the disciplinary board said."

"Even if he was involved, that doesn't give you the right to fabricate evidence now."

"I wasn't going to stand by and watch him get away with it again. It wouldn't be fair. He needs to pay for what he did."

"And you think he killed Carl?"

"Of course he did. Why else would he have hidden the body?"

"You hid the body. Does that mean that you killed him?"

For the first time Ashley seemed uncertain. "No, of course not. He was already dead when we moved him."

"What if Carl was already dead when Kevin found him?"

"Then why wouldn't he have said something right then?"

"Maybe he was trying to protect someone else."

Ashley looked back and forth between Dusty and I. "What are you trying to say? You're just trying to trick me."

I was fed up with Ashley, with all of them really, and I just shook my head. Dusty had been silent so far but now she spoke up and there was no mistaking the anger in her voice. "I think you're more interested in revenge than fairness. It never occurred to you that Kevin's motives might be more honorable than yours, even if his choice was unwise. I don't know if he was involved when you were drugged, but you haven't given us any reason to take your word over his."

Ashley turned sullen. "We did what we thought was right."

"And that worked out so well." Dusty gestured to the presumably empty cabin.

"Someone must have been watching us." Ashley turned her face away from us. "I didn't mean for this to happen." She shuffled her feet awkwardly. "So what happens now?"

I had no idea what to do, but I wasn't about to tell her that. "For the time being, we don't say anything. You go back and tell Emily to keep her mouth shut. Maybe the search tomorrow will turn something up. It's likely that the truth will have to come out at some point, but if we can figure out who really killed Carl, the police might be satisfied with that."

"It wasn't Emily's fault. She didn't want to do it."

"We'll worry about whose fault it was later."

She stood there indecisively for a minute, then nodded and walked off into the darkness. Dusty put a hand on my shoulder. "What are you thinking?"

"I wonder if we're the only two who didn't move Carl's body last night."

"Well, I certainly didn't, but you were off on your own for a while."

I laughed, but it was forced. "Let's go back to the cabin. I need to think about all of this."

We managed to get all the way there without anyone stopping us to confess that they'd moved Carl's body during the night. It was a small victory but I cherished it. Dusty opened a bottle of wine that we'd brought with us and put out some cheese and crackers we had picked up locally while I found the notebook I habitually carried and started working on my timeline. Everything was approximate since no one had bothered to actually look at a watch but at least the sequence was presumably correct.

The fight between Carl and Kevin had happened around 8:30 and Carl had stormed off. That was the last time anyone admitted having seen him alive. An hour to ninety minutes later, Laura had gone down to the beach and found him – presumably dead – slumped in a beach chair. She hadn't seen Kevin since then – I would have to check and see if anyone had been with him during that interval. Fearing that Kevin had killed Carl in a resumption of their fight, she had dragged him down to the waterline and over to the lifeguard tower, roughly concealing him inside. At about half past ten, she returned to the cabin, retrieved a towel, and went to take a shower. I couldn't imagine that took more than thirty minutes.

While Laura was returning from the beach, James Brock walked down toward the water, saw the drag lines, and subsequently discovered Carl's body. James and Kevin are friends but James jumped to the same conclusion as Laura and decided her hiding place was inadequate. He started to move the body, thought better of it, panicked when he heard someone coming and placed it in the dumpster. Kevin, meanwhile, had spotted Laura crying and with blood on her hands. He remained in hiding until she was gone or a little longer, trying to figure out what to do, then decided to see if he could follow Laura's trail backward in order to determine what had happened. He was the one whose presence had startled James, who ran off. Kevin then found the body and concluded that Carl had confronted Laura, a struggle had broken out, and Carl had somehow fallen and hit his head. This was at about eleven or shortly afterward.

A few minutes earlier Ashley and Emily had gone skinny dipping at the beach but cut their visit short because it was too cold. On their way back they heard someone coming, concealed themselves, and saw Kevin hide Carl's body in cabin 4B, which was unoccupied. Ashley, who believes that Kevin was an accomplice to her rape when they were in college together, claims not to have wanted him to escape justice this time so she convinced Emily, who had had too much to drink and who was easily swayed even when sober, to help her move the body to the other empty cabin, 9B. They are overheard "talking" to the corpse by Dennis and by Tina. Ashley probably intended to plant some evidence to implicate Kevin in Carl's death before arranging for the body to be discovered. Ashley did not strike me as a reliable witness, and she had been on her own for at least part of the time in which Carl was attacked. She had known him previously, not well according to Emily, but that would also have to be checked.

Somewhere around six the following morning, Kevin checked cabin 4B and discovered that the body wasn't where he had left it. At some point in the next hour or so, Laura returned to the lifeguard station and James looked in the dumpster, both making the same discovery. At ten o'clock, everyone had gathered at the chapel for the wedding, but Ashley left partway through the service, presumably to plant evidence implicating Kevin, but her plans went awry when she also discovers that the body had been moved. The wedding ended after an hour and a quarter. Constable Parish arrived in answer to our call and searched Carl's bedroom, discovering a bloody handkerchief. James, who looked in the room early that morning, insists some of Carl's things have been moved.

The only people I could think of who had time and opportunity to go through Carl's room were James, who could have done it any time during the night, and Ashley, who was alone after she left the wedding. I couldn't think of any motive for either of them to do so. Ashley would more likely have searched Kevin's room and since the cabin assignment diagram was still posted on the bulletin board, she would not likely have made a mistake. None of the cabins were securely locked so it needed no sophistication to break in.

I made a separate little timeline for the bloody handkerchief. It was almost certainly the one Kevin had loaned to Laura and which she had used in an attempt to clean the blood off her hands. She could have dropped it at any point that evening, but my guess was that she left it on the beach. I couldn't come up with any reason for anyone to plant it in Carl's room except possibly to suggest that Carl hadn't been dead after all when Laura found him, that he had returned to his room without waking James. There didn't seem to be any plausible reason for doing this, but then again, murderers don't always act rationally, particularly in crimes of the moment, which is what this appeared to be.

Another unresolved question was the identity of Carl's island friends. Presuming that he hadn't just invented them, why hadn't they come forward?

We drank some wine and Dusty read through my notes. "I have another question for you. Why haven't we told the police about most of this?"

"It's my overgrown sense of responsibility. If it wasn't for me, none of us would be here and Carl would still be alive."

"Not necessarily. Whoever killed him might have done so anyway. Ashley strikes me as pretty cold blooded. Not that I'm accusing her."

"She may have more of a motive than is apparent."

"And Emily didn't see her for almost half an hour."

"Which means that no one knows where Emily was during that period, or what she was doing. Do you think she could have killed Carl?"

"I suppose she could have hit him a moment of rage, but I don't think she could keep it secret for long. She'd break down the first time someone looked at her the wrong way."

"That leaves Kevin and Laura. I don't think either of them would have planned a murder, but an argument could have gotten out of control."

"Without anyone hearing anything?"

Her point was a good one. We couldn't hear people talking normally on the beach from our cabin, but we could tell when they were shouting.

"Who could have moved Carl's body this last time?"

"Assuming it was the last time, it could have been anyone. It happened between midnight and six, and everyone claims to have been asleep."

"But how would they know to look in cabin nine?"

That was another good question. It had to be someone who was still up shortly after midnight. "It appears that someone isn't telling the complete truth."

"Isn't that always the case?"

"Yes, unfortunately."

The wine was gone. My mind was numb. And a little while after that we were asleep.

It was overcast in the morning, which suited my mood perfectly. Uncle Ted had picked up three dozen assorted donuts and muffins and there was coffee brewing in the office. I counted heads and everyone was there although the Brubakers weren't really up to traipsing across the countryside. I finished a bran muffin and tried to decide how I was going to face Parish without revealing that I possessed guilty knowledge, but I was spared that trial because he sent one of his part time deputies instead.

Hiram was a heavy set man with a high pitched voice who accepted a cup of coffee and looked us over with an obvious lack of enthusiasm. I introduced myself and he explained that the constable was leading the search of woods around Little Salty and into the fringe of the preserve. "It's pretty rough going up there." Two boats were making their along the shoreline in opposite directions, checking the tiny inlets and rocks which couldn't be seen clearly from the land. "This group will cover the farms. Most of the fields have already been plowed so we can cover a lot of ground pretty quickly. There are clumps of blueberry and raspberry thick enough to hide a body...a person I mean...so we'll have to poke into each one of them as we go along."

He organized us into teams and gave us simple instructions. "Try not to walk where the ground is turned up. We grow most of our fresh vegetables here on the island. It's too expensive to bring them over from the mainland."

Hiram pretended to be satisfied with his preparations and led us out of the campground and up the road to where we could see that the land had been pretty thoroughly cleared. They were isolated stands of trees scattered about and more frequent clumps of brush. We were going to walk between the plowed fields and over the unplowed ones. "Someone lying down doesn't make much of a silhouette, so pay attention and don't rush to get to the next field just because you can't see anything right off."

We arranged ourselves in a staggered line per his instructions and then he waved and we started forward.

It was every bit as dull as it sounds, and I began to feel guilty about holding information back, but the body had to be somewhere. This was just as good a place to look as any. But what if the killer, or the last bodynapper, had simply thrown Carl off one of the bluffs? Would he be thrown back ashore or carried out to sea?

Fortunately my crisis of conscience was short lived. Hiram had a radio and he got a call around nine o'clock. I was too far away to hear what he shouted to us, but he was obviously waving for us to come to him and I knew that there could only be one reason to call off the search. Carl's body had been found at last.

It was in the last place I probably would have looked.

Hiram wasn't saying much. He told us that Carl had been found and wouldn't even say whether he was dead or alive, although at least half of us knew that he wasn't and most of the rest probably guessed the same. We could see the flashing lights before we reached the campground and I saw Constable Parish and Ted Welch standing near the car. Someone was in the backseat, hunched over, which I didn't understand at all. Other than the Brubakers and Steve, none of our party had remained behind and those three seemed unlikely criminals.

Parish spotted us and came out to the end of the driveway. "We found him."

"So I gathered." I waited for an explanation but he was obviously in no hurry. His expression suggested satisfaction and confusion simultaneously. "Is there anything you can tell us?"

Parish picked his words with obvious caution. "We've made an arrest. It's a local person, I'm afraid. We don't understand exactly what happened yet but he had the body stashed in his room." He glanced toward the police car. "It's Oliver Reynolds."

"The bearded guy in cabin nine?"

He nodded. "I've known for a while that we were going to have to do something about Ollie. He hasn't been right since his daughter died. But everyone liked him and I guess we just didn't see how much he'd deteriorated."

Ted Welch joined us. He looked miserable. "I'd been meaning to have a talk with Ollie about the way he's been acting lately, particularly after the trouble with the Sanfords. And then Mrs. Brubaker came by and told me she thought there was some kind of terrible argument going on in his cabin so I decided that I couldn't put it off any more."

Parish looked uncomfortable. He was probably trying to decide whether or not he should be allowing Welch to speak freely, but he couldn't think of a good enough reason to interfere.

"I could hear it before I got there. Ollie was in one of his rages, throwing things around and cursing at the top of his voice. At least the Sanfords weren't around. Anyway, I knocked on his door and he kept right on screaming so I opened it and there he was. It was pretty awful." Welch shook his head and turned away. I could see his hands shaking.

"Oliver had the missing boy in his cabin. Apparently he thought he was still alive. When Ted looked in, he was whaling on the body with his fists."

"I could tell he was dead. There wasn't much blood, not that I could see. Ollie didn't even notice me at first and I didn't go inside. He's a pretty big man and I didn't want him taking a swing at me. I ran back to the office and called Mitchell. Told him to come right over and he did."

Parish nodded. "He'd pretty much run out of steam by the time I arrived. I got him to calm down and come outside. We haven't moved the body yet. The state police launch is on the way and they'll have some forensics people with them."

"Are you sure it's Carl?"

"Mrs. Brubaker peeked in at my request and identified him."

Dusty stirred. "I'll go see if she's all right." She walked off.

"Any idea what got into him?"

"Apparently he thought the boy was the one his girl was sneaking out to see the night she died. He always claimed that the boyfriend killed her. Celucci looks a lot like the young lad Ollie assaulted last year, one of the tourists. That's probably what set him off."

"What was the cause of death?"

"Officially, I won't know until the state people tell me. Unofficially, the back of his head is caved in. I'd say that killed him. And he's been dead for a while. The blood was dried hard."

"Since Friday night?"

"Could be. Again, I have to wait on the state."

I glanced at the car again. It did not appear that Reynolds had moved since we'd arrived. "How is he?"

"Pretty much out of gas. He didn't resist, didn't even say much. Just something about how someone had to pay for his daughter's life."

"Are you going to lock him up?"

Parish shook his head. "Launch should be here in an hour or two. I'll keep him right where he is unless something changes."

"Did he admit anything?" I was trying to process this new situation while I spoke. I had not accounted for Reynolds in my timeline. He was one of those people whom we try not to see, so it was entirely possible that he'd been wandering about on the fringes of our group since we'd arrived. As far as I knew, he might well have killed Carl on the beach, and later spotted one or more of the subsequent attempts to conceal the body. It was likely that he was the one who had removed it from the other side of this same cabin. I remembered Ted Welch mentioning that he was storing some of his things in the vacant room. He may have decided that he'd failed to kill Carl earlier, or perhaps he didn't remember their first encounter. It seemed likely that Reynolds would be declared incompetent regardless of the precise chain of events, unless there was something else we didn't know. And there's always something else we don't know.

The state police would conduct a cursory investigation, but I knew what the outcome would be. Reynolds had been caught red handed, he had a motive or at least what he believed to be a motive. It would be easiest just to let the momentum carry them along and tie things up nicely. The good news was that it meant the various shenanigans that had gone on Friday night might never come out. The bad news was that it was entirely possible that Carl's killer was breathing a big sigh of relief.

The rest of our group was milling around, obviously wanting to know what was going on. I glanced at Parish. "How much do you want me to tell them?"

He sighed, obviously out of his depth. "Tell them their friend is dead and that the circumstances are under investigation. They should stay away from cabin nine and cooperate with the state police when they arrive. I'm sure they'll want to do some interviews." He glanced at Welch. "I assume it's all right to use your office."

"Sure. No problem."

"They'll want to talk to you first, probably, since you're the one who found the body."

"All right."

"I'll try to keep my people out of your hair." I glanced at my watch. "It's probably a good time to send everyone out to lunch."

It was a pretty subdued group who listened to my condensed summary. They broke up into small groups, eventually starting toward the downtown. I noticed that Maria was crying and that she ran off toward her cabin instead, and I also noticed that Ashley was alone and that Emily had attached herself to Eric and Claire. I felt a twinge of sympathy, but only a twinge. Dusty and the Brubakers emerged. Merrilee did not look traumatized, but I hadn't expected her to. I suspect that she was the toughest person among us.

Dusty touched my arm. "We're going down to get something to eat. Coming?"

I wasn't feeling remotely hungry. "I might grab something later. I think I'm going to hang around for a while."

Ted Welch had gone back to his office. Parish was standing by the patrol car talking into his radio. He couldn't have heard us speaking but Dusty lowered her voice anyway. "Are you going to tell him what happened?"

"Not yet. It's not going to be his investigation."

It was another hour or so before the state police arrived. Ted offered coffee and I took it gratefully. Parish did as well and the three of us stood around ostentatiously not talking about the thing we were all thinking about. Hiram had been sent down to the dock with his van to meet the mainlanders, two homicide detectives and two technicians with their bags. I knew the lead detective, Sasha Bullard. She was smart and conscientious, though sometimes in too much of a hurry to get things over with. To be fair, there was always pressure to close cases as quickly as possible.

She raised her eyebrows when she saw me but didn't say anything. The other detective and the two techies were set to work at cabin nine while Parish and Bullard disappeared into the office for a confab. After a couple of minutes, they called Ted in. I watched the technicians from a distance for a few minutes, but there really wasn't anything to see. A rather aged ambulance from the local clinic arrived and two uniformed attendants got out, but the detective whose name I didn't know told them they'd have to wait.

Parish and Bullard reappeared after a while. Other than a trip to the restroom, I'd kept myself available. Bullard spoke to the other detective briefly, then came over to where I was standing. She was my height, a bit taller, and almost as smart. Maybe smarter.

"Long time no see." She took out a pack of cigarettes and offered me one. I waved it off and waited while she lit up. "You and Dusty still together?" They'd met once, way back when we were still just dating.

"She's living with me now. She's in town getting lunch."

"I understand the victim worked for you."

"Most of the people who work for me are here. It's a kind of prolonged company picnic."

"A little more exciting than most company functions, I imagine."

"Not in a good way."

"Any thoughts about why Mr. Reynolds there would have it in for your boy?"

I shook my head. "As far as I know, they had never even spoken to one another. Carl supposedly had friends on the island somewhere, but he didn't mention any names and no one came forward when he went missing."

"Was he a nice kid?"

"A little rough around the edges, maybe." I mentioned the fight with Kevin and its root cause. Bullard didn't seem interested, but then she never did. It was a useful mask.

"Any reason why I shouldn't accept the constable's theory?"

"I don't know what his theory is."

I could have guessed it though. Parish had suggested that Carl – like the tourist a year earlier – had resembled the dead daughter's boyfriend closely enough to trigger a violent reaction. He might have seriously injured the tourist if they had been alone. Parish figured that he'd stumbled across Carl at the beach and something had set him off. Carl was drunk and belligerent and might have said the wrong thing, or Reynolds might just have had a short fuse. He'd struck Carl with a stone and moved the body under cover of darkness, perhaps not even aware that Carl was dead. Or maybe he'd just forgotten about it by morning.

"I don't know anything that would prove Reynolds didn't do it," I said carefully. "But I have problems with that scenario."

One of the technicians came up to us and indicated that they were ready to move the body. "I need to watch this," said Bullard. "We'll talk more later."

Carl's body was transferred to a stretcher and loaded into the ambulance. Reynolds caught sight of it and grew agitated, and after a brief conference one of the EMTs administered a mild sedative. Bullard tried talking to Reynolds for a few minutes but clearly wasn't getting anywhere. Parish and the other detective got into the patrol car and headed down toward the town wharf, where Reynolds would be loaded onto the police launch for transfer to the mainland. The technicians began packing their equipment back into the van.

Our party started returning in small groups. Bullard started to question Eric and Claire, who were the first to arrive, then decided to wait until there was more of a quorum. "I don't have time to conduct a dozen interviews. We have to get back." She had glanced at the sky, which was growing prematurely dark as clouds began to gather. We had already heard some distant thunder.

Dusty and the Brubakers returned along with almost everyone else in one group. Bullard decided not to wait for the stragglers, asked mostly questions about Reynolds, whom none of us knew. Barry was the only one who provided anything concrete. Apparently he had been keeping an eye on him ever since their brief confrontation on the beach. "I saw him prowling around from time to time, but he seemed more interested in the girls." No one had seen him with Carl.

Several people confirmed that Carl had stormed off after the fight with Kevin and no one admitted having seen him later. Bullard asked what had caused the fight and Kevin answered truthfully as far as I could tell. She might have pursued this line of questioning, but Parish got a call on the radio. "The chop is picking up and your people are getting nervous. They say if you don't leave now, they may have to weather it out here."

Bullard had no intention of remaining on the island. She asked me how long we were staying and I told her we were going back the following day. "Can you send me a list of names of everyone in your party?"

"Of course. And I think you and I should probably talk about this."

She was already starting to walk away. "We'll do that. Maybe over lunch. I'll call you tomorrow."

I was actually rather relieved. I'm not sure how much I was going to tell her about Carl's circuitous journey to Reynolds' cabin, but at least now I could say that I'd made an effort. It might not even matter. Reynolds could have killed Carl, mistaking him for the man he believed responsible for his daughter's death. At a minimum he was seriously disturbed and needed to be under a doctor's care. But I wasn't satisfied that he was the killer, at least not yet. I didn't know anything that suggested otherwise and it was quite possible that the simplest explanation was the correct one. It just didn't feel right to me.

The storm hit us half an hour later. The launch was ahead of it but I doubted they'd make shore before it reached them. The day's events would have cast a pall over us all even if it had been bright and cheerful. The rain drove us back to our individual cabins. Dusty and I were both lost in our own thoughts and I suspect the same was true of most of the rest of our group. Dusty told me that Dennis and his girlfriend had been arguing during lunch and that Emily and Ashley apparently weren't speaking. "On the other hand, Kevin and Laura seemed much happier than they were yesterday."

The rain thoughtfully paused early in the evening and there was a general exodus for supper. Most of us ended up at the Pirate's Den, which was as crowded as I'd seen it. A few of the conversations were animated but I thought they sounded forced, although Dusty later told me I was projecting. We sat with Tina, Barry, and the Brubakers. Tina was starting to talk about work again but this time I made no effort to derail her. Truthfully, I was anxious to get back myself.

It rained again during the night, quite heavily in fact, but the morning sky was clear. We all packed up and Captain Wayne called Dusty around nine to tell us she was on her way. There was no hurry but we all made our way to the wharf anyway. Emily was the first to spot our ride; she and Ashley were ostentatiously not together. I turned and glanced back toward the interior of Black Island. It had not been a pleasant stay and I told myself I was never coming back.

But I was wrong.

We weren't going to open the office until Tuesday morning but as soon as I had unpacked, I told Dusty I was going to run by to check the mail. When I arrived, I was not surprised to see Tina's car in the lot, but I wasn't expecting Barry to be there as well. His little red sports car was snuggled up to the front door. I felt an odd sense of relief as I unlocked the door and went inside. If the weekend had been meant as a vacation, I suppose it worked because for the first time in a while I was feeling actively enthusiastic about being at work.

Tina didn't even look away from her terminal when I called a greeting. Barry was in his office and was a bit more sociable, but he clearly wanted to get back to the spreadsheets lying on his desk. I disengaged and went to my office after checking the mail, which was of little consequence. Once there, I consulted my digital address file and called Jason Rudnick. Jason was a freelance operative who had connections with the faculty at the University of Rhode Island. I had sent him a couple of referrals and sometimes subcontracted surveillance jobs, since he was one of the few people in the business who seemed to enjoy them.

"So what's up?" he asked after he'd gotten an update about Dusty and I and I had heard the latest about his kids.

"I was wondering if you could look into a disciplinary case at URI a few years ago." I described the incident involving Ashley and Kevin. "I don't know the name of the fraternity or the exact date, but it can't be more than six years or less than three. One of the victims was named Ashley Sternberg and one of the accused was Kevin Wise."

"So which of them are you most interested in?"

"Wise." Kevin had seemed like an upright person, but if he really had been involved in some form of date rape, I wanted to know. It might not be enough to make me fire him, but I'd be concerned about his access to confidential information. "I know that they didn't find him guilty of anything, but we both know how this kind of scandal gets swept into a closet whenever possible. He works for me now and I want to know how far I should trust him." I was going to leave it at that, but I decided to indulge my curiosity as well. "But I'd like to know more about Sternberg too. I don't think she's lying about what happened, but she might not be telling the whole story."

"Does she work for you too? Sounds like bad chemistry."

"No, but she's close to someone who does." Although I wasn't sure how close they were now. I hadn't seen them together on the trip back aboard the *Calamity Jane*.

"I'll see what I can find out. Is this a rush?"

I thought about it. "No, but don't forget about me."

Bullard called a few minutes later. "Free for lunch tomorrow?"

"Sure." We picked a place and time. "Did you get anything out of Reynolds?"

She laughed humorlessly. "Oh, he likes to talk. He didn't like your boy, or some boy anyway. He doesn't seem to have known his name or much of anything else about him. Blames him for his daughter's death."

"You know that Reynolds' daughter died in a boating accident?"

"Yes, as a matter of fact I have the case file sitting on my desk even as we speak. I haven't read it yet except for the summary sheet and Reynolds' testimony."

"Was there any reason to believe that it was anything other than accidental?"

"The investigating officer and the Coast Guard didn't seem to think so. She was supposedly well qualified but the skiff was old and not in the best repair. There was no obvious reason for it to capsize but she had the sail up and the favored theory is that a freak wind knocked it over."

"And the body was never found?"

"Nope. But she was quite a way from land."

"She had a boyfriend on the mainland. She was on her way to see him."

"I read her father's statement. He didn't know she'd gone and hadn't given permission. But she never got that far. There were rumors that they'd been seen together on shore, but he had a pretty good alibi."

"What's the boyfriend's name?"

"I haven't gotten to his statement yet. Hold on a second." There was a pause. "Shit!"

"What is it?"

Bullard didn't answer at first, maybe because she was processing what she'd just read, maybe because she wasn't sure she should tell me. But finally she made a decision. "Keep this to yourself for the time being, Paul, but the boyfriend was Carl Celucci."

The case against Oliver Reynolds now seemed complete. I should have been happy to know that the killer wasn't one of the people who worked for me. But I still felt that something was wrong, that this was too neat, and that I'd overlooked something that I shouldn't have.

I told Dusty about it over supper that evening. "You're not relieved to hear it," was her immediate response.

"I should be. If Reynolds is guilty, by reason of insanity most likely, they'll lock him away and close the case. It will be tragic for Carl's family and sad for Reynolds' friends, I suppose, but at least my employees won't be looking at each other and wondering if the guy, or gal, at the next desk is a murderer rather than just a bodynapper."

"Did you tell the police about that yet?"

I shook my head.

"Are you going to?"

"Yes. I'll tell Bullard tomorrow. I'll try to play it down and convince her to look the other way. I'll promise a stiff lecture for all concerned. She's in homicide; she doesn't want to have to do the paperwork for a handful of minor charges that won't draw any jail time."

"Are you sure of that?"

"No, but I think it's better to clear the air."

But I didn't get the chance. Bullard called first thing in the morning to cancel our lunch. There'd been a triple murder on the East Side. "I'll give you a call when I have a chance," she promised.

But she never did.

I have to admit that for the next few days, I gave little thought to the matter. We had a fresh influx of work, including a rather large scale operation to discover who was stealing freight from the docks south of Providence. Steve was still on vacation and we brought in a temp to sit at his desk, but Steve wasn't going to be gone long enough to train her as anything other than a greeter and that's all she did. Dusty took a week off to go visit her brother and his family – he and I couldn't stand each other and his wife was a cowed nonentity – so I had no one to talk to except by phone, which only reinforced my sudden loneliness. There had been a time when I relished my privacy but those days were gone.

Monday's mail brought a report from Jason Rudnick. We had a round of meetings scheduled so I tossed it into my briefcase unread. Oliver Reynolds was no longer in the news. He'd been remanded for psychiatric evaluation and there was no indication that the police were looking at anyone else. Merrilee had replaced Carl with a young woman with the widest eyes I'd ever seen and Mandy gave us two weeks' notice because he'd had a job offer doing mechanical drawings for an engineering company. James had been busted for smoking pot and we'd terminated him. Emily told us that he'd had some with him on Black Island, which explained his reluctance to have the constable in his cabin.

Our final meeting of the day ran late and I picked up a meatball sandwich on my way home. It was the last night before Dusty was due back and I had made a note to clean the house that evening, so it was almost bedtime before I remembered the envelope in my briefcase.

Jason was a thorough man. In less than two days he had accumulated an astonishing amount of information including a transcript of the disciplinary board meeting, a list of the members of the fraternity involved, and a cover letter which summarized everything and left me to draw my own conclusions. I read this first. Jason had spoken to one of the professors who had officiated. There was even a short biography for each of several people involved.

There was little question that Ashley and her friend, Margaret Large, had engaged in sex with one or more partners on the night in question, probably while drugged and/or unconscious. Neither of them had ever filed a similar complaint and Margaret, though not Ashley, had asserted that she had not been sexually active prior to the night in question. They had notified the university rather than local police and had waited so long that there was no chance of detecting the specific drug used, but their stories were consistent with that explanation and there had been previous allegations – though no formal complaints – about the fraternity in the past. Neither woman was able to identify the person or persons who molested them but Ashley had insisted that they had received their last drinks – beer – from Kevin Wise. They also identified several other young men with whom they had subsequently been talking but insisted that they had never put down their drinks so no one else had had an opportunity to add anything to them.

Their testimony was contradicted by at least half a dozen people, some of them female, who said that both of the victims had been dancing intermittently, that they had not only left their drinks unattended but had actually become confused about which were which. Kevin had admitted that he'd served drinks to almost everyone at the party, although he claimed not to remember Ashley or Margaret. There was supposedly someone checking student IDs at the door and no one under drinking age was supposed to have been allowed in, but he admitted that he didn't think they were really screening attendees very well. The university had declined to punish anyone individually but had suspended the fraternity for the balance of the term along with various other sanctions that didn't interest me. They might have done more but neither Ashley nor Margaret appeared at the final hearing.

Professor Gillian, who had chaired the board, had told Jason that while someone undoubtedly spiked the drinks and raped the women, she was reasonably certain that Kevin had not been involved. He apparently manned the bar throughout the evening and was cleaning up when the two victims recovered and came downstairs. Gillian believed that everyone involved had displayed bad judgment, that some fraternity members were clearly guilty or rape, and that others were protecting their friends. There was, unfortunately, no way to determine the identities of the rapists.

I read through the transcript next and could find nothing to contradict Gillian's opinion. The biographical sketches were all short and succinct. Kevin had finished his degree but had permanently moved out of the frat house. Margaret Large had dropped out of college, had an abortion, and moved to California, where she worked for an insurance company. Ashley Sternberg transferred to Bryant and graduated a year later. Kevin had given no indication that he had recognized Ashley, although she obviously remembered him. I made a mental note to ask him about it and clear the air.

I almost didn't bother with the rest of the documents. There was a photograph of the fraternity house, notes about the various board members, a summary of two alleged incidents that had occurred the previous year involving the same fraternity. Kevin had not been a member until the following year. And finally there was a complete list of members of the frat at the time of the rape. On impulse I scanned through them, not expecting to find anything.

Surprise! Carl Celucci was also a member.

I stared at his name for a long time. It might be just another coincidence. Stranger things have happened.

The following morning I very deliberately drank a cup of coffee at my desk while I thought about the report some more. When

I was done, I picked up the phone and called Merrilee's desk. "Is Kevin in today?"

"Yes he is."

"Could you ask him to come down to my office?"

"Is he in trouble?"

"I don't know. Probably not. But a question came up. Do you know if he and Carl knew each other before they came to work here?"

"Not that I know of. They hit it off pretty well back before Laura entered the picture, but not right away."

"All right. Have him come talk to me. I'll fill you in later."

Kevin arrived promptly, looking nervous. I told him to have a seat and waited a few seconds. I figured I'd get more if he was on edge.

"I understand you had a little bit of trouble during your junior year at URI."

He looked puzzled for a second, then nodded. "You heard about the party."

"And the rape charges."

"I wasn't involved with any of that, Mr. Birch, I swear. I was just handing out beers. And I dropped out of the frat right afterward."

"One of the victims named you specifically."

"I know that, but she was wrong. Maybe I was the only one she remembered. There was a lot of drinking going on. I didn't drug anyone and I didn't go upstairs at all until after everybody was gone and I'd finished cleaning up."

"But you know who did."

He shook his head. "I've got a pretty good idea but I didn't have any proof. My parents never found out, thank God. They won't even have alcohol in the house."

"Did you know either of the two women who brought charges?"

"No. I mean, I probably saw them at the party, but there were lots of girls there and I was pretty busy. I was going steady then but my girlfriend was out of town that weekend. That's why I volunteered to work the bar."

"Do you remember their names?"

"No. One of them was Maggie something, I think."

"The other was Ashley Sternberg."

It took a few seconds to sink in. Then he nodded. "So that's why she was so antagonistic. I didn't recognize her at all. I think she had real short hair back then, but I just don't remember. It's not one of my favorite memories."

"Did you know Carl when you were in college?"

"No. He was in the same frat but he didn't live at the house. He had a girlfriend over in Warwick and she had a whole house. Parents with money. I didn't even know he was a brother until we went out drinking after work one night and compared notes."

"Then you never met the girlfriend?"

"No, never."

"You don't remember her name by chance?"

"I don't think I ever knew it."

I sent Kevin back to work with assurances that his job wasn't in danger, that I had just wanted to clear the air. In fact, I should have been feeling much better all around. It didn't seem likely that Kevin was involved in the fraternity rape, despite what Ashley believed. There was now a powerful motive, or at least it seemed so, for Reynolds to have killed Carl. There was some coincidence involved, but after all the secretive comings and goings and moving of Carl's body, a little coincidence was pretty easy to accept. Everything seemed to have been tied up at the end, if not very neatly. Bullard would be happy with her case, Reynolds would be institutionalized, and life would return to normal.

So why wasn't I comfortable with the situation?

I tried calling Bullard again but she was out of the office. I left a message but she didn't call back and when I tried again late in the afternoon, I was told that she was unlikely to be back before morning. "Her caseload is pretty heavy at the moment, Mr. Birch." She wouldn't be happy if I suggested that she should look more closely at one she probably already considered closed.

It was the following Monday before I finally got through to her. I could hear the irritation in her voice when I told her that I still wanted to talk to her but I promised to buy her a nice lunch if she'd bring along the case file on the Reynolds girl. "Why?"

I was ready for that. "A couple of my people are peripherally involved because of their relationship with Carl. I just want to reassure myself that they aren't hiding something that might suggest their integrity is questionable."

"Everybody's integrity is questionable." But she agreed to bring the file.

We met at Alforno's. Bullard brought me up to date quickly. Reynolds would not be going to trial any time soon if ever. He had stopped speaking and did not seem to be aware of his surroundings most of the time. "The doctors also say he has brain cancer. Probably inoperable. We'll know more in a day or two."

I decided to clear the air. I gave her a brief account of what I'd learned about the night Carl had died. She listened without changing expression but I thought I saw a hint of a smile tugging at the corners of her mouth. "I don't think any of this affects your case directly, but I didn't want you to think I was suppressing evidence."

"Took you a while to get around to it."

"I tried to tell you out on the island but you took off. And I had an appointment the following day and you cancelled."

She granted my point. "You know that I should be charging them all for interfering with a police investigation, unauthorized movement of a dead body, and so forth and so on."

"None of them actually lied to you. You didn't ask the right questions. They did tell me and they knew I was going to pass on the information at the first opportunity."

We haggled a bit, but she didn't want to be bothered with the paperwork, and she didn't want to spend any more time on a case that seemed to be resolving itself smoothly. Our food arrived just as she was handing me the case file. "You'll have to read it here."

"You didn't make me a copy?" I knew she wouldn't have.

"You can take notes."

I read it while I ate, skimming parts that didn't interest me. I found Carl's address in Cranston and the name of the girl he was living with. It was not Reynolds' daughter unless she was using a fake name. I hadn't expected it to be. I jotted down the names of people the police had interviewed who had confirmed Carl's whereabouts at the time the girl presumably died, although with no body, there was certainly plenty of leeway there. His roommate hadn't known that she had competition and there was a note that she was hostile and uncooperative.

The Coast Guard appraisal confirmed the accident theory. It had been gusty that day and the foundered skiff had not been rigged appropriately. Too much sail and not properly balanced. Someone had walked the piers along the coast with a picture and no one on the mainland remembered seeing Alyson Reynolds on the day she disappeared, although a couple of them knew her face. Reports of a couple roughly matching the description were too vague to be definitive. There was no indication that she had ever reached the mainland.

Carl's story was a bit odd but not implausible. He said that Alyson had called the previous afternoon to say that she was coming over in the morning and that he should meet her in Galilee at noon. He didn't have his own car so he'd tried to get a ride from a friend, but the friend called back at the last minute and cancelled. He took a bus and a cab instead, arriving almost half an hour late at the coffee shop where they were supposed to meet. She wasn't there so he stayed around for a while, then decided she'd left in a huff believing that he had stood her up. He said that he called her cell phone but that she hadn't answered.

The interview with Oliver Reynolds had not gone well. He had clearly been distraught and asserted that it was all Carl's fault, that the girl knew better than to take the skiff without permission and had been tempted into disobedience. He refused to believe that it was an accident, insisted that he'd taught his daughter how to manage the skiff and that she would never have made such a foolish choice of sails. He evidently believed that the two had met in Galilee, that Carl had killed her for reasons unknown. He had no explanation for how the skiff had been found capsized well out to sea but was convinced that Carl must have arranged it somehow. Nothing in the file supported his version of events.

It all seemed pretty straight forward, but I still wasn't satisfied. "No one actually saw the girl leave the island," I pointed out.

"But she told her boyfriend she was coming and it wasn't the first time she'd taken off like that without letting her father know."

"Still…"

Bullard sighed. "You've been around long enough to know that there are almost always some loose ends that don't get tied up neatly at the end."

"The investigating officer only spent two days on the case."

"What would you have had him do that wasn't done?"

I didn't have an answer. I scribbled down a few more notes while we had coffee and dessert and then handed the file back to Bullard. "Thanks for this, and for forgetting about my ill-advised employees."

"Crack the whip a little harder and we'll call it even."

When I got back to the office, I took the time to type a summary of what I had just learned and print out a copy. I re-read the text before putting it into my briefcase and decided I was just being foolish. It was, after all, none of my business. Even if Carl had somehow contributed to Alyson Reynolds' death, it didn't matter anymore. He was past being punished. I told myself to forget about it.

But naturally Dusty asked me that evening about my meeting with Bullard and I offered to let her read my summary.

"No. Tell it to me. You're always meticulously neutral in print. It's only when you're talking about a case that I get a real sense of how you perceive it."

'Okay. Here's what we know, or think we know. At some point in 2010 Carl Celluci visited Black Island where he probably met Alyson Reynolds for the first time. He told the police they hooked up in the bar at the Moby Dick. Oliver Reynolds was unhappy about their relationship. Carl says that her father was overly protective and didn't want her seeing anyone, even though she was twenty years old. The police talked to some islanders who apparently were sympathetic to Reynolds, but even they suggested that he was old fashioned and refused to recognize that his daughter was a grown woman. On the other hand, he doesn't seem to have objected to her dating some of the local boys, so he may have had a specific reason to dislike Carl."

"There are a lot of overly protective parents." Dusty's father had never been physically abusive, but he firmly believed that he was entitled to make all the decisions for his family and he still tried to dominate her, which was why we so rarely saw her parents.

"Anyway, on October 4 Alyson and her father had a major fight when he demanded that she break things off. She and Carl had been dating for about three months at that point, but it seems to have been pretty casual. Sometimes she went to the mainland, sometimes he came out to island, but they didn't meet more than a couple times per month. When they were on the island, they always avoided Oliver because on the one occasion when she had introduced them, it had nearly ended with an actual fight."

"But he had to know about them being together," interrupted Dusty. "It's too small a community."

"Maybe that added a little zest to things. It's not clear how serious they were. Carl was in fact living with another woman at the same time," I consulted my notes, "Connie Meikle. Carl says they had an open relationship, but Connie apparently was unaware of that loophole. She says she never knew about Alyson until the police came to see her. They checked around a little and didn't find anything to contradict her story."

"Gives her a motive though."

"Yes, but she threw Carl out that same day, which suggests otherwise."

"What did Carl say? About Alyson, I mean."

"He says they were just friends, admits they had sex a few times, but they had been meeting less frequently and, according to Carl, he was planning to break it off. In fact, according to his story, he had cancelled two consecutive planned trips and that was why Alyson was so determined to meet him on the day she died."

"When she came to the mainland previously, did she take the ferry or the skiff?"

"During the season the ferry runs more frequently so that's how she traveled most of the time, although she did take the skiff across by herself at least twice before. She'd been sailing back and forth since she was sixteen, so she obviously was experienced. But once the season ended October 1 the ferry was unworkable unless she planned to stay overnight, which on this occasion at least she did not. Carl says they rented a motel room once but he discouraged overnight stays because he didn't want to have to answer questions about why she couldn't come to his apartment."

"She didn't know about Connie."

I nodded. "So she called Carl and arranged to meet him at a coffee shop in Galilee. Carl told her that it was bad timing because he couldn't borrow a car that day, but he talked a friend into giving him a ride down, called her back, and the meeting was set. Then the friend backed out for reasons unknown - although he confirmed

Carl's story – and Carl had to make other arrangements. He arrived half an hour late, waited around for a while, claims that he walked the waterfront looking for her skiff before calling a cab. He said that he figured her father had forbidden her to take the skiff, which in fact was the case, but she had ignored him."

"He never tried to call her?"

I searched my memory. "He made at least one call to her cell phone, but she didn't answer. I don't know if he ever tried again."

"But you said that he and the father did know each other."

"Yes, they'd met only once according to Carl and Oliver never said otherwise. He knew that Carl hadn't been out to the island for awhile and that his daughter was anxious to see him, so he forbade her to use the skiff without permission. That was confirmed by another islander. Father and daughter had a big blowout about it because she'd apparently used a lot of her own money to buy new sails and some other equipment."

"They both had jobs, I assume."

"She was a waitress during the season and did some part time secretarial work the rest of the year. Oliver was an electrician and sometimes tended bar. He stopped working shortly after his daughter died, sold his house, and rented a cabin from Ted Welch."

"Where was he the day she died?"

"Installing a new generator for one of the locals. He said that Alyson was apparently still in bed when he left the house in the morning, but was gone when he came back around mid-afternoon. He didn't think anything of it until around supper time when he went down to the pier and found the skiff missing. Called her cell phone, but she was probably dead by then. One odd thing is that no one else saw her that day and no one saw the skiff leave, so we don't know what time she set out."

"No one else noticed that the boat was gone?"

"There's no mention of that in the report. Some of the private piers are pretty secluded though. And even if someone passed by and looked, there'd be no reason for its absence to stick in their memory. A lot of the islanders, including Reynolds and his daughter, sailed over to the mainland to shop or take care of other business."

"Who found her boat?"

"A couple of guys out fishing called the Coast Guard and reported it. They were still looking for survivors when a Coast Guard rescue cutter showed up but they didn't find anything. They towed the boat back. No significant damage, no bloodstains or other signs of violence. In their opinion it was an accident probably due to misrigging."

"But Reynolds didn't accept that."

"No, he did not. According to him, Carl somehow lured her to her death. Alyson was too good a sailor to make that kind of mistake. She shouldn't have gone out on such a windy day. His accusations don't make a lot of sense and sometimes contradict one another."

"Grief isn't always logical."

"No. The facts support the ruling that her death was accidental. I suppose it's possible that she ran into an unfriendly boat en route and whoever was on it somehow overturned her skiff, presumably killing her somewhere along the line. But it was clearly impossible for Carl to be in two places at once so he couldn't have done it."

"What if she's not really dead?"

I hadn't considered that possibility. "Faked the accident and skipped out on her father? I suppose it's possible. But why would she do it? She was an adult and according to the police report she had a nice little nest egg tucked away. She could have left the island any time."

"Maybe she was afraid her father would come after her. He's obviously the obsessively possessive type."

"I suppose it's possible, but it doesn't seem likely lacking some other, deeper motive." I thought about it some more. "But it wouldn't hurt to ask a few questions."

"You like asking questions."

"Not really. I like getting answers."

It was easy to tell myself that I was going to look further into the presumed death of Alyson Reynolds but it wasn't quite as simple in practice. Merrilee had Eric track down Carl's old girlfriend, who was now living in San Diego. I had noted the name of the Coast Guard officer who filed the accident report – a Lieutenant Javier Hernandez – and left a message that I would appreciate if he called me either at home or at work. I also put in a call to Constable Parish, who was obviously surprised to hear from me.

"What can I do for you, Mr. Birch? I thought all the loose ends were pretty much tied up."

"They seem to be, but I found a little fraying around the edges and thought I might be able to clean them up."

"What did you have in mind?"

"I thought I might come out one day and talk to some of the people who knew Alyson Reynolds. Her friends, the people she worked with."

"You could do that, but I don't know how much they'd be willing or able to say. Alyson was pretty much a loner, you know. She wasn't really close to anyone on the island."

"She must have dated, hung around with the girls."

"Not so much. Oh sure, she went out with the local boys a few times but there was never anything serious about it. She was just waiting to get off the island."

"Why didn't she then? She was twenty."

"Probably waiting for the magical twenty-one. I know she was salting away most of the money she made. Her heart was on the mainland. Some people are born islanders. Some aren't."

"Well, I'd feel better if I made the effort. Could you give me a list of names and contact information?"

"Let me have your email address and I'll see what I can come up with."

"I'd like to talk to people who knew her father well, get an idea of her home life."

I could feel his hesitation. "You might run into some resentment. Despite his faults, Oliver had lots of friends and we islanders tend to stick together."

"Nothing I can do could hurt his case, and it might help."

"Well, just so you know. Anything else? You want me to tell these people you're coming?"

"It's no secret but don't go to any trouble. And I don't know just when I'll be able to find time for the trip."

"Are you working on some theory or just fishing?"

"Fishing, mostly. But I did want to ask you something. Did you or anyone else ever suspect that Alyson Reynolds wasn't dead after all? They never found her body, and the accident – if that's what it was – could have been staged."

"The Coast Guard officer asked the same question. But we couldn't figure out any reason for it. She didn't clean out her bank account and she could have left any time if she'd wanted to."

"Might she have been afraid of her father?"

"Alyson? I don't think that young lady was afraid of anything. Oliver always had a bit of a temper but it was nothing compared to hers."

"Interesting. All right, I've taken up enough of your time. Thanks for humoring me."

"No problem."

Connie Meikle did not call that evening or the one following. I thought about leaving another message or sending a letter, but I was busy enough that I didn't do either. I did hear from Lieutenant Hernandez who sounded quite pleasant, if a little puzzled. He was going to be in Providence on Saturday giving a lecture on boat safety at a local country club. "It's open to the public so you could meet me there. I'll look up my notes on the case before I come."

That Friday night I was undressing when the phone rang. It was Meikle, calling collect as I'd suggested. Her accent said Cranston, Rhode Island, and her tone said she was wary but curious. I had said that I wanted to talk about Carl Celluci but I hadn't mentioned that he was dead and, as it turned out, she hadn't known.

"Well, I guess I'm sorry to hear that but I'm not particularly surprised. How did it happen?"

I gave her a simplified summary of the official story and she responded with a nervous laugh. "I guess he finally pissed off the wrong person."

"Was he that hard to get along with?"

"Not at first. He could be charming when he wanted to. I let him stay with me six months rent free, you know, so he must have had something. I'm not the soft hearted type."

"How did you meet him?"

"In a bar. We were pretty casual. He was around and I was looking for company. We never pretended it was love at first sight or anything but we had some good times."

"Did you know any of his friends?"

"Not really. He never mentioned any and I got the feeling he was kind of lonely."

"But he lived with you for half a year." I hoped I didn't sound critical, or old fashioned.

"Yeah, but even if he hadn't been cheating on me, it would have ended pretty soon. I already had a line on a job out here and I wasn't going to renew my lease."

"You never met Alyson Reynolds?"

"Was that the girl he was seeing? No, I never even heard her name before."

I wasn't finding out anything I didn't already know. "Carl told people he had friends on Black Island. Did he ever mention any of them?"

"I knew he'd been out there a few times. I told him maybe I'd go with him and check it out but he told me I wouldn't like it. So I guess he must have been cheating all along because that was right after he moved in."

"He never mentioned anyone else that he might have known out there?"

"I think he said something about a bartender he talked to a few times but if he said the name I don't remember."

"Did he ever stay overnight?"

"Yeah, sure. Two or three times. Once he called and told me he'd missed the last ferry boat, and once he said he was feeling sick and was going to bed." She laughed unpleasantly. "He probably was going to bed."

"Did he stay at one of the hotels?"

"No, he was too cheap for that. Now that you mention it, he said he was bunking with a friend. I always figured it was a guy but I guess it was probably that Alyson person."

I tried a few more questions but Connie didn't know, didn't remember, and probably didn't care. Her only hint of sympathy was right at the end when she asked if she should send flowers to the funeral.

"There wasn't one. Carl was cremated." His parents had arranged it all from Florida. "Did you ever meet the parents?"

"No. Carl wasn't speaking to them. He said they threw him out of the house because he wouldn't pay them enough to stay there."

"Do you know where they lived?"

"East side of Providence, I think. They had money. It wasn't as if they needed for him to pay rent."

"Maybe they thought it would teach him some responsibility to pay his way."

"Yeah, I guess." Connie obviously saw no logic in that.

I thanked her and hung up and wrote up everything I had learned. It only took a minute or so.

Dusty was finishing up the final edit of her novel that weekend, so I left her to it and went to Bristol alone. The Bristol Waterfront Country Club was small but the building and furnishings were impressive. I figured there were a few million dollars worth of yachts in the adjoining marina and a few millionaires in the crowded little bar. Signs guided me to one of the piers where a uniformed Coast Guard officer was talking to a handful of teenagers. Apparently the adults already knew everything they needed to know about safety on the water and they were all inside consuming an alternate liquid. I hovered on the fringe of the small crowd, not really paying attention, and after a few minutes there was some scattered applause and they dispersed.

I walked over to introduce myself to Lieutenant Hernandez, who seemed not much older than his recent audience although it turned out he was nearly thirty. "You must be Mr. Birch."

I admitted my identity and shook his hand. "Is there someplace we can talk?" I glanced toward the mob scene in the bar.

"There's a little place across the street that sells fried clams and fritters."

"Sounds great."

Twenty minutes later we were sitting in a cramped booth in an overcrowded diner, but the clams were great. Hernandez had a briefcase in which he'd brought a copy of his investigative notes, although as it turned out, he never had to refer to them. "So what would you like to know about the Reynolds case and why are you interested?"

I explained about the connection to Carl Celluci and gave him a very heavily edited summary of the events surrounding his death. "On the surface, it all seems to make sense, but a couple of things bother me. For one thing, they never found the body."

Hernandez dipped a French fry in catsup. "You think the young lady may have faked her death?"

"At this point, I don't think anything. I'm just trying to gather facts and see what fits together."

"Well, the missing body is annoying but not that unusual. She was still pretty far from shore and the water is deep there."

"But don't bodies float to the surface once they start to deteriorate?"

He nodded, nibbling a bite of fried potato. "Normally, if they're not caught on something or eaten by something before that happens."

"But if it did make it back to the surface, wouldn't it have ended up on shore somewhere?"

"From where we found the boat, I'd say the odds were about fifty-fifty. I would have preferred to find her, but I wasn't much surprised when she didn't turn up."

"How about the boat? Was it really windy enough that day to blow it over?"

"Not as a matter of course, but it was gusty and there was too much sail on the skiff. If it caught her just right, then over she'd go."

"My understanding is that she was an experienced sailor. She went back and forth to the mainland fairly frequently. Why would she make such a dumb mistake?"

He gave a short laugh. "You'd be surprised by some of the dumb things done by experienced sailors. They think they know enough to get away with breaking the rules. The tentative sailors are the safest. They double check and triple check and don't take chances."

"So there was nothing suspicious about the accident."

"Oh, I didn't say that. There were a couple of things that bothered me. First of all, why put up sail in the first place? She wasn't out fishing or sightseeing. She wanted to get to the mainland and see her boyfriend. So why not just use the outboard and go for it?"

"Would that have been faster?"

"Considerably."

"That didn't raise a red flag?"

"Not by itself."

"How hard would it be to have intercepted her boat?"

Hernandez sat back. "It wouldn't have been impossible but it would have taken some planning. I looked into the possibility that she'd been followed but since no one saw her leave, obviously no one would have seen a second boat in her wake."

"Was there anything suggesting what time she set out?"

"Nothing definitive. The father claimed that she was still asleep when he left for work that morning, but he didn't actually see or hear her. The door to her bedroom was closed and apparently he wasn't allowed in without an invitation. The young lady was famous for her temper." He grinned and then popped the last of his fries into his mouth.

"So she might already have been out of the house."

He nodded. "Which means she could have left at any time during the night or early morning. She had a cell phone so we don't know where she was when she called the boyfriend. We tried to trace the phone's location by GPS but no luck. The accident – if it was an accident – might have taken place while she was en route to the mainland, or coming back, or traveling between two other points."

"Did you check to see if she'd been seen anywhere that morning?"

"Not personally. We asked the state police to make some inquiries, which they did, but nothing turned up. The most likely explanation is that she left the house and the island some time after her father went to work."

I was just about out of questions so I thanked him for his time but he made no move to get up. "There's one other thing that you might find interesting."

"What's that?"

"We couldn't find a mooring rope on the skiff."

I thought about it. "The boat capsized. I imagine anything loose on deck was lost."

"Correct. But why would the mooring rope not have been secured." He leaned forward across the table. "The rope is tied to a ring set in bow of the skiff. The loose end gets tied and untied every time the boat is moored or cast off. But why would anyone untie the opposite end?"

I thought about it. "There might have been a reason. It might have come loose and she didn't bother to retie it."

"Or it could have been frayed and she planned to replace it. There were a couple of other suggestions. They're all plausible but they're also all improbable."

"What does it mean?"

"I haven't the faintest idea, but it bothered me."

"So now two of us are bothered."

"Right. But does it do either of us any good?"

"Too soon to tell." I found myself liking Hernandez, so I decided to tell him something I hadn't planned to reveal. "I have a problem with the death of the boyfriend."

"It sounds straightforward enough," he said noncommittally.

"Yeah, but the morning after he disappeared, the local police checked his cabin. They found a blood soaked handkerchief."

"Might not be related."

"Except that we know it was. A young woman found the body on the beach the previous night and thought he was still alive. She tried to clean the wound with that very same handkerchief."

"You're sure it was the same one?"

"Pretty sure. It was distinctive."

"She didn't tell anyone?"

"It's complicated, but once she realized he was dead she found herself shielding someone else."

"Could she have gone to the cabin for some reason and left it there?"

"She says she didn't and I believe her. There was no reason for her to lie."

"Is there any chance that he was still alive, recovered, and went there himself?"

"No. Trust me on this one. He didn't go anywhere on his own after she found him."

The food was gone. Hernandez sat back and stretched his arms over his head. "I'd say you have quite the little problem there. Do you have a working hypothesis?"

"Not really, but I'm convinced the two deaths are connected in more ways than the obvious ones. I think Carl knew something – or was perceived to have known something – about Alyson Reynolds that some party unknown – and not her father – wished to suppress."

"It's been a couple of years since the girl disappeared. Why now?"

"Maybe Carl just recently discovered or realized what he knew and confronted whoever killed him. Maybe they were involved in a long standing conspiracy and it broke down or the other party just decided not to risk it anymore."

"Do you think it was someone on the island then?"

I shook my head. "Not necessarily. No one keeps track of who comes and goes on the ferry or when they do it. Someone could have followed us over from the mainland."

"Or preceded you if they knew about your excursion."

"Which wasn't a secret. And that doesn't even account for the various private boats owned by the islanders, or the visitors who moored there during the day. I suppose I could get a list from the harbormaster."

"Don't bother. It's on a cash basis. He might remember the names of some of the boats but it's been a couple of weeks. I wouldn't trust his memory."

"Nothing is ever easy."

"Tell me about it." There was a prolonged silence and Hernandez reached for his wallet.

"No, lunch is on me."

"On the expense account, you mean."

"Not this time. I don't have a client. This is personal."

"You liked the kid?"

"Not particularly. I just don't like being played for a fool."

"Neither do I. Let me know what you find out."

"I'll do that."

I had kind of hoped that Hernandez would provide me with some answers but I had also kind of expected that he'd only have more unanswered questions. I should have felt discouraged by our conversation, but I didn't. I wasn't the only one who thought something had been missed and now I had more reasons – admittedly very small ones – to think that I was right.

Later that day, I called Bullard to see if she had contact information for Carl's next of kin. She did and she read it off to me. "I don't suppose you found anything interesting among his possessions?"

"Not even slightly. Nothing at his apartment except some cds and a rather impressive selection of rather unimpressive clothing.

Nothing personal at all. No photographs, correspondence, everything generic and nothing out of the ordinary."

"What about his pipe? He claimed it was an antique."

"Didn't find one. Wait a second." I waited. "There's no pipe listed in the inventory. Are you sure he had it with him?"

"Yes, but it probably doesn't matter. If he had it on the beach with him, it might have been washed out to sea after he was killed." I thanked her, thought about it, and decided it wasn't important. But I made a note anyway.

There was another long distance telephone call that I needed to make, but I'd been putting this one off. Robert and Gayle Celluci lived just outside Coral Gables, Florida, in a condo complex catering to the elderly. Carl had been an only child and his parents had both been in their forties when he'd been born. I wondered whether the pregnancy had been a late life quest for proxy immortality or a very unexpected surprise.

I called from the office on Monday morning and got a gruff but not unfriendly male voice. "I'm looking for Robert Celluci."

"You've got him. What can I do you for?"

"My name is Paul Birch. I run the agency where your son Carl was working when he died. I wanted to call and tell you how sorry I am about your loss."

"Thank you for your concern." The voice had lost some of its heartiness.

"I wondered if I might ask you a few questions."

"What kind of questions?"

"I'm investigating the circumstances of his death."

"I thought the police had already done that. They told us the man responsible has been arrested."

"They've arrested a suspect and at this point it appears likely that they have the right person. But there are some unanswered questions that I'm trying to resolve."

"What's your interest in this, Mr. Birch?"

"Carl was an employee and I feel a certain obligation to him. And if Mr. Reynolds is not in fact responsible for his death, I want to make sure that whoever did kill him is apprehended." I was a bit surprised to hear some hostility in his voice. "I know it won't bring your son back, Mr. Celluci."

I could hear the sigh. "Listen, Mr. Birch, I'm sure you're trying to do the right thing, but I may as well tell you now that neither my wife nor I had spoken to our son in two years and there was little prospect that we would ever have done so again."

I wished that I had been able to see Robert Celluci at that moment because body language is sometimes very important. "I understand that there was some estrangement."

He laughed, short and ugly. "Do you have any children, Mr. Birch?"

"No, I'm not married."

"Well if and when you ever do get married, give some serious thought to remaining childless. I know they can be a blessing but they can also be a curse."

I didn't know what to say, but Celluci continued without waiting for a prompt.

"Our son was troubled right from the start. The psychologists called it an 'affect disorder' or something like that but the problem wasn't something he had. It was something he didn't have - a conscience."

"Sometimes it takes a while for children to develop a sense of responsibility."

"Carl didn't know right from wrong, Mr. Birch. He only knew what he wanted and once he wanted something he calculated the easiest way to get it. The rights of others, or any other kind of consideration, weren't just secondary. They were nonexistent. He stole from his friends, from the neighbors, and from us. It started when he was very young and it never stopped." He paused for breath and I decided to let him resume on his own.

"He never denied it when he was caught. He didn't seem to understand why people were upset. He became angry, sometimes violent. We felt both relief and apprehension when he went off to college. For a year or so it seemed to do him some good. There were no incidents that we knew of, but then again, we gave him a handsome allowance. Not handsome enough, apparently, because my wife discovered that he had somehow learned our password and was tapping into our retirement account. She was so furious that she confronted him without waiting for me."

I started to say something but he cut me off.

"The little bastard knocked her down and kicked her. Broke two ribs. I found her lying there when I came home from the golf course. She spent two days in the hospital and she still hasn't gotten over it. I wanted to call the cops but she wouldn't have it, so we sold the house, changed our passwords, and moved to Florida. I suppose he could have found us if he'd wanted to, but I never heard anything from or about him again until the police called to tell us he was dead."

I didn't know what to say so I said "I don't know what to say."

"I don't know if this Reynolds person killed our son or not. But if it was someone else, then I say good for him. He did us all a favor. The world's a better place."

I don't know how much of that he meant, but it was obvious that he wasn't going to be able to tell me anything about Carl's recent activities. "Thank you for talking to me, Mr. Celluci."

And I hung up.

Constable Parish had emailed me a list of names – three boys Alyson had dated plus the woman who employed her as a part time office worker and a man who had hired her occasionally as a waitress. There were addresses and telephone numbers for each person, or in some cases, for a married couple. I separated these into two categories. Those who were friends of the family – most likely the father's age – I would attempt to reach by telephone. I just wanted background from them and considered it unlikely they could, or would, tell me anything significant. The second list of names consisted of people who had known Alyson more intimately. These people I wanted to talk to in person. You can often learn as much by watching expressions and body language as you can from the actual words people speak.

The following morning I walked upstairs to Merrilee's domain and asked people to gather around. I explained that I was doing some follow up concerning Carl's death and wanted to know if anyone – including those who hadn't gone on our excursion to Black Island – could tell me anything more about Carl's friends on the island. Jeff Mikulski immediately raised his hand. "He told me once that he had stayed with a friend there a couple of times but hadn't been back in a couple of years."

"Friend or friends?" I asked.

"I'm pretty sure he said friend, and it was a guy. That's all I remember though."

I thanked him and asked everyone to keep me in mind if they thought of anything else.

Later that same day I called Tabitha Short. I knew Tabitha professionally. She ran a smaller version of my own operation down in the southwestern corner of the state and we competed for business from the insurance industry in Hartford. Fortunately there was enough of it to keep both of us and a couple of other competitors comfortably occupied. Tabitha also did divorce work, which I avoided, and had a deserved reputation as tough and resourceful. I had never subcontracted anything to her in the past because I could get better rates from the independents, but this time I wanted some work done that I preferred to keep secret from anyone in my organization, formally or otherwise.

We exchanged greetings, promised each other that we'd get together for lunch sometime even though we both knew that we probably wouldn't, and then I moved on to the business at hand. "I want you to do some focused background checks on about a dozen people."

"Isn't that your line of work?"

"All of the people on the list work for me."

She digested that. "All right. I gather you don't want anyone to know that you're doing this."

"I don't want anyone to even know that it's being done."

"That makes it a little harder, but not dauntingly so. Focused how?"

"I want to know what connections, if any, they have to Black Island or any of the residents thereof. Family relationships, previous job experience, college roommates, romantic entanglements, anything that seems to establish a link."

"How far back?"

"They're all in their twenties. Let's not bother with their parents or siblings, at least not for the moment."

"Anything in particular that we're looking for?"

"Probably, but I don't know what it is." I gave her a brief summary of Carl's murder and the death or disappearance of Alyson Reynolds. "Any connection to the Reynolds family would be of particular interest, obviously."

"How fast do you need this?"

I wanted it yesterday, but I wasn't willing to pay the premium she'd ask for that kind of service. "There's no rush, but I don't want it to gather any cobwebs."

"Who do we bill?"

"Me." I gave her my home address. "What's your email? I'll send you the list along with their birth dates." I could get that from the computerized personnel file.

I made up the list right away. While I was adding birth dates and social security numbers, it occurred to me that technically Steve, my secretary, should also be there. He was the only one I absolutely knew had connections on Black Island. I thought about it and decided to leave him off. I couldn't see any possible way that he could have taken his wheelchair down across the soft beach sand to kill Carl Celluci, and even if he had, he would have left a highly visible trail. More importantly, even though Steve had worked for me for less than two years, I was no more willing to accept the possibility that he was a killer than I was of Tina, Barry, or Merrilee. My judgment of people has been faulty in the past, but never of anyone I've known as well as I knew Steve. I didn't add his name.

Another weekend passed before I returned to my phone list. Dusty picked up a bad cold somewhere and passed it on to me. I spent a day and a night and the following day mostly in bed or on the couch, marveling at how much fluid my sinuses were able to produce. Dusty recovered first and nursed me that last day, but I slept so much that I was up late in the evening reading, unable to sleep even though I felt considerably better. That was Saturday and I have an aversion to bothering people on Sunday, so it was Monday again before I called the first name on my list.

Harold Cabot answered the phone so quickly he must have been sitting right beside it. I identified myself and explained that Constable Parish had given me his name as someone who might be able to tell me a little about Oliver Reynolds and his daughter.

"Are you a reporter?"

"No, sir. I'm an investigator looking into the circumstances surrounding Mr. Reynolds' arrest."

"Everyone says he must have done it."

"Sometimes everyone is wrong, but I'm not working for Mr. Reynolds or against him. I'm just trying to establish what really happened."

"Can't tell you anything. I haven't talked to Oliver in almost a year. He got pretty strange when his little girl was lost."

"They were close then?"

"Father and daughter. What do you expect?"

"I understand Alyson had quite a temper."

"Wouldn't know about that."

We went back and forth for a time before I realized that if Cabot knew anything interesting, he wasn't going to tell me. Parish had warned me that people might not want to talk, but I told myself Cabot might just be more close mouthed than most.

Henry Todd, Gloria Taplak, Annette Wilson, and Wolfgang Barth were equally uninformative. The Barkleys did not answer their phone.

The last name on my list was Agnes Tillotson, a widow, and despite my weariness I dialed her number. It ran for a long time and I was about to hang up when there was a click and a thready voice answered so softly that I almost couldn't hear her. I ran through my identification and reason for calling again, and asked if there was anything she could tell me about the Reynolds family that might help me understand why the elder Reynolds had been so despondent. Agnes not only could, but she was ready to discourse on the subject in such intricate detail that the call lasted well over an hour.

Stripped of all the irrelevant gossip, her story was considerably shorter. Oliver Reynolds had been an islander all of his life, as had his wife, Gwen. I don't think Agnes quite approved of Gwen despite her frequent praise. Gwen was devoted, obedient, a good homemaker and mother, quiet and unassuming. Perhaps too quiet and unassuming. She had been totally dominated by her husband, who made all the decisions about the household, would not allow his wife to continue with her part time job or charity work after they were married, and who rarely engaged in an active social life. Agnes implied that Gwen was virtually a prisoner but never seemed to mind, and that's where Agnes expressed her carefully guarded disapproval. "She never had time for her old friends any more, or actually she did have time but Oliver didn't think it was proper for her to have a circle of friends of her own and she never questioned him." Gwen had died of cancer about six years after giving birth to Alyson.

Their daughter was another person entirely. Alyson proved rebellious even before her teen years, was constantly sneaking out to play with the boys, and at fourteen was involved in the theft of a neighbor's sailboat. "There was her and three boys on it when the constable – it was Bill Parker back then – overhauled him and made them come back. Bill and I played bridge together and he told me that Alyson was the brains behind the operation. She always was a smart one, too smart for her own good."

During adolescence, Alyson dated casually, never had a steady relationship, and began telling everyone that she was going to leave the island as soon as she was old enough. "We all kind of expected her to run off after she got out of high school, but she got herself a couple of part time jobs and stayed with her father."

Oliver, meanwhile, had tried unsuccessfully to manage Alyson's life the same way that he had managed her mother. It had been like setting sparks to tinder. "I'll give the man credit. I don't think he ever laid a hand on her. That wasn't his way. But I could hear them shouting at each other sometimes when I walked down Merchant Street, and that's two blocks away." The storm had not diminished with the passage of time and Alyson's chaotic emotional life had occasionally erupted elsewhere. "She was in some fights at school, nothing serious but she got suspended at least twice that I know of. And one time Bobbie Stone tried to make a move on her and she hit him with a lamp hard enough that he needed stitches."

Alyson had, however, acquired some self control by her late teens. She held a succession of part time jobs and did well at all of them. "She used to make up rooms at the Breakwater and she always got bigger tips than the other girls. Alyson always made an effort to talk to the tourists and convince them she was interested in them personally. It was really the tip she was interested in but people go on vacation to live in a dream, so it's not wrong to help the illusion along, is it?"

Agnes didn't think that Alyson had any close friends. "She and Linda Bettis hung around together for a while, but then it wasn't very long. I'm not sure if she had any special friends toward the end. I haven't been able to get around as much as I used to. The doctor says I need to have my knees replaced, blames it on all the years I was a waitress. I suppose he's right but I don't much like the idea of having gears and things inside my body. Isn't natural."

She did know a bit more about Oliver's collapse after his daughter died – Agnes was certain she was dead. He went to pieces right away. He'd been the same way when Gwen went, but he had the child to look after and came out of it pretty quickly. This time there was no one left. His brother had died a few years earlier and he didn't have any other relatives that she knew of. "He started drinking at first, but that didn't last long. Stayed at home, wouldn't see any of his friends, and he did have friends. Say what you will about the man, he was generous and helpful. He loaned money to Art Baldwin to set up his dental practice, and he was always willing to give advice to anyone who asked for it."

The drinking was followed by a deepening apathy. "People would hire him to do a job and he wouldn't show up, or he'd start it and then wander off for days. He stopped attending town council meetings even though he was a member. He'd pass old friends in the street without a word and he talked to himself sometimes. Then there was that problem with a tourist."

The tourist had been an apparently inoffensive college student from Deming, New Mexico, who was on break from Providence College and came over to the island with a few friends. Oliver had encountered him on the street and had flown into a sudden rage. "I guess it took everyone by surprise because he really hurt that poor boy before they pulled him off. Broken ribs, banged up face, stuff like that. Young Parish was the Constable then. He locked Oliver up and talked the kid out of pressing criminal charges, but he went to court for damages and won. That's when Oliver had to sell the house and his boat and pretty much everything else. He rented a cabin from Ted Welch and people kind of pretended he wasn't there. He wasn't the man we used to know."

I thanked Agnes profusely, promised to come see her if I was ever out on the island, a promise I had no intention of keeping, and then called the last name on my list, the one I hadn't given Parish. Ted Welch answered immediately and when I identified myself, asked after the rest of my party. With the civilities out of the way, I told him I was looking for background on Oliver Reynolds and his daughter. "I gather they had a stormy relationship."

"Well, you'd have to understand Oliver. He was pretty set in his ways, and his ways were a little old fashioned." His description did not vary significantly from the one Agnes had provided although he was a bit more sympathetic to Alyson. "He wanted her to go straight to school and straight home again and not speak to anyone except the teacher. I thought he was going to have a stroke the first time she decided to go out with a boy. But he knew better than fight about it, and she was never serious about anyone so I guess it didn't bother him as much as it might have."

Ted also confirmed that Oliver had never physically abused his daughter. "He's not a small man but I never heard of him ever touching anyone else in anger until the day he opened up on that young tourist. It was like all his strength was in his voice and when he stopped talking to other people, well, that strength had to come out some other way."

He couldn't remember the tourist's name, but I knew I could find it if I wanted to. I made a note, thanked Ted for his time, and promised I'd come out to the island again soon, a promise I did mean to keep.

The battered tourist was named Nelson Train and he was now in his senior year at Providence College. The school wouldn't give me his telephone number but it was in the book so I called, got an answering machine, and left a mildly cryptic message that I hoped would entice him into calling back. He took the bait, but not until the following morning.

I explained who I was, asked if he had heard the news about Oliver Reynolds. He had. "They should have locked him up a long time ago."

"I'm just trying to develop some context that might have a bearing on what happens to him. I wondered if you could tell me exactly what happened the day he attacked you."

"What's to tell? I was walking down the street all by myself, not bothering anybody, when this raunchy looking guy suddenly grabs my arm and asks where his daughter is. I figured it was, you know, mistaken identity, and I told him I didn't know his daughter. I was already starting to walk away when he hit me. Never saw it coming. There were some steps there and I tripped or I might have hit him back, but he was a big guy and he pinned me down and just kept hitting me and screaming. And then some other guys pulled him off but I was pretty much out of it by then."

"You hadn't seen him before?"

"Might have passed him on the street. We'd been on the island since the night before – slept on the beach until they chased us off."

"Was this your first time on Black Island?"

"First and last. You couldn't pay me to go back there."

And that was that. I looked through the notes I had taken during better than four hours of telephone calls. There wasn't much more than a single typed page. With wide margins. Hopefully my trip to the island to talk to people personally would be more productive.

I spent the weekend helping Dusty dismantle the world of Pullemia in our attic. The fantasy series was done, the publisher had accepted the manuscript for the final book in the series, and she was already playing with ideas for her next project. "I'm considering doing a western with something supernatural going on."

"*The Good, the Bad, and the Really Really Bad*?"

"Someone's already doing that. I was thinking more like something that lives in a silver mine and kills the workers. Or maybe I'll just give in and do another Craig Daniels thriller. The publisher keeps asking for one. We could take a trip to Japan or somewhere to do research and charge it as a business expense."

"Or just build a scale model of Tokyo."

"Or both."

By Sunday night, Tokyo had won out over the Old West.

Another week passed before I felt I could spare time for a day trip to Black Island. I started calling people on my second contact list, trying to set up times when we could meet. Both of Alyson's former employers were easy to reach and amenable to talking to me, although both seemed somewhat guarded and one told me outright that they'd heard through the island grapevine that I was poking around. I assured her that my intentions were not malevolent.

Alyson's friends, such as they were, presented a more difficult challenge. One of the boys had left the island a year earlier and his present whereabouts were unknown. His father was unhelpful and expressed his lack of interest in his son's present location or situation. Another was in Afghanistan. The remaining two boys were, conveniently enough, sharing a room at the Oceanview where they worked, one as night security and the other as kitchen help. I talked to the former, whom I had apparently gotten out of bed, and he vaguely agreed to a time and thought he might be able to get his roommate to come along. I promised to buy them a meal.

Parish had also given me the names of three young women whom he believed were as close to friends as Alyson allowed. The first flatly refused to talk to me. "I hardly knew her and I never met her father. She was kind of a bitch and I wouldn't waste my time on her. That's all I got to say."

Fortunately the other two were willing to meet me for lunch as long as I was buying. I scheduled an appointment with the woman who owned the restaurant where Alyson had been a waitress for the morning, since she didn't open up until noon, and with the manager of the Oceanview for the afternoon. It looked like I could easily manage everything in a single day and take the evening ferry back.

Dusty expressed some interest in going. The day before she came home from the library with a substantial pile of books about Tokyo and a smaller one about Fukushima. "Craig uncovers the truth about what really caused the Fukushima meltdown and he has to hide in Tokyo because the bad guys don't want him to reveal the truth."

"You're not going to spread radioactive materials around in the attic, are you?"

"No, but I might buy some phosphorus." I couldn't tell if she was joking.

"I'm going over to Black Island on Thursday. Want to come along?"

"Are you going to get into trouble?"

"Probably."

"Then I guess I should probably go along to rescue you."

"Or you could just send Craig Daniels."

"He's going to be busy and I'm more fun anyway."

"Can't argue with that."

As it happened, Dusty didn't go with me after all. When she told her new agent that she was starting a new Craig Daniels novel, he set up a meet with his contact at the publisher and Dusty took the early train to Manhattan, planning to get in a little shopping as long as she was there. After dropping her off, I drove down to Galilee and took the eight o'clock ferry, which gave me just enough time to have coffee and a cruller before heading over to The Moby Dick, which was open now that the season was underway. It was fancier than The Pirate's Den, empty when I arrived and knocked on the door. A couple of teenagers were filling salt shakers and arranging place settings and I could hear voices from somewhere in the rear, presumably the kitchen.

Margaret Taylor was probably in her sixties but looked a decade younger. She was tall, carried herself well, and radiated self confidence. She opened the door for me, asked if I wanted coffee or tea, and led me to her office. "So what can I do for you, Mr. Birch?"

I repeated my stock explanation for asking questions. "I understand that Alyson Reynolds worked for you."

"She was a waitress for two seasons."

"Good at her job?"

"Very. She knew how to be friendly enough to get a good tip without being so friendly that it caused trouble."

"Do you often have trouble?"

"Not very, but a disproportionate number of my customers are young, unattached males. The island has become something of a destination for singles. Some of them drink too much."

"Was Alyson friendly off the job as well as on?"

She frowned slightly. "Alyson wasn't unfriendly, but she tended to keep to herself. The other girls sometimes went out together but she never went with them as far as I know."

"Did you ever meet her father?"

This time she allowed herself to laugh. "This is a small island, Mr. Birch. I doubt that there is anyone living here that I haven't met at all, and I probably know all but a handful by name. Yes, I knew Oliver Reynolds. He was an occasional customer and he went to school with my younger brother. He always had a stick up his butt and I don't think he approved that I managed this place on my own, but we weren't unfriendly. I was sorry to hear of his troubles, all of them."

"Do you think he killed the Celluci boy?"

She thought about that. "I think he was capable of it."

"You said Alyson didn't hang around with the people she worked with. Did she have friends outside of work? A boyfriend?"

"She had met someone from the mainland but I never met him or heard his name. I know that he came over to the island a couple of times but I never saw them together."

"Was there anyone with a reason to wish her harm? A jilted boyfriend? A jealous rival?"

She laughed. "Well, she sure came equipped to have either. Alyson was a real looker, or whatever the term is nowadays. But she never let any of the local boys get close. She wanted off Black Island and she didn't want anything, however tenuous, to hold her here. Alyson had a temper but she knew when it was appropriate to let it loose and when it wasn't."

We talked some more. She told a couple of anecdotes and I realized she had felt considerable respect for Alyson Reynolds. I revised the picture I had been developing and wondered what Alyson had seen in Carl Celluci. He certainly wasn't her ticket off the island and he wasn't strikingly handsome. She was probably making more money than he was while they'd been dating.

It was close to noon before Taylor started to get restless so I thanked her for her time. "I'm meeting a couple of Alyson's friends here for lunch. They said you serve the best food on the island."

"I do, but Perry over at the Den makes the best scampi I've ever eaten."

The two young women arrived right on time. They were both in their early twenties but that was about the only thing they had in common. Kristin Coyle was trying a little too hard to be sexy, too much makeup, a tank top one size too small for her, and an affected air of sophistication that wouldn't have fooled a wino. Carrie Wayland was plainly dressed and wore no makeup at all as far as I could tell. She seemed ill at ease and restless. The hostess brought them to the booth where I was nursing a lemonade and we introduced ourselves.

Carrie had worked with Alyson cleaning rooms and had seen her intermittently up until her disappearance. "After I got a full time job at the emergency room, I didn't have as much free time. We were never that close anyway."

Kristin had gone off to attend the University of Rhode Island, dropped out during her sophomore year, and was back living on the island. "But not for good. I'm just getting my act together. Alyson and I always said we were going to leave, even back in grade school."

"Why didn't she?" I asked.

Kristin shrugged, her nose stuck in the menu. "She had a plan. Alyson was always organized about things. She had figured out how much money she needed as a stake and set herself a deadline. On her twenty-first birthday, she was packing up and leaving and wasn't ever coming back, not even to visit. She kept saying it was the final chapter in the book of her childhood and she was anxious to get on with the sequel."

"What do you think happened to her?"

"She screwed up. It wasn't the first time she'd taken a chance out on the water. My dad's not the brightest guy in the world, but he taught me to respect the ocean. It can kill you in a heartbeat if you don't."

I turned to Carrie. "How about you? What do you think happened?"

She shrugged. "Everyone says it was an accident. Alyson took chances sometimes."

I ran through most of the same questions I had put to Margaret Taylor. Did Alyson have enemies, had she been more secretive in the days preceding her death, did they know the boyfriend from the mainland? If these two had been Alyson's closest friends, then she was one of the most closed in people I had ever encountered. Carrie hadn't even known that Alyson was seeing someone, and Kristin knew but hadn't met him, hadn't even known his name.

"She might have told Lynda about him," said Kristin. "They were pretty tight for awhile."

"Who's Linda?" No one of that name had been on my list.

"Linda Bettis. She used to work at the Oceanview." Kristin looked uneasy, as though she had revealed some dark secret, but Carrie was unconcerned. I remembered now that Agnes had mentioned the same name.

"Yeah, she and Alyson were pretty tight. Not best friends forever, or anything like that, but they hung out after work sometimes."

"Can you tell me how to get in touch with her?"

They shook their heads in unison. "Linda left the island about a year ago, after her mother died. Sold the house to some real estate guy who still hasn't found a new buyer." Kristin made clear her disdain for the realtor. "I heard she was in Providence, but that was awhile ago."

I jotted down the name in my notebook. "Does she have any other family on the island?"

"No," said Carrie. "Her father died in a boating accident when she was a little kid."

"He got drunk and fell over the side is the way I heard it," added Kristin. "If you're a hotshot detective, how come you didn't know about Linda?"

"Constable Parish didn't give me her name."

She thought about it. "Yeah, maybe he didn't know. They kept to themselves. Rumor has it they were a couple for a while but it didn't work out."

The food was good and all three of us had appetites. Carrie asked at one point if it was exciting being a detective and I gave her the short version of my prepared speech about how it was relentlessly boring most of the time.

"It's pretty dull out here too. When Mr. Reynolds killed that guy, it was the most excitement we've had in a long time. Mrs. Grayson had me jumping through hoops." Mrs. Grayson, it turned out, was the Registered Nurse at the island's aid station. The two local doctors were technically always on call but most of the time it was flu shots, cuts and scrapes, and the occasional hypochondriac. "Anything serious gets sent over to the mainland." The nurse also ran the island pharmacy which was incorporated into the emergency room. She hadn't been born on the island and according to Carrie was counting the days until she could retire and leave.

" When Mrs. Grayson heard someone was missing and possibly injured, she had me running around like crazy getting things ready. And it was all for nothing."

"Still better to be prepared."

"Yeah, I guess. But she could at least have let me make some coffee first. The second I walked in the door she handed me a list of things to do."

We finished lunch. I didn't learn anything else. Carrie thanked me politely and I gave one of my business cards to each of them. "If you think of something else, I'd appreciate a call."

Arthur Bushnell, manager of the Oceanview, was a complete washout. He was abrupt, irritable, and uncooperative. He was willing to give me Alyson's dates of employment, grudgingly admitted that she'd been an exemplary employee, but he didn't know anything about her friends, habits, or potential enemies. "We don't pry into the private lives of our employees."

I tried a couple of roundabout questions, hoping he'd open up a little, but if he knew anything – and he probably didn't – he wasn't going to tell me. I was there less than a half hour.

That left me with four hours to kill before my appointment with the two boys Alyson had dated, and from whom I expected to learn little if anything that I didn't already know. A picture of Alyson had formed in my mind. She had been a strong willed and intelligent young woman, organized and with a specific goal she was working toward. I had the impression that she was very disciplined, although the suggestion that she sometimes took chances when out on her boat seemed to contradict this, and it also made the ruling that her death was accidental somewhat more reasonable. She didn't seem like the kind of person who would pair up with Carl Celluci, but perhaps she was just using him for something. Or maybe he was great in bed.

With nothing else to do I wandered through the shops, a couple of which had not yet opened when I'd last been here, and I was bored enough that I bought a little miniature pagoda in a gift shop. Dusty might be able to use it in the mock up for her new book. I had a cold drink and an ice cream cone and finally found a bench facing the water where I could watch the occasional boat drift past. That's where I was when Constable Parish spotted me.

"I heard you were on the island today." He sat down beside me with an exaggerated sigh. "Find out anything useful?"

"Not much. I didn't really expect any startling revelations. Television shows to the contrary, I'm in a boring business. Most of the time I'm sifting through paperwork. Today I'm talking to people who generally aren't interested in helping trying to find some information the nature of which I don't pretend to know and which might not exist in the first place."

"Sounds grim."

"It beats working for a living."

"I hear you. Do you know why I'm Constable Parish instead of Chief Parish?"

"An attempt to be quaint?"

He laughed. "We're overstocked on quaint. The town can't afford a real police force. Outside of a couple of college courses, I have no formal training. We couldn't afford to pay an experienced, qualified person. But that's okay because I'm really more of a bouncer than a police officer. I corral the drunks, make a run past the beaches every night to keep kids from sleeping there, come back early in the morning to chase off the ones who sneak back, search for lost dogs, mediate arguments between neighbors, and call for help whenever anything more complicated comes up."

"Probably pays a princely sum as well. What keeps you here?"

"I'm an islander. It's in my blood. I never feel quite easy when I'm on the mainland."

"The rhythm of things does seem different out here."

"How'd it go with Art Bushnell?" He was grinning so I figured he had a pretty good idea already.

"He's not the most forthcoming witness I've ever interviewed. Margaret Taylor was much more helpful."

"Peggy's a peach, all right. She chairs the town council in her spare time. Formidable woman. Serves a good meal too, not that she doesn't have competition. It's either the Dick or the Den if you want to eat well out here."

"That sounds vaguely obscene."

He chuckled. "It used to be called The Pirate's Booty."

"Ouch!" I paused appreciatively. "I'm meeting Devin and Karl for supper. Maybe they'll have something for me."

Parish looked doubtful. "I wouldn't get my hopes up. It's been close to three years since either of them actually went out with her."

"She might not have been exclusive with Carl."

He nodded. "Good point. But if she'd been seeing either of them, even casually, it would have gotten around."

"Small island," I said.

"Very small."

"Alyson Reynolds didn't like it here very much."

"We lose better than half our young people. There's no potential for growth here, and most of the jobs available to them are part time or low paying. If they have the training and aptitude for something better, they go off to the mainland. Can't really blame them."

"But you stayed."

Parish glanced out toward the water while he thought about that. "You know, to be honest with you, I never actually thought about leaving. Some people have the island mentality and some don't. I'm no hermit. I go over to the mainland every week or so. I used to date a TA from the university but she went off to grad school a few months back."

"You're lucky. Not everyone gets to stay in a place they love, if they even know where one is."

"It's not so much that I like it as that this is where I belong. I couldn't stand to be away from the ocean for more than a couple of days. That boat of mine cost nearly as much as my house is worth. It's fast, comfortable, and powerful enough to pull a good sized sailboat off a sandbar. Half the year it's my home, the other half it's my refuge, and I'm honest enough to admit that it's a big part of my self image. Over there," he gestured vaguely toward the distant shore, "I'd just be another guy trying to get along."

"What's the story about Linda Bettis?"

"Linda?" He gave me an inquisitive look. "Where did her name come up?"

"Someone said she and Alyson were pretty close."

"Maybe, for about half a minute. Linda isn't into men and for a few weeks Alyson thought that might be the life for her, but it blew over pretty quickly. I'd forgotten all about it."

"She left the island, I understand."

"Went off to make her fortune. She definitely wasn't the island type. The first time she ran away from home was when she was twelve. Stole her mom's grocery money to buy a ferry ticket. The Galilee police picked her up right away. The next time she was gone for a week before she turned up at a shelter someplace in

Warwick. Settled down a bit after that, but there was never any doubt in anyone's mind that she'd leave as soon as she was able."

"Sounds like she stayed longer than she might have."

"Her mother got sick and Linda stayed with her till the end. I give her credit for that. But she sold out right afterward, paid off all the medical bills, and took the ferry with all her luggage. I haven't heard anything from or about her since she left. I don't think she'd be much help to you."

"Even so, I might try to track her down. Can you ask around and see if anyone knows where she ended up?"

"I can do that. Don't know that it will help."

Dinner with Devin and Karl was not a tremendous success. Both young men seemed ill at ease. Devin, the security guard, talked too much and Karl said almost nothing. Both men admitted having dated Alyson "years ago and for about two minutes" according to Karl. They couldn't remember having so much as spoken to her during the year preceding her disappearance and they both assumed that Oliver Reynolds had killed Carl justifiably.

"If it wasn't for him, Aly would still be alive. She should have known better to hook up with an outsider." Devin's argument was somewhat flawed since he later admitted he was semi-engaged to a girl from Cranston.

When I asked about Linda Bettis, they exchanged looks. "She's a dyke," said Devin. "And she always thought she was too good for the island. No one was sorry to see her leave."

"I understood she and Alyson were pretty close."

Neither of them met my eyes and Karl was actually blushing. "I never heard anything about that. You'd have to ask her," suggested Devin.

"I don't suppose you'd know how I could get in touch with her?"

"Sorry, man. I got no interest in dykes."

I thanked them, paid the check, and made my way down to the ferry. The trip hadn't been a complete waste of time, but I was still disappointed.

Monday morning I stopped by Merrilee's desk and asked her to see if someone could track down Linda Bettis for me. Frankly at this point my interest in the deaths of Carl Celluci and Alyson

Reynolds had waned considerably. Oliver Reynolds was clearly incompetent and would never be tried. Despite some odd elements, his daughter's death had probably been an accident. Neither Carl nor Alyson had left behind any obviously grieving friends or family. Worst of all, I had nothing even approximating an interesting line of inquiry. On the other hand, good investigators are thorough and there were still a few loose ends, however unpromising they might be.

Merrilee was poised to take notes. "Social security number?"

"Don't have it."

"Date of birth?"

"Unknown. Her parents were living on Black Island at the time. I think."

She pursed her lips. "Job training?"

"Waitress." I gave her what little employment information I had.

"She might have married and taken her husband's name, you realize."

I shook my head. "I don't think Linda is the marrying type."

"Well, let us take a stab at it."

I managed to successfully put the entire matter out of my mind for the balance of the day, which was moderately busy. There had been a series of break-ins on the East Side and the home owners' association wanted an independent evaluation of alarms and surveillance systems.

Then I had a late afternoon meeting with a client in Scituate and I forgot about it even though Steve had reminded me twice. Since I hate being late, I rushed out to my car and that's when I spotted Ashley Sternberg, sitting in an unfamiliar dark green Honda in one of the visitor's spots. If I'd had more time I would have spoken to her, but as it happened, I didn't even acknowledge her and drove away wondering what had brought her to my office. Merrilee had told me just a day or two earlier that she and Emily were no longer a couple. But the meeting was important, I started rehearsing my presentation, and I forgot about the incident until later events made it seem more sinister.

Merrilee came down to see me the following morning. Steve brought us coffee and I asked after her husband, who was suffering from gout. Then she opened a folder and took out a single sheet of paper.

"Linda Bettis worked as a cocktail waitress at Buster's Bar and Grille for three months last year. That gave us her social security number and a home address, an apartment house on the south side of Providence."

"But she's not there any longer, I assume."

"Nope. She gave notice with no explanation, worked out her remaining time, and cashed her final check. She also moved out of the apartment. The landlady says she left no forwarding address and there's no record of one at the post office. Unless she's working under the table, she hasn't had a job since. No telephone listing for anyone of that name in Rhode Island except an elderly woman in Westerly who never heard of our missing person. She could have gone underground, or moved out of state to live with a boyfriend – or girlfriend, or…"

"Or she could be dead," I finished.

"All sorts of possibilities. Does this have to do with Carl?"

"Sort of. I'm not sure." I explained the connection. "Thanks for the help." Merrilee started to rise as I asked, "Do you know if Emily and Ashley are back together?"

"Not that I've heard of. That girl has been moping around ever since we got back. She's one of our best, when she's concentrating on her work. Any reason why they should be?"

"I don't know. I thought I saw Ashley in the parking lot the other day. I might have been mistaken." But I knew I wasn't.

Dusty's reconstruction of Tokyo and Fukushima was well underway. She had accepted my pagoda thoughtfully, looked it over, and rejected it. "Thanks for the thought, but that's a Tibetan pagoda. It's not Japanese."

"Since when are you an expert on Asian architecture?"

"Since I read the label on the bottom." Given her substitutions in the past – the cooling towers at Fukushima were represented by wine bottles – I thought she could have stretched a point. The next day I visited a toy store and was rewarded by a shout of laughter when Dusty went upstairs the following morning. She must have found the plastic Godzilla I'd placed in downtown Tokyo.

My visit to Buster's was not very productive. I arrived half an hour before they opened and rapped on the door until someone came to tell me they weren't open yet. I explained that I just wanted to ask about a former employee and eventually I was ushered into the presence of Buster himself. Buster was a roly-poly guy with a shaved head and a face that looked positively evil, but he was reasonably cooperative.

"Sure, I remember Linda. Good worker, knew how to deal with the problem customers. She was only here a few weeks but I was sorry to see her go."

"She didn't leave a forwarding address?"

"Nope. What'd she do? Some guy called just last week asking about her."

"That would have been one of the people from my office." I gave him my card. "She's not in any trouble. We're just looking for information she might have about a boating accident."

"I'm not going to be much help. I don't ask about their private lives."

"Was she particularly friendly with anyone else who worked here?"

Buster rubbed his chin. "She and Angela got along pretty good. Angela's been with me ever since I opened this place."

"Do you think I could talk to her?"

"As far as I'm concerned, no problem. But you'll have to wait until next week unless you want to fly to Wisconsin. She took a week's vacation to go to her sister's wedding in Madison. She'll be back on Monday."

"Maybe I'll do that." But I didn't think I would. Even thoroughness has its limits.

Tabitha Short called me a few minutes later. None of the names I'd given her appeared to have Black Island connections. "I can dig deeper if you want, but I don't think I'm going to find anything."

"No, I'm satisfied. Thanks."

In retrospect, this might have been the end of my involvement in the case. I had accomplished virtually nothing and halfway believed that the official explanations of both deaths were accurate in the main although probably deficient in some details. I had no leads, no alternate hypothesis, no client, and no other external incentive to spend further time on the matter. As Dusty would say, I had no dog in this race, and didn't like dog racing anyway.

But then something happened that gave me a fresh and powerful incentive for discovering the truth. Someone fired a gun at Dusty.

It was the morning of the day Angela the waitress was supposed to return to work, but her name wasn't even on my tentative schedule for the week. We were moderately but not excessively busy, but Tina was on the warpath because someone had introduced a virus onto "her" network and even though her preventive measures had isolated it for extermination, she wanted everyone to know that this was unacceptable. Steve looked so abashed that I thought he might have been the guilty party, but then I noticed that everyone else had the same sheepish expression. Tina's occasional outbursts have that effect. I probably looked guilty myself.

I was considering that possibility when the phone rang. It was Dusty. "Come home. Now." And she hung up.

I did as I was told.

There were three police cars with flashing lights in front of my house, but no ambulance or anything with the word "coroner" on it. Nevertheless, I was having an anxiety attack while I identified myself to the uniformed officer standing guard over my front yard, which was sequestered behind yellow tape. "What happened?"

"Shots fired. No one hit as far as we know. The sergeant said to let you through."

Sergeant Scott of the local police was in the living room with his partner and a uniformed female officer. I knew Bill Scott quite well; he was straight as an arrow but lacked imagination. Dusty was sitting on the couch with her legs crossed. She appeared calm but I could tell by the severely neutral expression on her face that she was anything but. I asked her if she was all right and she nodded. "Somebody shot at me."

"Three times as far as we can tell," said Scott. "We found all three rounds."

"Who was it?"

"We were hoping you might have some suggestions. Whoever it was parked at the curb, fired through the passenger side window, then drove off."

"What kind of car?"

"Dark green or grey," said Dusty without looking up. "That's all I noticed. You know I don't pay attention to cars."

"Where were you?"

"I had just come outside. I had planned to go to the flea market. I was turning to lock the door and something hit the wall right beside me. I didn't realize it was a bullet until I turned and saw the car at the end of the driveway. There were two more flashes and I dove into the hedge. I had my cell so I dialed 911, then called you."

"What happened to the car?"

"It drove away."

"Did you see the shooter?"

She shook her head. "Not even a silhouette. Just a kind of dark shadow in the window. It didn't seem like a good time to introduce myself."

"Miss Rhodes insists that she doesn't have any enemies," explained Scott. "Not even an impassioned reader upset that her hero didn't end up with the right girl. It might have just been something random or a case of mistaken identity." Scott didn't believe either of those explanations and neither did I.

"This wasn't about her."

"A disgruntled client? Someone you showed up or got fired?"

I thought about it, but shook my head. Only one of my recent cases had resulted in anything more than mild embarrassment, and the exception was currently locked up. I supposed it could be a friend or family member, but it didn't seem likely. On the other hand, if I told Scott what I suspected, it wouldn't do any good. "I'll give it some thought."

There were a few more questions and a few more cautions. Photographers and technicians went over my front yard and trampled some of the flowers. Dusty endured it all with a set face and it wasn't until they were finally gone that she began to shake. I held her for awhile. "That must have been scary," I ventured at last.

"Scary?" She pulled away from me, but slowly. "I didn't have time to be scared when the shooting started and there's no reason for it now. But I'm mad. I'm furious. I want to go out and buy a handgun and learn to use it. I want to hunt that bastard down and rip his throat out with my teeth."

"Or her throat," I suggested.

"Whatever. Why would someone want to shoot at me?"

I hesitated, but I hadn't lied to her ever before and I wasn't going to start now. "I don't think it was you. I think someone is unhappy that I'm asking questions about Carl Celluci's murder, or the disappearance of Alyson Reynolds. Or both."

She considered that for a few seconds and nodded. "That makes sense. But why shoot at me and not you?"

"I think it was a warning. The shooter could have waited until you came down to your car. They couldn't have missed from that distance. And I saw where the three shots hit. Either our mystery visitor is the world's worst shot or you weren't really in any danger."

"That doesn't make me feel any better."

"No, I didn't think it would. But maybe you should go visit your brother for a few days."

"Because you're not going to stop asking questions."

"Actually, I had just about decided to drop the whole thing. Now I'm more convinced than ever that Reynolds is innocent and I don't think that his daughter's death was an accident either."

She digested that. "First of all, I'm not going anywhere." I hadn't thought for a second that she would allow herself to be frightened away, but I had had to make the effort. "Second of all, I want to help."

I didn't like that idea much but I decided not to argue the point. Dusty was going to do whatever it was that she was going to do. I would just have to see that she was as safe as possible while she was doing it.

"So who knows that you've been looking into the two deaths?"

I thought about it and winced internally. "Well, everyone at the office, because I've had them checking a few things." I thought about my request that Constable Parish talk to people on Black Island and my own conversation with Agnes. "And probably just about everybody out on the island. And at least a few in the Coast Guard, the State Police, and a few miscellaneous categories."

"A real stealth operation."

"I didn't see any reason why it should be, and given the situation, there was no way to keep things under wraps in any case."

"You've been at this for almost a month. What did you find out recently that changed things?"

I gave it some thought but I couldn't think of a thing. I had run into a number of dead ends and turned up a few minor discrepancies, but none of them had been secrets and none pointed toward any individual. It probably wasn't what I had learned but what I might learn, which meant that somewhere out there was a clue that could unravel the truth, and I must have brushed against it even if I hadn't realized it at the time.

"I'll get all my notes together and we'll go over them together. Maybe a fresh set of eyes will help."

I won't lie to Dusty but that doesn't mean I tell her everything. If I even suggested a bodyguard, she'd go ballistic. Sergeant Scott had promised increased patrols in the area for the time being, but I knew that was more for show than results. There were a couple of people I employed off and on for surveillance who could handle themselves, but unfortunately Dusty had met both of them. On the other hand, there was a newcomer in the area who had just relocated from Dallas. I couldn't remember his name but he had sent me his card looking for business and I'd checked his background. His reputation was good and he had worked with the witness protection program. I made a note to call him in the morning.

Parts of my notes were just my personal variety of shorthand, memory triggers rather than detailed summaries. I've always had the ability to replay conversations in my mind. That made them less accessible to others though, so I ended up talking for most of the evening, repeating just about everything that had been said to me since the beginning. Dusty was particularly interested in what Lieutenant Hernandez had said. I did edit out a lot of the sidebars I'd heard from Agnes.

Then we went over everything that had happened during the excursion to Black Island. I had constructed a rough timeline of events and Dusty added several details. There wasn't a single person from our party that we could rule out absolutely, although she agreed with my exclusion of Nina, Barry, Steve, and the Brubakers.

"Do any of the others have any connection to Black Island or the Reynolds girl?"

"Not that we know of," I admitted. "Tabitha is always thorough. But that doesn't mean that none exist. Any of them could have gone to the island at some point in the past, or have met someone from the island while they were on the mainland."

"But they all worked with Carl. Why wait so long to kill him?"

"The motive, whatever it was, might not have existed previously. The killer might just have learned something about Carl. One of the guys might have been Alyson's secret lover and he might have decided that Carl was in fact responsible for her death."

"Did she have a secret lover?"

"If people had known, it wouldn't have been a secret."

Dusty shook her head. "It doesn't sound right to me."

It was late by the time we decided to call it a night. The only potential source of information that hadn't been pursued was Angela, the waitress at Buster's. I wasn't optimistic that she could help. It seemed unlikely that Linda Bettis could tell me anything of substance that I didn't already know, but she might be able to suggest another area of inquiry. I also needed to talk to Constable Parish again, just to see if he had turned up anything on Black Island. And while I was at it, I decided to call Detective Bullard and tell her about the shooting incident. It might spur her into taking another look at the Celluci case.

I was very careful to ensure that all the doors and windows were secured before we went to bed.

Dusty seemed to have shrugged off her scare by morning, but I knew her well enough to understand it had not been forgotten. We spent the morning at home and I noticed that she kept the curtains drawn, but occasionally peeked out toward the street when she thought I wasn't looking. Once she tensed for a couple of seconds, then relaxed. I asked what was wrong and she gave a nervous laugh and said a dark car had just driven past the house and it had startled her. So I took her out for lunch and we spent most of the afternoon in the Providence Place Mall. The shooting had almost certainly been a warning so I wasn't seriously concerned that someone would shoot at us, but I couldn't entirely dismiss the possibility and my nerves were on edge all day.

Monday morning I called Bullard, who pointed out that there was no evidence that Dusty's scare was in any way related to her now closed case. I had to admit that logically she was right. "But it does suggest otherwise."

"Maybe. But not strongly enough to reopen the Reynolds file." She hesitated. "But watch yourself and Dusty as well."

The next order of business was the bodyguard. The name I had was James Coleman and he answered his own phone. His voice was deep and confident. I told him who I was and asked if he was available for some clandestine surveillance. He was. "It might involve some physical danger."

"That's always the case."

I explained what had happened. "It might be related to a matter I'm investigating. I'm interpreting it as a warning to back off."

"Which you're not going to do."

"Which I'm not going to do."

"They'd get better results if they shot you rather than your girlfriend."

"That thought had also occurred to me." I had taken my brand new Kel-Tec P11 semi-automatic out of the office safe and it was now sitting on my desk. I would keep it with me until the situation was resolved. "I'm taking precautions."

"It would be easier if the young lady was aware of my presence."

"If it was easy, I would have called someone with a lower fee."

"All right. I need a picture, address, and so forth."

"I can email you everything you'll need." I copied down his email address, asked a few more questions and answered some of his. I sent off a scanned picture of Dusty along with everything else Coleman was likely to need. It made me feel marginally better.

Constable Parish didn't answer so I left a message on his voicemail. Buster's wasn't open until the afternoon, so that was pretty much all that I could accomplish immediately, and I had a staff meeting to conduct. There were no surprises there, but when we were done Merrilee stayed seated and we waited until the rest were gone.

"You asked the other day about Ashley and Emily?"

"I wondered if they were back together."

"Well, they're not, but it seems that Ashley isn't happy with the situation. She's been calling Emily at work and following her when she goes home."

"I was pretty sure I spotted her in the parking lot."

"She asked if there was anything we could do to help."

There wasn't a great deal, but I could make some suggestions. "Send her down to my office. I'll talk to her about it."

Emily looked uncomfortable when she arrived, almost tearful. "I'm really sorry about this, Mr. Birch."

"Don't worry about it. It's not your fault." I offered her some coffee, just to help her relax a little, but she declined. "Why don't you tell me about it?"

It wasn't a complicated story. They had met about a year earlier at a party given by a local artist whom they both knew. Emily was not inexperienced but had not come out to her family or most of her friends. She had been very careful about her previous encounters, none of which had ever evolved into a formal relationship. "Ashley was everything I wanted to be, or at least that's what I thought at the time. She was smart, confident, never uncomfortable about who she was or who knew about it." Emily was still living with her parents and while she often stayed the night at Ashley's apartment, she had not actually moved in. "It wasn't a big deal. Ashley offered and there was room enough but I told her I wanted to go slow and she respected that."

Her parents, however, were adamant that they meet their daughter's new friend and inevitably when Ashley finally came to dinner, they realized the nature of her friendship with Emily. "It was really uncomfortable. They told me afterward that they thought I should get my own place. I think they were afraid it was going to rub off on my younger sister."

This had all happened just a few days before the trip to Black Island so the situation had been unresolved, although Emily had decided that there was no reason not to move in with Ashley. But things had started to unravel on that Friday. "Once Ashley spotted Kevin, she was like another person. She told me that she knew he was a rapist, and I said I found that hard to believe, and we had our first argument. For a while I didn't want to even share the cabin with her and that meant I couldn't move in with her at all, but then she came back and apologized and I thought, well, sometimes I go off on someone for no good reason so I shouldn't be so judgmental."

"Did she tell you about the time she was raped?"

"Yes, but I don't know how true it was. She insisted that Kevin had drugged her drink and carried her off somewhere and that the university had covered it up. I got her to admit that she hadn't actually seen him put anything in her drink, and that she'd been unconscious afterward, but she started to get mad again so I dropped the subject."

They had both been quite drunk the night they'd moved Carl's body, but Emily was upset the following morning and suggested they tell someone what they'd done. Ashley had been furious and had cowed Emily into remaining silent. "But things just got steadily worse after that and I knew that I was going to break up with her." Emily had found herself an apartment of her own and hadn't told Ashley the address.

"She kept calling and I pretended I was still living at home, but that was a mistake because she started calling there and my parents got upset because they said she was very rude. So I called Ashley and told her I had my own place but that I didn't want to see her anymore and I thought that would be the end of it. But she must have followed me home from work because I started getting letters from her and a couple of times I saw her car driving by."

"Did you talk to her about it?"

"I tried, but she wouldn't listen. She kept insisting that it was just a tiff and that once I got over it, we'd be together like before."

"Has she made any threats?"

"No. Sometimes I think that's what scares me the most. She's not the cool and collected type."

"How much do you know about her past? I assume you're not her first partner."

"Oh, no. She's been around. But she said she was only in a serious relationship once before and that was a couple of years ago and didn't last very long."

"Another unpleasant breakup?"

"No, she said the other woman died in an accident."

Little alarms began to sound inside my head. "Do you know the other woman's name?"

She shook her head. "Ashley didn't like talking about it. She only mentioned it once and we'd been drinking. We drank a lot when we were together." Her face got a funny look, as though she'd never realized that before.

"Do you know what kind of accident it was?"

"I assume it was in a car, but she never said." She frowned. "Is any of this important?"

"Probably not." I had a new line of inquiry to pursue, however. "Have you considered getting a restraining order?"

"I don't want to make the situation worse than it already is."

"Ashley has no right to bother you. If you've made it clear to her that you don't want to see her anymore, and if she refuses to stop coming to your apartment and calling, then you have the right to protect yourself." It took a few more minutes to convince her, but eventually she agreed. I asked for Ashley's address, then told Steve to walk her through the procedure for a restraining order. She thanked me – and she was crying now - and then I was alone with my thoughts.

Was it possible that Ashley's lost lover was Alyson Reynolds? The odds were against it, but if it was true, then she had a motive to assault Carl, and Emily admitted that they had split up for a half hour on the night he died. Her callousness regarding the body fit with that theory. And now that I thought about it, Ashley drove a dark colored car and so had the person who had fired shots at my house. I called someone I knew who worked for the state and asked if they could tell me if Ashley Sternberg had a firearms permit. They said they'd get back to me.

I was actually in a pretty good mood after that. At least I had another subject into which I could poke my nose a little. Ashley and I were going to have a conversation.

I got my call back. No firearms permit had been issued to Ashley Sternberg, which didn't mean she didn't own one.

Parish called back a little later. I asked him if he'd turned up anything new. He sounded tired and a bit distracted and he really didn't have anything new to tell me. "It's not really likely that anything significant was going on behind the scenes. This is a small community and we're pretty isolated. Everybody knows everybody else's business."

"She seems to have kept her romances away from public scrutiny."

"Not really. No one knew Carl very well but it was common knowledge that she had a boyfriend on the mainland, and a couple of people saw him when he came out to visit."

"But no one spoke to him? I find that hard to believe."

"Other than her father, who can't help us, that seems to be the case. They kept pretty much to themselves. There are places you can go and be alone. From your description, Carl didn't seem like the sociable type. His interests were probably more physical than conversational."

"Well, keep me in mind."

"Will do, but the season is in full swing. I'm pretty busy meditating disputes, escorting drunks back to their rooms, and chasing away kids who want to sleep on the beaches."

"Sounds exciting."

"Yeah, and it pays well too."

I did a little research on Ashley Sternberg on my own because I didn't want anyone upstairs to know more about Emily's business than they did already. There wasn't much to find. No criminal record, not even a parking ticket. Her parents had both died young and she'd spent her adolescence in foster homes. Had a full scholarship to college and got good grades, but dropped out of Bryant College about a year after the rape incident. She had worked as a clerk in a convenient store for a few months, then switched to a non-profit advocacy group concerned with women's issues. She had an apartment in Providence.

That afternoon was free for me and I had already decided to drop by Buster's to talk to Angela. I wrote down the address of the advocacy group. I'd stop there on my way back and ask a few questions. Ashley would probably be unhappy about that, but her harassment of Emily justified a little obnoxiousness on my part.

Buster's had just opened when I arrived and Buster was behind the bar. He recognized me and waved me over as soon as I came in the door. "Still looking for what's her name, I gather?"

"Linda Bettis. I was hoping to ask Angela a few questions. I won't take up much of her time. I assume she's back from Wisconsin."

"She's back, but she's not here today. Monday is her day off."

"Maybe I could catch her at home. Could you give me her address?"

He looked genuinely sorry as he shook his head. "Sorry, but I don't think I can do that. We have to be very careful giving out personal information about our waitresses. We get all kinds in here. I'm sure you're okay, but it's our policy."

"No problem. She's working tomorrow?"

"From one to eleven. Tuesdays are slow so she'll have plenty of free time."

"Thanks again."

The offices of Women on the Move were in a rundown part of Cranston. There was a diner on the left and a check cashing service on the right. Their windows were so filled with posters that I couldn't see much of the interior but the sign on the door said welcome and I assumed that applied to me, so I opened it and went inside.

There was a receptionist, and a double row of cubicles stretching toward the back of the space. I could hear people on telephones and their voices had that cadence that I associate with sales calls or fund raising. The receptionist gave me a neutral look, neither friendly nor unfriendly. I ventured a slight smile in return. "Hi. I was wondering if I might speak to one of your staff members, Ashley Sternberg."

"With regard to what matter?' Her voice was absolutely toneless.

"I'm a private investigator." I offered her one of my cards, which she accepted, examined critically, and set aside. "Ms Sternberg has some familiarity with a case I'm working on. I don't have her home address," I lied, "and it will only take a moment or two."

"Ashley is on leave of absence."

I felt a flash of frustration. "Would it be possible to talk to her supervisor then?"

She considered that proposition for a few seconds, then picked up the phone on her desk and pressed a button. "There's a gentleman here who wishes to talk to someone about Ashley. Do you want me to send him back?" There was a pause. "All right." She hung up.

"Rose will talk to you. Follow that aisle all the way to the back. The office will be on your left."

It wasn't much of an office; it was just a slightly larger cubicle. Rose was an older woman, her hair tinged with gray, wearing a business suit. She shook hands as we introduced ourselves and she offered me a seat, actually the only seat other than her own.

Her desk was completely covered with paperwork, arranged in neat piles, although I don't know if that was cosmetic or functional.

"I understand that you want to talk about Ashley."

"Just in general terms." I mentioned Carl's death, Ashley's presence among our party, and my uncertainty about the conclusions the police had reached. "There's a possibility that Ashley might be called as a witness and I don't want to be surprised by any unforeseen revelations. I don't have any reason to suspect anything, but I would like to be reassured."

She thought that over. "I won't tell you anything really personal about Ashley, in part because I don't have the right and in part because I don't know much about her life outside this office. She is smart, hard working, well organized, and dedicated. She could easily make more money elsewhere. She has a good sense of humor, although sometimes it's a bit darker than I care for. She tends to keep her distance, at least while she's here, although I do know she has," she hesitated, "a romantic interest."

"I know that's she's gay," I told her. "She doesn't make a secret of it."

"Nor should she."

"I understand she's taken a leave of absence."

"That's correct."

"Did she give a reason?"

"No, and if she had, I don't think I would repeat it." Not unfriendly but firm.

"Can you tell me when she's due back to work?"

"Monday morning, unless she requests an extension." Her face softened slightly. "We rarely get talented people to work here for what we can pay. When we do, we're willing to be very flexible when they need time off."

"I understand." I couldn't think of anything else to ask and I'd accomplished my primary purpose in coming. Ashley would hear about my visit and get a taste of her own medicine. If she was as smart as she seemed to be, she might take the hint.

As it turned out, she found out well before Monday.

The following day I finally met Angela, the waitress. Buster had told her that I was coming and she came over to the bar when he gestured. "You must be the detective."

"Paul Birch." I shook hands.

    "Angela." Her grip was firm but she didn't offer her last name.

    "I'd like to ask you a few questions about Linda Bettis. She's not in any trouble. I'm just hoping she can help tell me something about a young woman she used to know." I glanced around. "Maybe we could sit in one of the booths."

    She shook her head. "Not a good idea. Buster doesn't want the customers fraternizing with the customers and it wouldn't look good. Come with me."

    She led me into a narrow room behind the bar where cases of liquor and cartons of bar snacks were piled up haphazardly. There was no place to sit except on the cartons themselves. Angela chose a case of Heineken and I perched myself atop some Smirnoff. "I understand you and Linda were good friends."

    "Good enough."

    "Do you have any idea how to get in touch with her?"

    "I might."

    I offered her a twenty but she shook her head. "I'm not looking for money. I need a reason."

    "Okay. I'm looking into the death of a young woman Linda knew when she lived on Black Island. The death was ruled accidental at the time but there is some reason to believe that might not be the case. I have no reason to think Linda was involved in any way, but since she and the dead girl were very close friends, I'm hoping she might be able to point me toward someone who would have a motive to want her dead."

    She pressed an index finger to her lips and pondered for a few seconds. "By very close, you mean that she and Linda were lovers, right?"

    "That's my understanding. But they were no longer a couple when she died. In fact, the closest we have to a suspect was her current boyfriend." I didn't mention that he was also dead.

    "I can get a message to Linda and ask what she wants to do. I don't think I should just tell you where she is without permission."

    I chafed at the thought of another delay, but I sensed right away that it would do more harm than good to argue about it. I handed her one of my cards. "She can call me at that number. It's my office, so if I'm not there she can leave a message. And this is my cell number." I took out a pen and added that on the reverse side.

"You didn't tell me her name. The dead girl, I mean."

"Alyson Reynolds."

Her eyebrows went up. "Linda talked about her a couple of times. Didn't she drown or something?"

"Supposedly. They never found the body."

"That sucks. Eaten by fishes. Fishes or worms, I suppose it doesn't make any difference. And you think someone killed her?"

"I think it's possible."

"Linda will want to help. I think. I'll call her during my supper break."

"I'd really appreciate it." We both stood up and I offered her the twenty again. "I've probably cost you a couple of tips."

This time she took it.

Dusty made dinner that evening. I'd arrived home a little early and called Coleman from my car to tell him he could go off duty until morning. I waited outside to see if a parked car would pull away but he wasn't that obvious and I had no clue where he was. Dusty and I avoided talking about what we were both thinking about until the meal was just about over. I was making coffee when she came up behind me and put a hand on my shoulder.

"So who do you have watching over me?"

"What makes you think I do?"

"The fact that you didn't ask if I wanted someone. You knew that I'd say no and that you'd have to lie or at least mislead me because you weren't about to leave me unguarded. So who is it? Anyone I know? If it's Lydia Perkins, she might as well come in and we can catch up. I haven't seen her since last Christmas."

"It's no one you know. He's new in the area, very good, very discreet. I didn't spot him when I came home even though I knew he was here somewhere."

"Want to invite him in for coffee?"

"No. He went home. I told him I'd cover things while I'm here." I glanced over to the sideboard where I had left my weapon.

"I don't think I'm really in danger. It was probably just meant to distract you."

"If so, it had the opposite effect. And it will be obvious very quickly that it failed. Whoever is responsible might decide to provide a more significant distraction."

"So who's watching your back? Killing you is the only sure way to stop the investigation."

"I'm being very careful."

And that's why I noticed that I was being tailed when I left work the following evening.

It's almost impossible to effectively follow someone with a single car and remain undetected. The dark greenish gray car that showed up in my rear view mirror was driven either by someone who was completely unskilled or someone who didn't care whether or not I noticed. It might have taken me a little longer to realize what was going on if I hadn't been watching for something like that, but I would have spotted the vehicle pretty quickly anyway. It stayed right behind me, slowed when I slowed to let it pass, never signaled for a turn until after I had done so. It was a Honda.

I eased my gun out of its holster and set it down on the seat beside me. I wasn't looking forward to a shootout. I waited until I was sure I had the license plate number memorized, then waited for an intersection with a light. I modified my speed so that I would arrive just as the light turned red, signaled for a left turn, braked as though I didn't have a care in the world. There was no traffic in sight in any direction. Then, at the last possible second, I pressed down on the accelerator and made a sharp right turn.

The driver was clearly not a professional. The car lurched forward, stopped abruptly, and then turned through the red light to follow me. I just caught sight of that before I took a left into a row of small business complexes, cut into a parking lot and pulled around behind a big blue dumpster. The dark car sped past a few seconds later. I waited to see if it would come back when it reached the next intersection and realized I was gone, but I didn't see it again. At least, not that evening.

I knew someone at the registry, but they'd be on their way home by now, so I called Bullard.

"Have you been pissing someone off again?" she asked when I told her what had just happened.

"Appparently."

"Is this connected to the Reynolds case?"

"Possibly."

"I'm not supposed to do this for civilians."

"Regrettably."

"But I don't always pay attention to the rules."

"Thankfully."

"I'll call you back."

The rest of the drive home was uneventful. When I called Coleman he said the day had been boring, just the way he liked it. He asked if I had any idea how long this was going to go on. "I need to stock up on some new cds if we go more than a few days."

"If nothing happens by Friday, we'll regroup."

I was just telling Dusty what had happened when my cell phone rang. It was Bullard. "Got a name and address that you never heard from me."

"I haven't even spoken to you today."

"The name is Ashley Sternberg." The address she gave was the same one I already had. "Do you want me to have someone ask her a few questions?"

"No, not just yet anyway. Thanks."

Dusty looked disbelieving when I told her. "I can't believe Ashley killed Carl or shot at me. I know she's a little tightly wound, but she just doesn't seem the type. She'd want to be in my face, not sneak around and shoot from ambush."

"I'm not ready to label her the killer either, but we have to recognize that she's a good candidate. We know she had another lover before Emily who died in an accident."

"We don't know that it was Alyson."

"No, we don't. I'm constructing a scenario, not gathering all the suspects together for the big revelation. If that is the case, however, she has a kind of motive for killing Carl, and we know that she and Emily were not together for part of the period during which we know Carl died."

"But she had to now that Carl wasn't responsible for Alyson's death. The police established that he wasn't with her at the time she died."

"Actually, we don't know what time she died. We can't assume that she drowned when the skiff capsized."

"But it wouldn't be rational for Ashley to blame Carl, and she seemed level headed enough."

"Each of us has moments of irrationality. Carl might have said something that infuriated Ashley so much that she picked up a rock and hit him with it. She might not have intended to kill him. In fact, it was her idea to go for a midnight swim, so maybe she was planning that she and Emily would find the body, report it, and muddy the waters."

"Then why the elaborate game with the body later on?"

I shrugged. "It could have taken her by surprise, and she was drunk by then. Maybe she thought it would just add to the confusion. Maybe she was suffering from a mild case of shock. What she and Emily did wasn't completely rational, regardless of who actually killed Carl."

Dusty considered that for a while. "But if that's the case, what happens to your theory that Alyson was murdered? Ashley wouldn't have reacted that way to Carl if she was responsible."

"Unless Alyson had told Carl something about Ashley and he accused her when they met privately on the beach."

"If they met on the beach."

I nodded, but my head was beginning to hurt. "The police never spoke to Ashley, never established her whereabouts. They didn't even know about her."

"If she was Alyson's lover."

"Too many ifs. I'm going to have to speak to her."

And then my phone buzzed. It was Linda Bettis.

"I almost wasn't going to call you," she confessed. "We're talking about a part of my life that is over with. I'm not sure I really want to resurrect it."

I told her I was sympathetic, that I didn't want to cause her any distress, and that the only reason I had been looking for her is because I thought Alyson Reynolds deserved to have her story told. "I never knew her, obviously, but she seemed to have had her life planned out methodically and realistically and it's not fair that she never got to enjoy it."

"Aly and I were friends for a while, but we were traveling in different directions."

"So I understand."

"All right. I don't really want to come into the city."

"I'd be happy to come to you."

She gave me an address in Managansett. "It's a farm. The house is set back quite a way from the road but there's an old broken down wagon right at the end of the driveway. And don't come before nine. I have dairy duty tomorrow."

"I'll be there."

I hadn't driven through Managansett in years but it looked exactly as I remembered it. Even the downtown seemed to have the same series of stores – none of them national brands. There was a shopping center right at the town line with the usual fast food places and familiar retailers, but none of them had made it to Main Street. I turned on Reservoir Road, which circled back around the main residential district, wound its way through some apple orchards and woodlots. Then it opened up and a series of farmhouses appeared, about half of them abandoned, almost all of them in need of some serious maintenance work. The broken down wagon was flanked by two rows of poplars that partially concealed a rambling house, fair sized barn, and a grain silo with gaping holes in its side.

The driveway was narrow and unpaved and led me directly to the house. A gray haired woman sat on the porch, knitting, and another about my age came to the door as I drove up. She walked to the edge of the porch as I parked and got out of the car.

"Hi. I'm looking for Linda Bettis. She's expecting me."

"She's out in the barn." Her voice was deep and commanding. "You're too late for breakfast but there's still coffee."

I declined politely, sensing that the offer was purely symbolic.

The barn could have used a fresh coat of paint, but it was otherwise in good condition, as was what I could see of the house. The double doors were wide open so I stepped inside, blinking while my eyes adjusted to the gloomy shadows. There was a row of stalls along the left, with a cow standing in each of those which I could see. The loft was full of baled hay. Most of the right side of the barn consisted of shelving and barrels, with tools hanging from that wall and the rear one. A twenty something woman in jeans and a plaid shirt was bent over one of the barrels when I came in.

"Linda Bettis?"

She straightened up and I saw that she'd been filling a bucket with some kind of grain. She wasn't conventionally pretty but she had strong, regular features. Her hair was tied back in a ponytail.

"Mr. Birch?"

We shook hands and I followed her out the rear door of the barn where a couple of dozen chickens were milling around in a small fenced area. She took a handful of grain from the bucket and tossed it among them.

"I thought commercial farming was impractical up here."

She nodded. "It is, other than apples, I suppose. We sell a little bit locally but most of what we grow is for us." She tossed another handful. "This is a woman's cooperative. There are six of us. Beth's name is on the title papers but we're all theoretically equal partners."

"It must be a lot of work."

"It's not as bad as you might think. We pay one of the neighbors to bring his tractor over and do the heavy plowing and tilling. Since we're only growing enough for ourselves and a little extra, there's only weeding and watering and harvesting to do. Plus the cows have to be milked every morning and the eggs gathered and things like that."

"Are you all vegetarians?"

She laughed. "No way. I need my burgers. And we have lots of chicken." She threw some more grain. "Beth doesn't eat meat but the rest of us are all carnivores."

"It kind of puts you off the radar."

"Nothing wrong with that."

It occurred to me that Linda Bettis had found herself another island, though she probably didn't realize it. "Pretty lonely out here."

"Oh, we have neighbors. Don't see much of them though. I don't think they approve. They probably think we're having nonstop lesbian orgies out here."

"Have you had any trouble?"

"Not trouble, but we're not on anyone's party invitation list. It's kind of funny because two of us have boyfriends and Beth is straight and I don't have a partner. Mary and Celeste are our only couple."

"Mary and Celeste?" I looked closely to see if she was kidding me.

"Yup. They were fated to be together, I guess. Actually, it's Elaine Mary and I think she was Ellie before she and Celeste got together. It probably started as a joke and stuck."

"So what can you tell me about Alyson Reynolds?"

"What do you want to know?"

By the time the chickens had been fed, she had confirmed what I already understood about Alyson, her father, her intention to leave once she was off age, and her lack of any strong ties to the island. "She and I had a thing for a while, but I guess you already knew that."

"Did the two of you still talk afterwards?"

"Oh yeah. It wasn't a big deal for either of us. Bigger for me probably because it was her decision. Alyson was still trying to figure out who she was and where she was going, and I guess she decided she wouldn't be going there with me. I liked her. She was fun and honest and I was sorry when we broke up, but I guess that wasn't really me either because I moped for a day or two and then started looking for someone else."

"You knew about the boy from the mainland? Carl?"

"The one who got himself killed? Sure, she talked about him. That was pretty casual too. She was trying him on like a new hat but the last time I talked to her she was partner shopping again. That was just before the accident."

"But she didn't break things off with Carl."

"You don't throw out the old hat until you have a new one. That's too cold, I guess. I would have told him to take a hike as soon as I found out he was living with another girl. Alyson didn't really care except that she was annoyed that he tried to keep it secret."

"She knew about Connie Meikle then?"

"Was that her name? Yeah, she knew. She read his phone messages once when he was asleep."

"Did you ever think that her death might not be an accident?"

Linda considered that one for a minute or so. "She was real handy with that boat. Almost everyone on the island can do some simple sailing, but she had a real gift for it. On the other hand, sometimes she got over confident and took chances. I wasn't surprised to hear that she died that way."

"Could she have faked her own death?"

"I suppose, but why bother? She wasn't hiding from anyone. She could have left the island anytime she wanted after she turned eighteen. Do you really think someone might have killed her?"

"I don't know. There were some odd things about the accident but they could have been coincidence. Was there anything else that was bothering her at the time? Maybe something she wouldn't talk about but might have hinted at in other ways?"

"Not really." Linda had suddenly turned away from me and I sensed that she was hiding something.

"If there was anything, it might be important. Had she argued with anyone recently?"

"I was already planning to leave the island by then and I was pretty busy with my own problems. Unlike Alyson, I didn't have a nest egg hidden away. All the equity in my mother's house went to pay for her medical bills and I just managed to scrape together enough for her funeral."

"Was there anyone else I could talk to? Had she ever been close to anyone else?"

"No." She said it quickly, too quickly, and I knew she was holding something back. I decided to edge around the issue and come back at it from another direction. I asked about Oliver Reynolds. Linda didn't think much of him but admitted that he'd loved his daughter and never would have hurt her.

"They fought like cats and dogs but it was just their way."

I mentioned the names of the boys I knew Alyson had dated. Linda knew them both but laughed when I suggested that anything might have been going on between them. "Alyson outgrew them in high school. If they hadn't been the only game in town, she'd never have given them a second look."

Linda had never heard of Ashley Sternberg and doubted that Alyson had ever taken another female lover. "I can't say that she wouldn't have gotten involved casually with another woman after me but she was definitely straight by preference."

I asked if there was any male on the island that she might have been interested in, even if it was someone inappropriate. "You mean like married, or old?" She laughed and it seemed genuine. "You can cross that right off your list of questions. Alyson wanted romance, a husband, a house of her own, and kids. She was more traditional than most people realized. But she didn't want any of that on Black Island. I don't think she'd have let herself get interested in anyone there. Not that she didn't get approached once in a while." She pressed her lips together and I realized she hadn't intended to say that last bit.

I tried a little longer because it was still obvious that there was something she wasn't telling me but it was apparent that she wasn't going to spill the beans. I contented myself at last by giving her my card, urging her to call any time if she thought of anything that might help, no matter how insignificant. She agreed and any reservations she had were invisible. She walked me back to the car and a few minutes later I was on my way back down Route 13.

It wasn't quite the washout that it seemed. Linda Bettis hadn't told me much about Alyson Reynolds that I hadn't already known and none of it seemed significant. But the fact that she had withheld information indicated that there was something to be found out, if not from her then perhaps from another source.

Speaking of which, I checked my GPS and set course for Ashley Sternberg's home address.

Ashley rented one floor of a three story house in Pawtucket. I found the address with no trouble, but parking was more problematic. I circled her block, then the two adjacent blocks, then several others before spotting a blinking signal light and slipping into a newly vacated space. During all that time I had not seen her car parked anywhere and there was no garage at the house, which suggested she was not at home.

There was a private entrance and bell with just the name "Sternberg" and I tried it. There was no response. I tried twice more before walking around to the front of the house. There were two names adjacent to two more buzzers, "J. Fearn" and "L. Fanthorpe", but I didn't have any better luck with either of these. I walked slowly around the house and decided that there was sufficient cover that I could pick Ashley's lock unobserved, but I decided against it, at least for the time being.

With two strikes under my belt, I called the office to tell Steve that I would be there on time for the one o'clock meeting with a new client, only to find out that he had called to reschedule. "All right then, I'm going home for lunch. I'll be in later."

But when I turned into my block, I spotted a dark greenish gray Honda parked in front of the house and I didn't need to read the license plate to know it belonged to Ashley Sternberg.

Now what I should have one at this point was call Coleman and find out what he was doing. I confess that I never even thought of that. The sight of that car parked at the curb, while Dusty's was in the driveway, triggered something primal. I almost pulled up onto the lawn intending to storm the house. I was at least sensible enough to realize that would be pretty foolish, so I continued past the house, turned the corner and parked. Then I hot footed it through my neighbor's yard, climbed the fence, and dropped down beside our not tremendously successful vegetable garden. My weapon was in my hand and if anyone had spotted me, they would be calling the police.

I ran across the open space to the back of the house. I couldn't hear anything from inside, but the windows were closed and the air conditioners were going so that didn't mean a lot. The back door would probably be locked, but I had brought my key. I eased the screen door open carefully, holding it with one knee, while I carefully unlocked the door, turned the knob, and pushed it open. Drawing a deep breath, I slipped inside, closing both doors behind me as gently as possible.

I was in the kitchen now. There was a short corridor that led to the front of the house and I peaked around the corner. I could see Dusty sitting on the couch, apparently all right, and my heart slowed from frantic to just racing like crazy. She didn't see me. Her expression was neutral to serious and she said something I didn't catch to someone I couldn't see, presumably Ashley. She would be to my right if I came down the corridor, which was pretty much my only course of action. Unless she moved, she wouldn't be able to see me until the very last moment.

With both hands on my handgun, I forced myself to breathe more naturally, then turned and moved quickly along the length of the corridor. Dusty had her head turned to one side but she must have caught movement out of the corner of her eye because she spotted me just before I burst into the room.

Ashley was sitting in my favorite chair just to my right, sipping from a cup of coffee. A man I had never seen before was in the other chair, or rather he was out of the other chair, dropping to the floor and rolling behind the far end of the couch. Almost immediately his hand held what I was pretty sure was a Glock and it was pointed at me.

"Relax, everyone," said Dusty quickly. "We just had this room replastered and I don't want bullet holes in the walls."

The other man slowly rose from behind the couch, but he didn't put his weapon away until I had reholstered my own. Dusty looked solemn but I could tell by her voice that she was amused. "Paul Birch, meet James Coleman. And you already know Ashley."

It took a few minutes to get everything straightened out. Coleman had seen Ashley drive up and get out of the car. By the time she had started toward the house, he was behind the shrubs at one corner. "I didn't know who she was or if she had a weapon in her bag, but she looked upset so I had to play it by ear."

Dusty had answered the door and had been greeted by a barrage of angry shouting. That had tipped the balance and Coleman had stepped out and quickly introduced himself to the two women.

Dusty hadn't realized that Coleman and I had never met. "I thought you always interviewed people personally before hiring them?"

"I was a little pressed for time," I explained.

Coleman was more impressive in person than he had been on the telephone. He was bigger than I am, solid, and his eyes were in almost constant movement, analyzing his environment, sizing up everyone in the room. But I didn't get to talk to him very long because as soon as the shock of two drawn weapons wore off, Ashley blew her top.

"You went to my boss and asked questions about me!" She stayed in her seat but her shoulders were tensed and both hands were clenched tightly. "What right do you have to stick your nose in my business?"

"I was acting on behalf of a client." I made a mental note to tell Emily that I had taken her as a pro bono client following our conversation.

"What client? What are you talking about?"

"You've been acting in a way that could be construed as threatening. My client is considering taking legal action against you. I went to your place of business looking for you, hoping that we could settle the matter informally."

Ashley appeared to be genuinely perplexed for a few seconds, but then dawning realization stole across her face. "Emily. It's Emily, isn't it?"

I didn't see any purpose in concealing the truth. "You've been stalking her."

"I have not!"

"You waited in the company parking lot and followed her home. As a matter of fact, you tried to follow me at least once."

"I wanted to talk to you. And I wanted to talk to her, that's all."

"My understanding is that she told you that your relationship was over with, that she didn't want to see you or speak to you again. Am I misinformed?"

She bit her lip. "Yes, she said that, but she didn't really mean it. Or she wouldn't if she'd just let me talk to her about it." Ashley didn't like being put on the defensive and she didn't stay there for long. "It's none of your business anyway. You can't just invade my privacy like that."

"Actually, I can." I didn't actually dislike Ashley, but she was starting to annoy me. "Just as you invaded Emily's privacy. There is a remedy for both of you. She can get a court order to make you stay away from her and you can do the same."

"This is bullshit! It's not like I was threatening her. I just want to talk it out."

"You've done all the talking to which you're entitled. If you don't leave Emily alone, she can and will take legal measures, some of which might get back to your employers. That's the simple truth of it."

Ashley was clearly having difficulty controlling her temper but she was at a disadvantage. She was on enemy territory, outnumbered, and judging by her frequent glances at Coleman, a bit overawed. Coleman was big and he projected even bigger, even though his expression was neutral and he didn't say a word. Suddenly Ashley was on her feet. "I won't listen to any more of this crap! I'm going. But don't think this is over because it damn well isn't."

Dusty followed her to the door but Ashley pulled it shut behind her without a word. We were staring at each other when we heard her drive off.

"Well that was special," said Dusty at last.

"Do you think she was the one who shot at you?" I asked.

"I don't know. I would have said she wasn't the type, but she's pretty worked up. And I never really saw the shooter. Sorry."

Coleman stood up. "I guess it's time for me to go."

Dusty never hesitated. "Are you married, Mr. Coleman?"

"Not even close."

"Then why don't you stay for supper? It's Paul's turn to cook but I promise you he's pretty good at it."

"It's nice of you to offer, but I'm just the hired help."

"Not when you're off duty," I said. "And it's about time we actually talked. I'm always looking for reliable people."

It took a little more effort, but Coleman finally agreed. He and Dusty sat in the kitchen while I put in some steaks and sautéed some mushrooms and fresh spinach. Coleman admitted to enjoying wine and Dusty opened a bottle. He sketched in a little of his background – brief stint as a police officer in Carmel after a tour in the Marines, legwork for a private agency for two years, the decision to move to the East Coast and set out on his own.

"I find enough work to pay the bills but I haven't gotten ahead of them yet."

Over supper, Dusty and I took turns telling him about Carl's murder and my subsequent suspicions about a connection to the death or disappearance of Alyson Reynolds. He listened attentively, didn't interrupt to ask questions, and when we ran out of steam he dug out a few things we'd forgotten to mention by asking us to fill in holes. He was sharp and I found myself liking him.

"You really don't have any evidence that contradicts the way the police reconstructed the crime, other than the shenanigans with the body, which don't seem to be relevant. All you have is a couple of things that don't support it."

I had to admit that he was right. "One being the fact that we never did identify the person or people whom Carl claimed were local friends of his."

Coleman nodded. "And the other being the bloody handkerchief."

"That's the one that actually bothers me the most. We know Carl never went back to his room, regardless of whether or not he was already dead when Laura found him. So how did it get there? And when? Oh, and he smoked a very distinctive pipe that's missing. I don't think he had it with him at the cookout, so it should have been in his room with his other effects."

"I could come up with reasonable explanations for all that. And your reasons for being suspicious of the boating accident are even more tenuous."

"Alyson was universally described as a very competent sailor."

"But one who took risks."

I nodded to acknowledge his point. "And then there's the missing mooring rope."

"Which is odd but doesn't suggest anything sinister. Not much as the basis of an investigation. Do you have any suspects for either death?"

I shook my head. "Except maybe Ashley. If Alyson was in fact her one time lover, she might have wanted Carl dead. She has a temper and it does look like a crime of impulse."

"Does she have any other connection to Black Island?"

"Not that I know of." I thought about it for a moment, then retrieved my cell phone and called Merrilee Brubaker at home. Yes, her husband had indeed taken a lot of pictures that weekend. Yes, she was quite sure some of them were of Ashley. Yes, she would bring them into work in the morning so that I could look them over. I thanked her and hung up.

"I'm going over to Black Island tomorrow," I said quietly. "I'm going to see if I can find anyone there who knows Ashley Sternberg."

Dusty announced that she was going with me, but then changed her mind. "I've got too much to do here and I'd just get in the way."

"You're never in the way," I answered gallantly. "But I'd feel better if you stayed behind closed doors as much as possible until we get this all sorted out."

Coleman got to his feet. "Sounds like I'm working tomorrow, so I'd better get on home and catch some sleep."

We walked him to the door and at the last minute Dusty caught his elbow. "There's no reason for you to lurk in the bushes all day. You can probably watch out for me better if you're in the house. I'll have coffee ready in the morning if you bring the doughnuts."

"I can manage that."

Merrilee presented me with quite a variety of pictures, but not surprisingly there were no shots of Ashley alone. I found one in which she and Emily had their arms around each other but were facing the camera. I borrowed it and then called Parish, a courtesy call to let him know I was coming out on the mid-morning ferry.

"Find out anything interesting?"

"Not really. One of my employees might have had some previous business out your way so I'm going to take her picture around and see if anyone knows her."

"Sounds like a long shot."

"Sometimes that's all there is. Busy out there?"

"It's the season for it. A few drunks, a shoplifter, and I spent part of yesterday winching a good sized cabin cruiser off a sandbar. You'd think after spending that much money on a boat people would have the sense to learn how to read a chart."

"Actually, it doesn't surprise me at all. I'll give you a call while I'm out there. Maybe we'll get lucky and you'll tell me you arrested this young woman for assault."

I almost missed the ferry thanks to road construction, heavy traffic, and a fender bender, but I reached the lot, ran to the terminal, and boarded just as they were about to close things up. I spent the trip going through my notes, which I'd brought along, and wondering why I felt such a strong compulsion to spend my time on an investigation for which I would not be paid and in which I had no stake.

Everything looked pretty much the same except that there were more people in the shops, on the streets, and using the beaches. On the other hand, none of the shops or restaurants were crowded, the ferry had been at less than half capacity, and the moped rental place only had four empty slots out of three dozen. I started at one end of the commercial district and made my way systematically from one shop to the next, showing the picture to staff members, asking if they had ever seen Ashley before. About half of them barely looked. The ones who did all shook their heads. After two hours, I was pretty sure I was going to strike out.

I was also hungry by then so I returned to the Moby Dick for lunch. There was no wait for a table and I was enjoying fish and chips when Margaret Taylor spotted me. "Couldn't stay away?"

I smiled. "The food here is so good I just couldn't resist."

"Business or pleasure this time?"

"Business, I'm afraid. Not that I seem to be getting anywhere." I pulled out the photograph and handed it to her. "I have reason to believe that the young woman on the right had been out here in the past, maybe more than once."

She frowned at the photograph. "Can't say that she looks familiar to me, but we get a lot of faces passing through."

"No one else remembers her either."

"I know the other one though."

I almost choked on a mouthful of fish. "You've seen her before?"

"At least once. She came in with one of the local guys a couple of years back. They were both pretty drunk and they started to argue. They gave the waitress a hard time when she tried to quiet them down and she called me down. I arrived just in time to see her break a pitcher of beer over his head. Cut his scalp open. Lots of blood. She would have hit him again but another customer grabbed her. The guy wouldn't press charges so they bandaged him up and Parish put her on the ferry back to the mainland."

"Is that the last time you saw her?"

"I think so."

"What about the boy?"

"Fred Gertz. He's a pretty dim bulb. Enlisted in the army last year. I think he's in Japan somewhere."

"I wonder if Constable Parish might know more about her."

"It's possible, but not likely. You have to understand something about Black Island, Mr. Birch. We don't have a healthy economy. We can't afford a trained police force. Mitchell Parish has no formal training whatsoever and his deputies have even less. We're lucky that he's bright enough to figure out what he can handle and when he needs to call for help. I don't understand why he sticks with it."

"Maybe he just needs the money. And the work is steady."

Taylor laughed. "The salary we pay is a drop in the bucket for Mitchell. He's one of the three richest people on the island. He owns the only grocery store and he has a majority position in the Breakwater and The Pirate's Den. He's like his father – just salts the money away and lives pretty simply."

"But he rents out his house during the season." I was very confused.

"That's because he prefers to live on his boat. The house is just his winter refuge. If it wasn't so cold he'd stay on the boat year round."

"So why does he work as constable?"

"Beats me. Maybe he just likes being an authority figure. But he does a good job."

I considered retracing my steps to ask if anyone else recognized Emily, but I would have felt like an idiot. So I called Parish and asked if he had a few minutes. "I'm out on the water but I'm headed back now. I should be there in another ten minutes."

I was about a ten minute walk from his private dock so I told him I'd meet him there.

I'm not a boat person. I've never understood why anyone would be interested in sailing out onto the ocean, all of which pretty much looks like all the rest. Although I can sort of understand fishing, I've never been interested. It's far too passive. I suppose it might provide an excuse for reading a book or taking a nap, but then again, I've never needed an excuse to either. And frankly I'm rather frightened of the ocean. It's so implacable.

So I had never really looked at Constable Parish's boat before, but Margaret Taylor's comments had made it fresh in my mind and while I was watching it come in to the dock, after which Parish jumped off with a rope in his hand and tied it to a stanchion, I realized that it was bigger than I'd realized. *The Shark* was not as big as the *Calamity Jane*, of course. Parish could manage this one without a crew. But it was bigger and fancier looking than most of the others I'd seen moored in the main harbor, though I assumed that more impressive ones could be found at the country club marina at the far end of the island.

Parish greeted me warmly and I complimented him on his seamanship, although I had no idea if he'd displayed any particular skill in docking. "Lots of practice," he said. "And she's a sweet boat. Sleeps four in two cabins, six if two of them are willing to use hammocks. Twin engines, reinforced hull." He provided some more specs that I didn't understand at all but I nodded as though I knew what he was talking about.

"How did your investigating go today?"

I brought out the photograph and handed it over. He frowned. "Both of these women were with your party, weren't they?"

"Yes. But I have reason to believe that Ashley, the taller one, had some connection to the island which she hadn't told us about. If so, I couldn't find it. No one remembers ever seeing her before. On the other hand, Emily there popped up on Margaret Taylor's radar."

He looked at the photograph again. "She doesn't ring any bells with me."

"Apparently you arrested her a while back. Drunk and disorderly. Assaulted her date with a pitcher of beer."

His eyes widened. "I'll be damned. You could be right. One of the deputies brought her in and we put her on the ferry. It was dark enough that her face didn't really register, but this could be her all right."

"The boy was local."

"Fred Gertz, I think. He's gone now. Went into the service when his parents threw him out."

"I don't suppose you remember what the fight was about?"

He shook his head. "I don't think I ever knew. Didn't care, frankly. We get a lot of drunks and some of them are aggressive. If they don't back down right away, we ship them out. We don't want to actually have to arrest them. It's expensive, wastes our time, and what passes for a jail is actually a lockable room in the town hall basement."

I took back the photograph. "Can you think of anyone else I could try with this?" He suggested Agnes, whom I already had in mind, and a couple of others, whom I'd already tried.

"Sorry I can't be more helpful."

"Well, it is what it is and I can only do what I can do."

Agnes was my very last stop, because I timed it so I'd have an excuse to cut loose quickly in order to make the ferry. She insisted on making tea – I wouldn't have minded if it had been iced tea – but the peanut butter cookies she put out were wonderful. She stared at the picture for a minute, then went to get her glasses and stared some more.

"I've seen both of these girls before."

"Do you remember when and where?"

"The one on the left used to date Fred Gertz. That boy didn't have a brain in his head but he was good looking." She went off onto a history of the Gertz family and it took me a while to get her back on subject. "It didn't last long. They had a big public fight and Mitchell threw her off the island."

"How about the other one?"

"She was here for two weeks a couple of seasons back. Rented a room and spent a lot of time walking around town. I heard she was looking for a job but once the season started, all the temporary jobs were filled and the few year round positions didn't pay enough. It's more expensive to live here than you might think, because everything has to be brought over by boat. That's why so many of us are barely hanging on even though the property values are supposedly pretty high."

"Did she have any friends here? Was she dating anyone?"

"I don't think so. I certainly never saw her with anyone. "

I tried a few more questions but she couldn't remember anything else." I extricated myself as gracefully as I could, even though I had more than enough time, but as I was leaving I tried one last question. "You don't happen to remember who she was staying with, do you?"

"Of course I do. It was Elaine Bettis. She was too sick to work by then and she was renting out her spare room to try to cover expenses."

My mouth didn't quite drop. "Would she be the mother of Linda Bettis?"

"They were the last two in the family. Linda moved away after she died. I don't know where she is now."

But I did.

On the way back to the mainland, I tried calling Linda Bettis but there was no answer. I left a message on her voicemail and spent the rest of the trip trying to figure out if anything I had learned was going to be helpful.

That evening, back at the house, I called Emily Granger at home, and ended up leaving another message. On impulse, I called Ashley and got another recorded message. No one wanted to talk to me.

Saturday morning I considered a surprise visit to the farm in Managansett but decided there was nothing to be gained. If Linda Bettis wanted to tell me anything, she'd call. I didn't think I was going to be able to cajole her into revealing secrets. I tried Emily again with the same result. Although I had some misgivings, I'd thanked Coleman and told him to send his bill to my house, not the business office.

I hadn't been in the attic for a while so I wandered up and nodded appreciatively as Dusty identified things for me. I've been to Tokyo only once and didn't see much of the city so I don't know how accurate it was, but she'd created a rabbit warren of streets and parks and buildings – most of the latter were just cardboard boxes with some features drawn on the sides but a few were plastic props for train sets that Dusty had picked up at yard sales the previous summer. There was a separate section for Fukushima, which from a distance actually did look a little like a nuclear power plant, until you noticed that the cooling towers were spray painted wine bottles and that the radioactive waste was Christmas glitter.

"So how's the hero doing?"

"He's in hot water. He knows that someone is after him but he hasn't figured out who or why. I'm afraid I made him a bit slow witted this time since all the clues are there, but he's been busy dodging ninja assassins and making frantic love to Azumi, the geisha girl who knows too much."

"Frantic love sounds like fun."

"Let's find out." We did. It was.

We had an early lunch and Dusty went back to writing. I puttered around for an hour or so and then made a crucial decision. The new Stephen King novel could wait. I was more interested in finding out what was up with Preston and Child's Pendergast. I made it to page ten before the telephone rang. I was hoping for Linda Bettis. Instead I got Constable Parish.

"I forgot to ask you if you ever found Linda Bettis."

"Yes I did, but she wasn't any help. She confirmed that she and Alyson Reynolds had been intimate, but implied that it was casual and didn't last very long. She says she never saw or spoke to her again after she moved off the island. I had the feeling that she was holding something back and I might try her again, but I'm not hopeful."

"She came out to Black Island."

"She did?" Gears started to turn inside my head. "When did this happen?"

"I'm not sure. Probably late yesterday or the first ferry this morning."

"I'd be very curious about who she spoke to and what she did."

"Actually, I'm pretty curious myself, because I just finished pulling her body off the rocks on the east end of the island."

I'm not often stunned to silence and never for very long, but it took a couple of tries before I could speak. "Do you have any idea what happened?"

"Nary a one. She might have fallen, or jumped, or someone might have pushed her off the cliff. There's a path that runs along the edge there, but the brush is heavy and as far as I know there weren't even witnesses. If it happened last night some time, the cliff walk would have been closed off. There aren't any lights and it's not the safest place even during the day."

"No sign of other injuries?"

"Nothing obvious. The body was all banged up. The fall would have killed her anyway."

I looked at the time. I could just catch the last ferry over, but that would mean spending the night. And for that matter, what did I hope to accomplish? "What's happening with the body?"

"The state police launch is taking it over to the mainland for an autopsy. There's no next of kin that I know of."

"I know where she was living. I can pass on the news to her friends if you want."

"The state police said they'd be taking care of notifications."

"Who's the officer in charge?"

"Hold on a second." I could hear papers rustling. "Sergeant Donovan."

I didn't know him but I could call Bullard and have her pass on the address of the farm. "I don't suppose anything else happened out there in the last couple of days that might be connected?"

"We had a fire last night."

"Anything serious?"

"Not really. No one injured. It was a bit coincidental though."

"Why is that?"

"Remember the cabin where Oliver Reynolds was staying?"

"Sure." I couldn't recall the number off hand but it was in my notes.

"Well, the state police asked Ted to lock everything up until after the investigation was over. They gave him the okay to clear his stuff out a few days ago but he hadn't gotten around to it. Last night, someone broke in, spread something flammable around, and set it all on fire. By the time anyone noticed, it was pretty much gone."

"No suspects, I assume."

"Might have been random. We had some hard partying yesterday. I found half a dozen kids sleeping it off on the beach this morning. A couple of them mouthed off until I threatened to send them home early. "

"Is there any reason why I should come out?"

"I can't think of one offhand, but you're welcome to visit."

"I can't think of one either, but I'll keep it in mind. Thanks for the call."

For a change I got hold of Bullard easily and passed on my information about Linda Bettis. I also mentioned the fire on Black Island. "It does make you think, doesn't it?" she conceded.

"Someone is covering his or her tracks."

"That's speculation. Coincidences do happen." I didn't respond and I heard her sigh. "On the other hand, if something is going on and you find out something that might interest me, I'd like to hear from you."

"But you aren't going to do any looking yourself?"

"Don't have the time. Innocent or guilty, Reynolds is staying right where he is so there's not a pressing reason to reopen the case."

"Linda Bettis might not agree with you."

"Linda Bettis might have committed suicide or missed a step. I will ask the coroner to take an extra close look at the body, but that's as far as I can go."

"Every little bit helps."

Dusty' s reaction matched my own. "She knew something that got her killed."

"That seems likely."

"Which means that Alyson Reynolds did not die accidentally."

"If she is in fact dead." But I was pretty sure she was. I was also pretty sure that Linda knew, or at least suspected, the same thing. But two years had passed. Why had she waited until now to act on her knowledge? Obviously it had something to do with my visit, but what?

Dusty had the best theory. "She might have believed the accident story until you told her that you had doubts. Maybe she went out to the island to poke around, ask a few questions. You said they were friends once."

"I wish there was a way of knowing who she talked to out there."

"You could go ask."

"Yeah, but the one I need to know about is the one who isn't going to admit seeing her."

Sunday morning I drove up to the farm. There was no one in sight when I arrived, but the tall woman who'd greeted me before came out of the house and waited for me. "I was expecting you."

I introduced myself and offered my hand. "I'm Elizabeth Banks." She didn't take my hand. "I suppose you should come inside."

The front room was a cross between a conventional living room and a business office. There was an overstuffed sofa and a coffee table, but there were two desks, one at each end, and a filing cabinet in one corner.

"I was very sorry to hear about Linda."

She nodded, gestured for me to sit on the couch. She took an armchair facing me. Beth was older than I had first thought, maybe fifty. "I know that you're not directly responsible for her death, Mr. Birch, but if you hadn't come to see her, she would still be alive."

"Probably. And the same is true if she had answered my questions rather than going off on her own."

"I can't help you. Linda kept very much to herself. She didn't even tell us where she was going and I've never heard her speak of her life before she came to us except in the most general terms. She was trying to put it all behind her and make something new."

"Then you don't have any idea why she went to the island?"

There was an awkward pause. Beth clearly resented me and was disinclined to cooperate. "Did Linda tell you anything about our arrangement here?"

"Only vaguely."

"I bought the farm outright at a foreclosure sale four years ago. It's not commercially viable but managed properly it can generate a comfortable living for six people. In order to do that, I needed to raise capital since the initial purchase exhausted my savings. So I began to look for partners. I found four of them fairly quickly, each of whom bought a one sixth interest in the property. That allowed us to refurbish the house, repair the farm, and make some other improvements. Linda would have been the perfect final member of our group except that she had virtually no money. We kept her on because she was a hard worker, but she never felt fully a part of our group and it's not likely she ever would have. For that matter, at some point we will need another influx of cash and that would have forced us to look for someone else."

She fell silent and looked out through the window. I had a moment of prescience and when she spoke again I could almost anticipate what she was going to say. "Thursday, Linda told me that she was going to be gone from Friday afternoon until sometime on Sunday. She apologized for disrupting our work schedule but said that she hoped that when she came back, she'd be able to announce a change in her financial situation that would allow her to buy into the group."

"Did you ask her where she was going to get the money?"

"I did. She said that an old friend had died and implied that she had just discovered that she was entitled to a settlement from the estate. It sounded a bit odd, but as I said, Linda never told us much about her past and I assumed that the details were her personal business. Her death, however, suggests something else."

"It might have been an accident." Beth gave me a look for which the word "skeptical" is totally inadequate. "But I don't believe it was. I think she went to Black Island to blackmail someone and it got her killed."

Beth nodded. "Linda shared a common fault of youth. She was convinced that she was invulnerable. I don't know much about what you're trying to achieve but I assume that it now includes identifying whoever it was who killed Linda."

"If I'm right, she's the third victim."

"Then I wish that I could help you further. Would you like to look through her room? The police haven't bothered and there is no one that I know of who would object."

"That might be helpful."

Linda's room was orderly but almost impersonal. There were no pictures on the walls except for a calendar. Her clothing was good quality, well maintained, and completely practical. She had a few books, mostly nonfiction, almost no jewelry or makeup, and the only mail I could find was a seed catalog and a news magazine. I was looking in particular for a diary but didn't find one. There were a few photographs in a large envelope, one of which had "with Alyson, June 5" marked on the back. Linda was wearing a bikini, as was her companion. It was the first good picture I had ever seen of Alyson Reynolds, who was strikingly attractive. None of the other snapshots seemed significant but I took the envelope with me when I left.

Beth didn't see me off.

That evening, Dusty and I went through everything we knew for about the hundredth time. It didn't take long because we still didn't know much.

"Okay," she said at last. "We're assuming that Alyson Reynolds did not die in a boating accident. That means that someone killed her either beforehand or at the time the skiff was overturned, or she's not dead after all but in hiding or imprisoned somewhere. In the latter case, she had to have had an accomplice, but while we have lots of candidates – virtually everybody in fact - for either accomplice or killer, we have nothing pointing to any particular person. It could be someone from the island or someone she knew from the mainland. We know Carl couldn't have done it, but we can't eliminate anyone else. I don't suppose it would be practical to check alibis from that far back?"

I shook my head. "And our evidence is pretty flimsy. It was an unlikely but plausible accident scenario and the mooring rope was missing. We don't even know when it happened. Her father thought she was still in bed when he left for work that day, but she might already have been gone. For that matter, she could have left anytime that night."

"So let's look at Carl's murder. Who is on our list of suspects there?"

I sighed. "Pretty much the same. Purely objectively, Oliver Reynolds is clearly the prime suspect. He had motive and opportunity and he was found with the body."

"Could he have murdered his daughter as well?"

"Sure. Consumed by guilt, he went stark raving nuts, displaced his self loathing onto Carl, and killed him when he got the chance. I can hear Bullard presenting that scenario, if I could convince her that Alyson was in fact murdered."

"And now we have Linda Bettis."

"Whom neither of us believes slipped and fell to her death. But unless Parish comes up with something, and I don't think he will, we're no better off there. It could have been any of the islanders, or anyone who had the price of a ferry ticket. It was Saturday. All Merrilee's kids were off work and we know Ashley took a leave of absence."

"But would they have known that Linda was going to the island, if they knew about her at all?"

"We can't rule it out. We don't know of any direct connections with Linda, but there might be several. Emily and Ashley have both been on the island before and Ashley even stayed with Linda's mother for two weeks. She must have met Linda."

"Did you ask?"

"I didn't know about Ashley's stay out there at the time and I haven't had a chance to speak to her again."

"So opportunity doesn't give us any strong suspects. How about motive?"

I got up and retrieved a bottle of wine. Dusty got some glasses and we sipped a little before continuing.

"We can't even speculate about the reason why someone would have killed Alyson, or why she would have disappeared. The latter seems unlikely given that she abandoned her savings."

"Crime of passion?"

"The only lover we know of was Linda Bettis. I think we can rule her out."

"But there might have been others. You said that a lot of the island boys lusted after her. Maybe someone got jealous when she started dating Carl."

"All right, and that might even give them a motive for killing Carl when the opportunity arose. I'm pretty sure that was a crime of impulse. If someone had planned it, they would have brought something more formidable than a rock."

"And since Alyson played both sides of the record, it could have been anyone, male or female. Does it ever get easy?"

"If it was easy, Bullard would have cleared it up within hours. So why did someone kill Linda Bettis?" I already thought I knew, but I wanted to know if Dusty would come to the same conclusion without my nudging.

"Obviously she knew who the killer was, or had a pretty good idea. She was going to blackmail them to get her stake to buy into the farm, but she wasn't careful enough and got pushed off a cliff. But why didn't she act sooner?"

"I assume she didn't know what she knew. As far as she was concerned, Alyson died in an accident and Carl was killed by her bereaved father. "

"But something changed."

"Sure." I drank some wine. "I went out and talked to her and something I said triggered a shift of viewpoint."

"So what did you say that she wouldn't already have known?"

I had thought about this for quite some time. "Nothing substantial. The only thing I can think of is that I suggested Alyson's death hadn't been accidental."

"But you can't prove that."

"Nope. And neither did Linda. I think she was suspicious but had no proof so she went out to Black Island intending to get some. I think she was smart enough not to confront the killer in a situation where she might be in danger, so I'm guessing she gave herself away too soon."

"If the evidence was on the island, doesn't that eliminate your people?"

"It certainly changes the probabilities, but we can't eliminate anyone yet. I suppose I could try checking everybody's alibi for Friday night and Saturday. I can't do it without ruffling some feathers though. I don't have any reason to connect any of them to Linda Bettis."

"Except possibly Emily and Ashley."

"Which is where I suppose I'll have to start."

Dusty idly looked through my notes. "What's this?" She held up the envelope I'd brought back from the farm.

"Linda Bettis had some pictures. There's a good one of her with Alyson Reynolds."

Dusty took them out and started to look through them. Restless, I got up, walked around the table, and stood behind her. "There. That's the one." Linda had been cultivating a goth look at the time. Long silvery bangles in her ears, multiple shiny bracelets, black blouse and pants, several rings distributed on both hands, hair cut short. She had worn no jewelry at all on the one occasion when

I'd seen her. Alyson was more conventional, a bright red halter top, hair down below her shoulders, the only visible jewelry an elaborate seahorse on a gold chain around her neck.

"She was pretty." Dusty browsed through the others, most of which I had only glanced at previously. About a third of them had notes written on the back, and these confirmed that the older woman appearing in several of the photographs was Linda's mother. There was nothing remarkable about any of them and they all seemed to have been taken on Black Island. I spotted Margaret Taylor in the background once, and in another there was someone who looked like it might be Ted Welch talking to the minister who'd officiated at the wedding. Another one showed my old friend Agnes wearing a wide brimmed hat and holding an ice cream cone. Constable Parish showed up twice, once waving from his car window, once staring intently at a group of older teenagers which included Alyson Reynolds and Devin, the security guard who'd dated her at least once, although there was no indication that they were together here.

"Pretty random," commented Dusty.

"I don't think they meant much to her. The envelope is pretty beat up and some of the pictures were stuck together when I first went through them."

"Where exactly did you find them?"

"On the table beside her bed." I frowned as I realized there was a contradiction here. "Which suggests that she'd had reason to look through them quite recently."

"Do you think there's something important here that we're not seeing?"

"Maybe. Or maybe she found what she was looking for and took it with her."

My phone rang. It was Emily, who said she had just gotten my message. "I went out of town for the weekend. I wanted to get away, you know, someplace where Ashley couldn't bother me."

"She knows about the restraining order."

"Yeah, but she doesn't always do what she's supposed to do."

"Where did you go?" I tried to sound casual.

"A bed and breakfast in Vermont."

"You didn't go to Black Island?"

"God, no! I never want to go there again."

"Was our outing the first time you'd been there?"

There was a pause. Obviously Emily realized that I wasn't asking just to make conversation. "No, actually it wasn't. What is this all about?"

"There was another death on the island yesterday. The police are investigating."

"Who was it? It wasn't Ashley, was it?"

"No. Why would you think that?"

"No reason." She must have known how unconvincing she sounded. "It's just that I know she used to go out there sometimes. Or she used to anyway, back before we were together."

"Do you know why?"

"She said it was restful, that she liked being someplace where no one knew who she was and no one had any preconceptions about her."

"Did the two of you ever go out there together?"

"Only for the wedding. I'd been there a few times before, a long time ago. I was seeing someone, but it didn't work out."

I considered telling her what I knew but decided against it. "All right. I'll see you at work in the morning."

I tried calling Ashley again. Still no answer.

Dusty had put the photographs back in the envelope. "I think I know what the problem is."

"I would be delighted to hear anything you have to suggest. I have lots of little threads that don't seem to be connected to anything."

"That's because you're looking in the wrong place."

I nodded. "The answer is on Black Island."

"Almost certainly. All three of the murders took place there or nearby. Two of the victims were born there. "

"Then you don't think the killer is someone from my office?"

"I didn't say that. Any of them could have gone back and forth on the ferry. There's no passenger list. Bettis was killed on a weekend, Carl while we were all out there, and Alyson so long ago that we have no way of checking. And all of them are in the same age group, if that means anything."

"So I have to go back."

"Looks that way."

But I didn't go right away. The following day I got the name of Emily's bread and breakfast and confirmed that she'd checked in on Friday night and out on Sunday afternoon. But guests made up their own rooms so there was no way of determining whether or not she had actually slept there either or both nights. Kevin and Laura had spent all day Saturday at a cookout with Dennis Malden and his new girlfriend. Eric and Clair said they'd been together most of the weekend, so unless they were in it together, they had alibis. Maria, who had become increasingly withdrawn and sullen since Carl's death, didn't respond to a casual question and became upset when I pressed her. No one else had an alibi.

I checked my calendar, then called Parish on Black Island. "I'm probably coming out on Wednesday."

"My day off, but I don't have anything pressing. I have to ask, though, if you think this is going anywhere. I'm still asking questions when they occur to me, but I feel like I'm wasting my time."

"I've been asking myself the same thing."

"Some questions never get answered."

"You've put your finger on a fundamental flaw in the universe."

Then I called Bullard, who apologized not very sincerely about not getting back to me. "The coroner didn't find anything inconsistent with accidental death or suicide. No drugs of alcohol in her system, no unexplained wounds, no ligature marks. Doesn't mean she wasn't pushed but there's nothing to say either way."

"Anything on her person that might help?"

"No handbag found at the scene or on the cliff walk, but it might have washed out to sea. Nothing in her pockets except a return ticket for the ferry and some loose change."

"Wouldn't that tell us when she came over?"

"It tells us she bought the ticket Friday afternoon. Doesn't tell us if she came over then, or the next day. Tickets are general admission. They're not associated with a specific trip."

"So is anyone going to look into her death any further?"

"Other than you, I doubt it. The local authorities believe it was an accident."

"Murder would be bad for the tourist trade."

"Death by falling from their cliff walk isn't much better."

"Lesser of two evils."

I still hadn't reached Ashley by the time I took the Wednesday morning ferry and I was mildly concerned, if not actually worried. I called her boss on Tuesday, but all that she would say is that Ashley had not yet returned to work.

The sky was gray and the sea was unsettled, choppy little whitecaps that slapped the hull rhythmically and threw up a chilly spray that was not at all refreshing despite the heat. I spent about ten minutes on the observation deck before going inside and getting myself some weak, bitter, but warm coffee. I looked at the agenda that I'd prepared for myself and decided that it didn't look any better today than it had when I'd written it the night before. I had nothing concrete to pursue, no new questions to ask, and I wasn't even positive what I was going to do when I arrived.

Even more annoying was the sense that I was overlooking something. It's very unlikely that someone could commit three murders – if in fact all three were actually murders – without leaving some telling clue behind. Even criminal masterminds slip up on some of the details. At least two of deaths were almost certainly crimes of opportunity rather than premeditated, which made it even less likely that all the bases were covered. The bloody handkerchief in Carl's room was almost certainly one such oversight. The missing mooring rope might be another. Separately or together, they didn't tell me anything.

I remembered Dusty's comment about her fictional spy, Craig Daniels, and the fact that he knew the solution to his problem all along, but wouldn't realize it until just before the climax. Was I in the same position? Were any of the facts in my possession more damning than they appeared? If I assembled them in the right order, might I get at least a glimpse of the whole picture? Or was I just wrong? Maybe Alyson Reynolds died because she was incautious and put up too much sail. Maybe Oliver Reynolds attacked and killed Carl on the beach, then later stumbled upon the body again and convinced himself that Carl wasn't dead after all. And maybe Linda Bettis had some perfectly innocent reason to think she could acquire enough to buy a stake in Beth's farm if she talked to someone on Black Island, maybe asking for a loan. She might have fallen to her death, or perhaps she'd failed in her effort and, despondent, had jumped.

None of this put me in a cheery mood and then it started to rain while we were leaving the ferry.

I had another cup of coffee – this one considerably better – and waited out the rain while watching people scurrying along the sidewalk outside. The rain only lasted about twenty minutes, but the clouds showed no hint of breaking up and threatened to renew the downpour without warning. I decided to call Parish first, even if it was his day off. I'd buy him lunch in return for everything he could tell me about Linda Bettis.

He was on his boat. "Come on over if you want. I can take you out and show you where it happened."

When I arrived, he was already aboard, wearing a green rain slicker, and the engine was idling. He greeted me as I jumped awkwardly from the pier to the deck. "You could have picked a nicer day for this."

"I'm being punished for something I did in a previous life."

Parish provided me with a spare raincoat and we edged away from the dock, moving very slowly until we were well away from shore. "I can show you where she must have fallen from later if you want, but there's nothing to see. It's posted as dangerous but the tourists let their kids run along there unsupervised all the time. Makes my skin crawl."

He opened up the throttle and the *Shark* seemed to leap forward eagerly. It only took two or three minutes to round the protruding corner of the island and run under some pretty impressive cliffs.

"We still get erosion here but it's pretty minor compared to the other side of the island. The sandbars and rocks break up the wave action." He slowed the engines. "That's the spot coming up now. See where that tree is growing right out of the side of that cliff? She was almost directly below that, wedged between two rocks. We'll be able to see them in another few seconds."

Parish slowed to an idle and was silent while I looked up and down the cliff, not sure why I had even come out here. There was nothing to see. I had known there would be nothing to see. I guess it was just something to do. I think it was at that precise moment that I decided I had to let this go. I'll give it till the weekend, I told myself. If nothing promising comes up before then, I'll file away my notes and try to put the whole thing out of my mind. It wouldn't be the first puzzle I had failed to solve, nor would it be the last.

"Most visitors don't get to see this part of the island. That over there is called the Devil's Lookout." It was a ledge, roughly square shaped, that looked as though it had been cut into the rock about twenty feet above the water.

"What an original name."

"Islanders tend to be traditionalists."

"So is it natural or artificial?"

"A little of both. When I was a kid, there used to be a way to climb down to it from above, and we had clandestine drinking parties there. We cleared off the brush and debris and built a fireplace out of rocks. It's deserted now. Part of the cliff fell and now the only way to get to it is to take a boat in and climb up. But there are rocks and sandbars there. I draw too much water to go much closer than we are already, but at least once a year some tourist gets curious and I usually have to pull them off. A small boat might make it in, but even then they'd have to know the shoals pretty well."

Parish took me right around the island, pointing out other landmarks like the Witch's Cave, which apparently was only about ten feet deep, the Captain's Roost, a popular make out spot, and Whale Rock, which didn't look much like a whale but which was certainly a rock. Eventually we passed the cabins and the downtown and made our way back to his pier.

"Do you want to check out the cliffs from the land side?"

I shook my head. "I've wasted enough of your day off already. Thanks for the guided tour."

"No problem. Always welcome an excuse to take the boat out. Let me know if you learn anything interesting."

I assured him I would.

The rest of my day was almost equally uneventful. Margaret Taylor told me that Linda Bettis was a hard worker and bright with books, but not so great with people. "She seemed to have a blind spot dealing with others. She'd say something to a guest that she thought was perfectly innocuous but there'd be a complaint with her boss by the end of the day. It was as if she worked out a scenario for an interaction in advance and couldn't understand why things didn't work out that way. Her father was the same way."

One of the young women running a hat shop had known Linda and Alyson pretty well. "They were as thick as thieves for a while but then they stopped going around together. I don't think they had a fight or anything. Probably just got bored. It's easy to get bored out here."

The closest I got to an actual clue was from my old friend Agnes, who claimed to have known Linda's mother quite well. "I used to go visit regularly when Elaine was sick, and she was sick for a long time. Linda tried to be helpful but sometimes I think it all got to be too much for her. I wasn't surprised when she left the island. There isn't much here to keep the young people interested."

I had glanced at my watch and realized that if I hurried I could make the four o'clock ferry, otherwise I'd be on the island for another two hours of frustration. I was about to thank her and rush off when she said something interesting.

"I remember when she bought herself a diary and then told me a couple of months later that she was only on the second page because nothing had happened to her worth writing down."

"Linda kept a diary?"

"Back then she did. Carried it around with her just in case, but I don't suppose she ever had much excuse to write in it. Maybe after she moved to the mainland."

I hadn't found a diary in Linda's room and I had looked around pretty thoroughly. It might have been hidden somewhere, but more likely she had lost or discarded it at some point.

I just made it back to the ferry on time.

At work the next day, I told Steve that I didn't want to be disturbed, sat back in my chair, and closed my eyes. I have an excellent memory and I began replaying everything that I had experienced related to the case, starting with the voyage over on the *Calamity Jane* and ending with my recent trip to Black Island. I tried to remember everything that had been said or done by everyone involved as exactly as possible, searching for some clue that I had overlooked. A couple of times I sensed that there were false notes but whenever I examined a particular statement or action, I realized that my reservations were trivial or explainable. By lunchtime, I felt emotionally and intellectually wrung out and had pretty much decided to let the entire matter drop. I wasn't helping anyone and I had already invested too much time in a wild goose chase.

Dusty was glued to her keyboard when I got home and was back at it before I had showered the following morning. "I'm doing the big revelation scene where everything gets explained," she told me without looking away from the screen. "Craig Daniels just realized that Minister Fukuda was asking questions about the missing documents before he could have known that they had been stolen. It seemed natural at the time because the Tokyo police inspector was aware of the theft, but there'd been no opportunity for him to brief anyone in the government."

"Sounds like something he should have realized long before."

"Well, a lot was going on at the time. He'd been shot at, someone had searched his room, his local contact was missing, and the Yakuza had paid him a threatening visit."

"All in a day's work for a super spy."

I left her to it, went downstairs to brew some coffee, and while I was standing there thinking about what she just said, a few pieces of the puzzle rearranged themselves in my mind and I had a sudden flash of recognition that literally left me shaken. I pulled out a chair and fell into it, replayed the relevant incidents in my mind one more time, and then pulled out my notes and my cell phone. I dialed the number of Carrie Wayne, who answered promptly, and identified myself. There was loud music in the background.

"Yes, I remember you, Mr. Birch." I could barely hear her over the ambient noise. It sounded like she was in a bar.

"Could you tell me what time your shift starts at the emergency room?"

"My shift? Why do you want to know that?"

"I'm just getting some timing straight in my mind."

"Well, I don't work there anymore. I was sorry to leave but I make almost twice as much with tips and all."

I ground my teeth together. "What time was your shift when you did work there?"

"I was supposed to start at seven but I was usually there a little earlier so I could have coffee."

"Thank you." I broke the connection. Then I called Merrilee at home. "Remind me who tracked down Linda Bettis for me." She did so and I thanked her as well.

I knew who had killed Carl Celluci. I couldn't prove it yet, but now that there was a chink in the wall, it was only a matter of time until I pulled the whole thing down. I sat at the table and made a list of the anomalies which now seemed painfully obvious to me, then made another list, this time my guesses about missing parts of the puzzle. I still didn't know how Carl's death related to Alyson Reynolds, but it seemed entirely possible that he knew something about her death – and I was sure she was dead – that put someone else at risk. Linda Bettis might well have met Carl when he was dating Alyson. But if the two of them knew enough to put the killer in danger, why hadn't they been killed much earlier? Admittedly they both lived on the mainland, but they were hardly out of reach. The killer hadn't balked at shooting up my front yard.

The answer had to be that the killer hadn't been aware that they presented a threat until recently. Carl and Linda might not even have realized that they possessed dangerous information until just before they were killed. Certainly that seemed to be the case for Linda Bettis. Was there something in her diary that suddenly became significant or had my visit just stimulated a dormant memory? Had she run off to Black Island to confront the killer and extort money so that she could buy into the farm?

I went back upstairs. Dusty was sitting back in her chair with her arms crossed. "What's up?"

I kissed her. "You're a genius."

"Yeah, I know. What genius type activity did I just accomplish?"

"You gave me the key to the whole case." And I sat down beside her and talked for quite a long time and when I was done, she kissed me back.

"I knew you couldn't leave a puzzle alone. But how are you going to prove any of that?"

"I'm still working on that part."

But by the following morning, I had a pretty good idea how I was going to proceed. I would need some good luck and some cooperation from others, but even if things didn't go exactly as planned, I was pretty sure my quarry would be flushed from cover. Carl's murder had been particularly sloppy and it was embarrassing now to realize how much I had missed. Better late than never.

I started making calls as soon as I reached the office. Constable Parish sounded sleepy. "I'm coming out to the island again on Monday morning."

"Sounds like you should get yourself a season ticket for the ferry. Anything new turn up?"

"Yes. I'll explain everything when I get there but I think you might want to have your deputies on standby. With luck, we'll be making an arrest."

"Why the delay then?"

"I have a few loose ends I have to nail down first. Sorry to be so mysterious but there's still a chance that I'm wrong and I don't want to get some innocent person in trouble."

"All right. What time are you coming?"

"I'll take the ten o'clock ferry."

"See you then."

Next I called James Coleman, who didn't sound at all sleepy. I explained what I wanted done and he asked a couple of questions, hesitated a bit before accepting the job, but finally agreed. "Breaking and entering isn't officially part of my job description."

"I'd prefer you just do the entering part."

"I'll see what I can do and get back to you."

Then I called Bullard, told her more than I wanted to but it was the only way to get her cooperation. "That's not enough to convince a judge to give me a search warrant."

"I've got that covered."

"Better not tell me the details."

"I never even mentioned the subject."

"All right, I'll see what I can do. But you'd better be right."

The last call was to Lieutenant Hernandez of the Coast Guard. It took a while to get through to him but he was cordial and listened quietly to what I had to say. I didn't tell him a whole lot and I might not need his services at all, but I always like to have a fallback position. He agreed to talk to his superiors. "They might not want to respond to a civilian request without a good reason."

I gave him Bullard's number. "They can check with her if they think I'm just a nut. She's not officially involved, but she's taking it seriously."

I was impatient to get this over with, but I knew that it might be fatal to move too quickly. Coleman needed time to do what I wanted him to do. His part might not pan out, but it was the surest way to success if he found anything. If not, I might have to take some chances that I'd prefer to avoid.

The weekend passed with glacial slowness. I resisted the temptation to call Coleman every five minutes, tried to think about something else, failed miserably, and spent a good deal of time arranging and rearranging my notes and theories. Dusty had heard my projection of what had probably happened, twice in fact, and had pointed out that a lot of it was speculative and impossible to prove. I went through some brief moments of self doubt. It wouldn't have been the first time an apparently well constructed scenario had fallen apart on me, but I was quite confident that I knew most of what had happened and why. I just wasn't sure how much of it would sound convincing to a jury.

Coleman checked in early Saturday evening, but his news wasn't good. "Never had a chance today. Every time I tried there were people around and I couldn't keep showing up without someone getting suspicious."

"You can only do what you can do," I told him, but it made for a restless night.

His luck was bad Sunday as well, but he planned to try again first thing the following morning. It was cutting things close. I could go forward with my plans even without his information, but in its absence, I would have to bluff and I didn't like bluffing.

I arrived in Galilee much earlier than I needed to. I could almost have made the early ferry, so I found a local coffee shop and pretended to eat a bran muffin while I waited. There was a lot of fog and I expected a repeat of my last trip to Black Island, but by the time I boarded the sun was breaking through the clouds and the sea that day was quite calm.

We were halfway across when my cell buzzed. "Bingo!" It was Coleman and he was clearly pleased with himself. "I found a lockbox. Not a very good one. I could have opened it with a paper clip."

"Where was it?" He told me. "What was inside?" He told me that as well. It wasn't absolute proof, but it was pretty strong evidence.

"You put everything back the way you found it?"

"Of course. As far as the police are concerned, I was never there. You may have to tip them off about where to look." He cleared his throat. "I did, however, take quite a few pictures. I've been sitting here going through them and they're very revealing." He told me some more and another piece of the puzzle fell into place.

I thanked him warmly. It would be much easier to do what I had to do now that I knew beyond any doubt that I was right.

The ferry was more crowded than usual and when we arrived I saw that the shops were busy and the beach was crowded. I sat on a bench overlooking the piers and called Parish. He answered on the first ring. "I'm here on the island."

"Okay. How do you want to handle this?"

"Are your deputies ready?"

"They're on patrol but this is a small island. They're only a few minutes away."

"All right. I have a lot to tell you first."

"Let's meet at my boat. We probably don't want to be overheard."

That suited me perfectly and I told him I'd be there in fifteen minutes. I called Bullard before rising, just to confirm that she had taken care of her end of things. She had. Then I stood up and went to meet the constable.

Parish was standing at the end of the narrow dirt road that led to his private pier. We shook hands and walked down toward the water. There was a tiny unpainted shed with a padlock on the door and a couple of benches. Out on the water, two men sat huddled in a small boat with fishing rods in their hands, looking miserable and bored. Sometimes reality doesn't live up to our expectations. We sat down and Parish took out a pack of cigarettes, offering me one which I declined.

"Smart man. I've cut way back but I still get the craving when I'm tense. So I guess this one is your fault in a way." He lit up. "So what's up?"

"Oliver Reynolds didn't kill Carl Celluci, for one thing."

"You have someone else to nominate?"

"Yes, but to understand that, you have to go back a couple of years and look at the death of Alyson Reynolds."

"Are you suggesting that someone else blamed him for her accident?"

"No, I'm suggesting that someone else was responsible for her death. And I don't think it was an accident. I think she was murdered and I have a pretty good idea what the reason was. Carl was probably killed because he had recently realized – or at least suspected – the truth. He may have tried to blackmail the real killer. It's also possible that he didn't realize the significance of something that he knew and that was potentially revealing, and that he was killed preemptively."

"That sounds pretty uncertain."

"There's more. Carl may or may not have realized the truth but Linda Bettis certainly did. She came to Black Island specifically to blackmail the killer. I'm not sure exactly what her evidence was but it was sufficiently damning that she had to die."

"Why would she go out onto the edge of a cliff alone with someone she thought was a murderer?"

"I don't know, but I hope to find out before the day is over."

"So someone on the island is a three time killer, if your theory is correct. Someone I probably know pretty well."

"I didn't say it was a resident. I've found out that several people connected to Carl's death have been back and forth several times in the past year. There might well be others."

Parish looked suddenly exasperated. "So who is that you suspect then? I've never liked a tease."

"No, you haven't, have you?" I took a deep breath. "That's probably why you killed Alyson Reynolds. You and her father were friends and you spent a lot of time at their place. She was just a kid at first, but you watched he grow up into a beautiful young woman."

Parish had stiffened but his face was bland and without emotion. "What are you talking about?"

I turned to face him and let him see the weapon in my hand, which I am happy to say was not shaking at all. "First things first. I'd like you to remove your weapon from its holster – using your left hand if you don't mind – and drop it to the ground."

He opened his mouth and I expected him to ask if this was some kind of elaborate joke, but instead he smiled and avoided the cliché. Moving with exaggerated caution, he did as I had ordered.

"Now kick it into the water."

He seemed to be actually enjoying himself as he booted it a good ten feet across the ground. It almost came to rest on the very edge of the embankment, but then it tilted and slid down out of sight with a faint splash. "What's next, Mr. Holmes?"

"Now I tell you the whole story and you fill in the gaps."

"I've always wanted to collaborate on a piece of fiction."

"I'm not sure just when you started seeing Alyson as something more than an irritating kid, but it was certainly long before she died. Linda Bettis even noticed and she wasn't the most observant person in the world."

"Linda wasn't very bright and she's not around to make any such claims."

"No, but she mentioned it in her diary."

His face changed, only by the tiniest bit, and if I hadn't been watching for it I wouldn't have noticed. "Who says Linda kept a diary?"

"She had it at the farm with her the day I went to visit." I was going to skirt the truth a little, but not much.

"You never said anything about it before."

"I didn't know how significant it was at the time. I didn't realize that you had killed Alyson until a few days ago."

"Alyson Reynolds died in a boating accident."

"Really? Well, let's look at an alternate scenario. Let's say you made a pass and she rebuffed you. You've always been able to take pretty much anything you wanted out here. You inherited one of the largest fortunes on the island. You asked for the constable's job – according to Margaret Taylor – and they gave it to you even though you weren't really qualified. That let you order people around – tourists mostly but I imagine some of the locals got out of line from time to time. I imagine Alyson was flattered by your attentiveness at first, but she grew out of it. She didn't want any permanent connections to Black Island, and you were as connected as it was possible to be. Eventually she warned you to back off and that made you angry. I don't know whether you killed her accidentally because you were so furious that you struck out without thinking, or whether you raped her first and then killed her to keep her from talking."

"That's so clichéd. If I was really a killer, I would have been much more imaginative than that."

"If you had planned it in advance, I'm sure you would have been. Certainly you were inventive enough about covering it up. The obvious solution was to arrange it so that Alyson was lost at sea.

I figure she must have died the night before her boat was found. You couldn't have towed her skiff away during the daylight. Too much risk of being seen. Fortunately the Reynolds pier was only about a hundred yards away from yours. You attached the line from your winch to the mooring ring, discarding the one that was already tied there, and crept off into the darkness. At some point, probably after you were well away from shore, you over rigged the skiff so that it would look like Alyson had taken an unnecessary risk and paid the consequences. Then you probably used the winch to raise one side of the skiff and ensure that the wind toppled it over. Her father never checked to see if she was actually in her bedroom the following morning, but if he had, the story might still have worked. She could have gotten up earlier than he did."

"It's an interesting theory, but without any physical evidence you might just as well suggest that a flying saucer attacked her."

"Point taken. It would help if I could prove you had something of hers in your personal possession, like maybe a seahorse shaped pendant that she was fond of wearing."

This time Parish was unable to completely suppress his reaction. His face flushed and the slight sneer of superiority vanished. "I don't know what you're talking about. A lot of people on the island have maritime related pendants. There wouldn't be anything to show that a particular piece belonged to a particular person."

"Except perhaps the initials 'AR' engraved on the back."

His mouth opened, then shut as he crossed his arms and sat back. "I don't know what you're talking about."

"The best piece of physical evidence would be her body, of course."

"It was never found. Probably washed out to sea."

"Not if it was never in the water in the first place. You couldn't take the risk that it would wash ashore and that an autopsy would reveal the real cause of death. Did you break her neck? Shoot her? Beat her to death?"

"I never saw Alyson the day she died." He thought for a second. "Or the day before."

I ignored him. "So you had to dispose of the body in such a way that it wouldn't be found. I imagine you buried her someplace her e on the island, probably that same night. Is she near us now?" I glanced around the immediate area. The faint smile returned to his face and I knew this wasn't the place. "Or is she in the wildlife refuge somewhere? No one's allowed to dig there and there's not much chance of it ever being developed. You didn't have a lot of time though and the ground is pretty rocky. I don't imagine she's very deep. You'd be amazed how easy it is to find a buried body nowadays. The police have dogs trained to smell them out."

Parish had regained some of his self assurance and I sensed that I was on the wrong track. Not the refuge then, but where? And then I had it. "You made a big point of taking me out to see where Linda Bettis fell to her death, even though you knew there was nothing to see. So you must have had another reason. Was it to gloat a little? And you made a point of showing me the Devil's Lookout. It's almost completely inaccessible. You said that even though you knew the safe channel, you couldn't take your own boat in because it was too big. But I bet you could have gone out in her skiff and buried her there. "

His face told me that I was right. Parish glared with such fury that it felt as though he was physically touching me. I may even have swayed back a little.

"Did you pick that spot to push Linda over for its symbolism? The two lovers, reunited in death if only briefly. Or did she pick the spot for the meeting?"

"I never saw Linda Bettis after she left the island last year."

"Ah, then you couldn't possibly have her diary in your possession."

"No, of course not. I don't even know if one exists."

"Well, we'll come back to that later. Let's talk about Carl. You made a couple of mistakes there. Don't feel bad, though. I wasn't smart enough to pick up on them at the time."

He raised his eyebrows but didn't speak.

"For one thing, you mentioned that Carl had a friend on the island before I mentioned it to you. And then later you asked if Carl's parents still lived in the area. How would you have known to ask that question?"

"That's pretty flimsy. It was only logical to assume that Carl was from Rhode Island. And I think I heard someone talking about Carl having an island connection when I dropped by right after you arrived."

"And then there's the bloody handkerchief. It didn't point to you specifically, but it obviously meant there was more going on than appeared on the surface. Here's what I think happened. You came by on your evening beach patrol – which I had forgotten about until I started reconstructing things – and found Carl alone and drunk. I don't think you had any actual plan to kill him at the time, but circumstances made it necessary."

"I'd never even met him before. Why would I want to kill him?"

"Oh, but you had. You were the friend Carl was referring to. He stayed with you at least once, probably a few times. It's even possible that he met Alyson through you. I'll bet you weren't too happy about that. I'm sure you hadn't planned it that way. You were probably just as upset as Oliver Reynolds when they got together."

Parish's face had relaxed again but his body was tense. I could tell that he wanted to lunge at me so I raised my arm a bit so that he remembered that I was armed.

"You and Carl started talking and something he said pissed you off. I admit I don't know what it was. Maybe he figured out that you killed Alyson, although it's more likely that he never realized that. He would have done something about it sooner. Blackmail, I'd guess. No, I think he just said something that made you nervous, something that suggested he might eventually figure out what had happened. It was a spur of the moment thing but you were smart enough not to shoot him. You picked up a convenient rock instead and bashed his head in."

"If I'd been worried about what Carl knew, why hadn't I done something earlier?"

"You tell me. I'd guess that you didn't realize how much he knew, or that it never seemed dangerous before, or maybe it was just that you saw that you could kill him, that no one was watching, and you figured you could cover things up. The second murder is always easier than the first. So you left him on the beach and went about your business, waiting for one of us to find the body or report him missing. But Carl had his own room and people were avoiding him. To make things worse, someone moved the body." I didn't want too much of that part of the story to become public knowledge, so I skipped past.

"When no one had called by morning, you decided to go on your normal dawn beach patrol and discover the body yourself. But when you arrived, there was no sign of Carl. That must have been quite a shock. You did find the bloody handkerchief and picked it up, then slipped into Carl's cabin to see if he was there. He wasn't, of course. I don't suppose you stayed long because you didn't want to be found there, but you wanted a souvenir of your kill and Carl's antique pipe was sitting out in plain view, so you took it. And accidentally or intentionally, you dropped the bloody handkerchief in its place."

"Very creative. I don't suppose you can prove any of this?"

"I might. If that pipe turned up in your possession, it would be hard to explain. It's quite distinctive. But you made a bigger mistake than that. You were worried that Carl wasn't dead after all, that he'd recovered enough to wander off in a daze. Someone might have found him during the night, or might yet find him during the morning, so you called the emergency room to see if he was there and so that you'd be called right away if he turned up. The problem was that you called before we notified you that Carl was missing. They remember what time you called."

Parish hesitated, then shook his head. "They just got the time mixed up. I called them right after you called me. It's their word against mine."

"The phone company ought to be able to confirm that."

He didn't have an answer this time.

"The police were satisfied that Oliver Reynolds was the killer, so you relaxed. It must have been quite an unpleasant surprise when I told you I was looking into the case myself."

"I pegged you for a busybody right from the start."

"I've been called worse. But then you made your biggest mistake. You decided to scare me off and you did it by threatening the woman I love. You came over to the mainland – either on your own boat or aboard the ferry – and you got yourself a car. I don't think you'd risk renting one. That would leave a trail. No, you probably boosted one from a long term parking lot, drove to my house and fired shots at Dusty, then returned the car to where you'd found it and went back to the island. I'm not sure why you didn't shoot to kill but I suspect that you don't feel as powerful on the mainland as you do out here. This is your domain. You're king of the hill, a wealthy and respected man, an authority figure who carries a gun, the one with the most powerful boat. Out here you're invulnerable but over there, you're just another mortal."

His eyes told me that I had struck a nerve. "But it was really stupid of you because I had pretty much decided by then to drop the case. I was half convinced that Oliver Reynolds did kill Carl and more than half convinced that Alyson died in a boating accident. If you hadn't acted, you would probably have gotten away with everything." I sighed. "And Linda Bettis would still be alive."

"Bettis didn't know anything that I needed to worry about."

I nodded. "She couldn't prove anything but if she told people what she knew, it would have made life very uncomfortable. I slipped up there, incidentally. They told me at Buster's that some guy had called looking for Linda a few days earlier and I assumed it was someone from my office. But the person who called on our behalf was female." I paused. "How old was Alyson when the two of you first had sex together?"

He didn't answer.

"According to Linda's diary, she told you it was on her sixteenth birthday. You would have been twenty-five, right? That's statutory rape."

"That would have been hearsay even if it was true."

"Maybe. But enough hearsay can convict you in the court of public opinion if not a court of law. And Alyson had a very distinctive pendant."

"You mentioned that before."

"Who do you suppose bought it and had it engraved?"

Parish was silent.

"It was you, wasn't it? And I bet if I asked the right person the right question, I'd find out who did the engraving and he or she would be able to look up the invoice and find out who ordered it."

"But that pendant is probably at the bottom of the ocean somewhere."

"If she had died out on the ocean, you'd be right. But she didn't die there, did she? And I'd guess you'd reclaim the pendant as a trophy, just as you did Carl's pipe and Linda's diary."

"You can't prove that I have any of those things." But he looked nervous, which was what I wanted.

"Not yet. So finally we have Linda who decided to blackmail you. I think she could have been bought off easily. She only wanted enough for a stake in the farm where she'd been living. She probably was asking for so little that she figured you wouldn't consider her a threat. It was chump change as far as you were concerned. Linda wasn't very good about figuring how other people would react. You could never have been sure and it was safer just to kill her. She arranged to meet you to talk about the diary – she had foolishly brought it with her – and either you suggested the cliff walk as nice and private, or she chose it and made your job easier. It would have been simple enough. Just grab the diary and give her a push. She probably never suspected she was in danger until she was already falling."

Parish remained silent. I could tell that he was considering his options and decided it was time to provoke him further before he could compose a defense. "What's say you and I go aboard and see what we can find? I'll bet you have a box of souvenirs hidden somewhere. "

I turned my arm and gestured with my weapon even though we were sitting quite close together. Parish was quicker than I expected. He clubbed my arm up and lunged forward. I lost my grip and fell awkwardly backward and when I sat up he had retrieved my gun and was pointing it at me. "And I thought you were a professional," he said tightly. "A child could have disarmed you."

I started to rise and he shook his head. "No, you stay right where you are while I figure out what to do with you."

"People know that I came out here to see you. There's no way you can disguise my death as an accident."

"I'm working on that. The way I figure it, you told me you were going to confront the killer, I tried to talk you out of it, and somehow whoever it was took your gun away and killed you. I just have to decide where to put your body."

"Someone will hear the shots."

"Maybe." Without lowering his arm he backed over to the shed. There was a small generator beside it and he pressed a button on the side. There was a low hum and then a louder, irregular one. "Or maybe not."

His eyes narrowed and I knew he was going to shoot. "One question. Why did you kill Carl? The other two I can understand, but he couldn't have known anything that endangered you or you would have done something about it a lot sooner."

Parish nodded. "He still thought she'd drowned. I met him while I was off taking some courses at the university. Rules of evidence, chains of custody, things like that. We got along all right, so I invited him to come out and he took me up on it. Stayed on the boat with me. I even introduced him to Alyson and he was hot for her right away. She wouldn't date anybody local but he was from the mainland so she started going with him. We got pretty wasted one night and he told me she'd finally fucked him. He was bragging so much that I just had to tell him that I'd had her first, on her sixteenth birthday."

"Just like Linda said."

"Yeah. I had no idea Alyson had told her about it. I thought it was a deep dark secret. Anyway, I was doing my night patrol and Carl was there and we started talking about old times. Then he told me that he'd seen Alyson's old man, Oliver, wandering around the cabins. He thought it might be funny if he told him that he hadn't been the one who despoiled his daughter after all, that I'd done her a long time before that. He was drunk and half kidding, but he had a big mouth. He might have done it, and Oliver might have believed him. We were friends once but he got strange after Alyson was gone. I just couldn't take the chance that he'd cause trouble, that someone like you might take him seriously and ask more questions. The rock was there and he was looking the other way and it just seemed like the best way to handle things."

"And it felt good too, didn't it?"

"Yes, in fact it did. Almost as good as this is going to feel." And he raised his arm and fired twice, aiming directly at the center of my chest. I threw up my arms and fell backward.

Some of what happened immediately after that I didn't actually see. The rounds were both blanks, of course, but when someone shoots at you from close range, the instinct to fall away is irresistible. I had arranged for Parish's own weapon to be kicked into the water just to get it safely out of the way, and I had correctly anticipated that given a chance to disarm me, the constable would take it. If he had chosen not to say anything before shooting me, I'd have been no worse off than before, and I was reasonably sure that he would have to gloat at least a little bit before pulling the trigger.

The rest of my plan went badly awry. Coleman erupted from the shed as soon as the first shot was fired. The padlock was closed but he had removed the nails from one end of the hasp so that the door could simply be held shut from the inside. His gun was not loaded with blanks and he should have been able to stop Parish in his tracks. Unfortunately, the ground was uneven and strewn with rocks, one of which turned under his foot. He went down hard enough to drive the air from his lungs. If Parish had stooped to recover his weapon, we would both have been in an unenviable position, but he still hadn't realized that I wasn't bleeding to death.

I raised my head and saw him running toward the *Shark*, and in the distance I saw the two fishermen start their engine and head toward us. They were, of course, two of Bullard's people provided to make the official arrest. But they weren't coming fast enough. By the time I was back on my feet, Parish had jumped from the pier to the deck and was casting off the line. Coleman groaned and got to his knees, but the boat's engine roared to life a second later and it almost leaped away from the shoreline.

The outboard was trying to cut him off, which was foolish because they were far overmatched. Parish steered directly toward them, ignored the gun one of the policemen pointed at him, and made as if to ram. Both men realized their danger and went over the side just before their ride was struck a glancing blow that was nonetheless powerful enough to flip it over.

Coleman was back on his feet by then. He gave me an apologetic look and I shrugged. What was done was done and there was nothing we could do about it. Instead we went down to the pier and helped the two thoroughly soaked policemen up out of the water. Parish was making good headway. He was well away from shore but had turned away from Galilee.

"Lost our radio," panted one of the policemen. "I dropped it when we hit the water."

The other one turned and looked out at the rapidly diminishing wake. "He could go ashore anywhere from here, Connecticut, Long Island."

I already had my cell phone in my hand. "We haven't lost him quite yet." I made the call, a voice answered, and I spoke quickly. "He gave us the slip and he's headed your way."

Thirty seconds later a Coast Guard cutter emerged from around the curve of the island. I don't know if she was as fast as the *Shark*, but she had the angle on him and for the first couple of minutes he apparently didn't even see her. We watched as the two dark shapes seemed to converge and then there were three very faint, very distant pops.

Coleman whistled. "Sounds like he still doesn't realize he's firing blanks."

Then there was answering chorus of pops and from the cutter, whose crew didn't know that Parish wasn't actually armed. The two shapes merged into one from our viewpoint and then we had to wait for a while before Lieutenant Hernandez called me. "He's down. You can relax."

It was a while later before we heard the details. Parish had fired at the approaching cutter, which provoked a quick and deadly response. Only one round hit Parish, and I wasn't at all surprised to learn later that it had been fired by Bullard, who had hitched a ride. Parish was still alive, but unconscious. He died several hours later without ever opening his eyes.

It's not entirely certain that a jury would have found Parish guilty, so perhaps it's just as well that his injuries proved to be fatal. A lot of the evidence was circumstantial and even with Coleman's corroboration of what transpired during our confrontation, a good lawyer could have found soft spots in the case. And Parish, whose estate was in excess of ten million dollars, could have afforded very good lawyers.

Alyson Reynolds' body was found just where I had expected it to be. He'd buried her in a little recess that wasn't quite a cave. The coroner's report say that her hyoid bone was crushed, suggesting that she had been strangled. The lockbox on the boat was exactly where Coleman had said it was, fastened under a bunk in the forward cabin, and it contained Carl's pipe, Alyson's pendant, an elaborately carved piece of scrimshaw, and Linda's diary. As of this writing, no one has recognized where the scrimshaw might have come from, but the police are looking into deaths and disappearances on Black Island over the course of the last few years. Parish's fourth victim – if that's what this signified – may well have been a tourist in which case the truth may never come out.

Linda's diary didn't contain any shocking revelations other than the entry where Alyson had told her about her sexual initiation by Parish. Her entries were few and brief – she had only used half the open space over the course of almost ten years. There were a couple of remarks about Alyson mentioning that Parish was still bothering Alyson, and hints that he sometimes frightened her. A good lawyer might have laughed and dismissed it as an adolescent fantasy and public opinion would probably have turned against Linda. Even now, some of the islanders refuse to believe that Parish was a killer. He was very good at ingratiating himself with others, particularly the elderly.

That about wraps it up. The police and the lawyers are satisfied that Parish committed all three murderers, accepting my reconstruction as the closest they were ever going to get to the full truth. Justice had been done, although Linda Bettis had no surviving relatives to welcome it, Carl's family didn't care, and Oliver Reynolds had withdrawn so completely from the world that he would never know the truth. Parish probably set the fire to destroy Oliver's remaining possessions just to make sure there wasn't anything there that might implicate him. Or it might just have been a drunken tourist.

Life at the office got back to normal, or a new normal. Emily and Ashley are back together – in fact Dusty and I attended their wedding. Ashley is seeing someone about her anger problems and even apologized fairly gracefully for her uninvited appearance at our home. Alyson was not the former lover who had died after all. Laura and Kevin did not work out, however, and Laura filed for divorce after catching her husband canoodling with Donna Goodrich – Dennis Malden's ex-girlfriend – at a party.

James Coleman is now on my list of preferred subcontractors and we've already sent him a couple of jobs. He does fine work. Astonishingly, Tina and Barry seem to have developed some kind of relationship – I'm not sure how romantic it is. They still fight every bit as much at work as they used to, but that doesn't seem to interfere with their spending frequent evenings together.

Dusty finished her novel, which made it to number five on the New York Times Bestseller List. The publisher and her new agent both want the next in the series but Dusty intends to write a western. She bought a dozen small cactus plants and has started cleaning Japan out of the attic.

I got back to my usual routine, meeting with clients, evaluating security arrangements, arranging for surveillance or audits or whatever was necessary. It was good to be back.

And then, this morning, Steve buzzed me on the intercom. "There's a Miss Wells to see you."

"I don't recognize the name."

"She doesn't have an appointment but she insists that she needs to see you. Won't tell me why. She appears to be rather worked up."

Just what I needed, but I told him to send her in.

Juliette Wells was in her late twenties, mildly pretty, smartly dressed, and obviously upset. She sat down, crossed her legs, uncrossed them, recrossed them. "Mr. Birch, I need your help. I witnessed a murder yesterday."

"The police..." I started.

"The police don't believe me. They can't find the body. And Mr. Birch, I'm pretty sure the murderer knows who I am."

I sighed, took a pad and pen out of my desk drawer. "Why don't you start at the beginning, Miss Wells?"

www.ingramcontent.com/pod-product-compliance
Lightning Source LLC
Chambersburg PA
CBHW072057170626
46813CB00004B/1390